Darkest Hour
Liberation War Book 1

John Walker

DISCLAIMER

This is a work of fiction. Names, characters, business, places, events, and incidents are either the products of the author's imagination or used in a fictitious manner. Any resemblance to actual persons, living or dead, or actual events is purely coincidental. This story contains explicit language and violence.

Blurb

A massive sphere appears near Earth, defying all attempts to communicate or understand its purpose. Power outages plague key cities and military bases, causing wide spread panic and chaos. Only the Space Agency seems to have a grasp on the situation but with all their combined resources, they're baffled.

Captain Warren Miller races to join his colleagues in the Agency headquarters, hoping to convince his superiors to launch their latest space craft, the battlecruiser Leviathan, which may be able to defy this intruder. In the absence of communication, he hopes a little intimidation might bring about a conversation.

But then smaller objects descend upon the Earth, grabbing up people from all over the globe. Captain Miller never makes it back to base, forcing the Agency to scramble for a response. With the weight of an expectant world beating down on them and the alien threat looming above, they have no choice but to engage the enemy or simply witness history in the making.

Prologue

"Breaking news!" Dirk Reidel always wanted to be a news anchor, to deliver stories to millions of people. He never imagined he would be the voice of the world, bringing to light one of the most important events in human history. His first reaction was to feel honored but fear replaced it quickly enough.

"We have received reports of some sort of object entering our solar system." Dirk fought not to clear his throat, struggled with the fact he'd gone dry. He'd never sipped water while on camera but this time, he made an exception. The cool water soothed him enough to go on. "We'll have some photos to show you shortly but at this time, we don't know what it is."

He quickly read over the next portion of his report and directed his gaze at the camera. "Several parts of the world are reporting power outages in metropolitan areas. If you're listening to this on a radio, please know that crews are working on the problem. It may seem logical to blame the object but we do not have evidence of its involvement at this time."

One of the assistants stepped on camera and handed him a new stack of papers. Dirk nodded a thanks to them and looked down, reading as quickly as he could. His eyes widened, despite the fact he'd been trained *not* to react to information on a page. He couldn't help it. Every new detail that came in was more and more shocking.

"I've received an update," Dirk said, "the object is described as round, too smooth to be a naturally occurring rock or asteroid. Sources say it is stationary, sitting halfway between Earth and the moon. We are waiting on a press conference with our Space Agency officials. I'm sure I can speak for the world in saying, I hope they can provide us with some answers.

"At this time, people are being asked to stay in their homes and to not panic. We do not have enough information to make sense of what we're seeing or if it may even be a concern. Authorities urge everyone to remain calm. They are working quickly to make sense of this—wait. We're cutting to the press conference now with Wyman Jacks, Space Agency Administrator."

Dirk turned to watch the screen to his left. An image of an older man appeared standing behind a podium. His dark hair was gray on the sides and a craggy face made him look harsh and uncompromising. The navy-blue suit looked out of place on him. He was the type of man that looked at home in a military uniform.

The Space Agency did call in a lot of military people, Dirk thought. *They're almost as mysterious as this damn object!*

"Good afternoon," Jacks said, his voice firm and unafraid. Dirk admired him, especially when he hadn't been able to pull that off himself. "Less than an hour ago, an as of yet unidentified object was discovered near Earth. We are actively investigating to determine threat level and where it may have come from.

"Unfortunately, at this time we know very little. It does not appear to be of natural origin for several reasons. One, it is not moving at all. An asteroid or meteor would be in some form of orbital motion. Second, our initial scans have indicated the surface is perfectly smooth and made of a form of tempered metal.

"All that said, we do not want to jump to any conclusions and will provide updates as we have them. There is no cause for panic. Our top minds are unraveling the mystery. As you know, we are multinational organization and have the full support of our governments to conduct this investigation. Any questions?"

A string of people began shouting, news reporters that somehow arrived at the event quickly enough to participate. Dirk felt grateful to not be among them. He hated having to vie for the attention of the speaker, shouting louder than the person next to him to be heard. Worse, he was quite certain those events were rigged anyway.

The people who got to ask questions were predetermined.

Acting as an anchorman appealed to him far more than any other form of journalism.

Jacks pointed at someone. "Yes, go ahead."

"Mister Jacks," a man's voice asked the question. He sounded like he might be from Boston. "The Space Agency has been quite private in the past about … well, everything. Should we assume that this press conference means we're looking at a dangerous event? What has brought you out today?"

"You are right, we don't offer many updates. Most of our work is incremental and not particularly interesting on its own. We have a few major projects we would love to talk about but they were simply not ready. That said, we are in the best position to investigate this particular event and that's why I'm here today."

"Can you tell us if this object has anything to do with the power outages throughout the world? Are you planning a response?"

"We have not detected any signals coming from the ship," Jacks said. "But it stands to reason that it's somehow involved. This is at the top of our research list and we hope to have an answer soon. If it did cause these power interruptions, it did so in a way that we don't know how to detect yet but we should not make assumptions. Facts are coming soon and yes, we have a plan for a response."

"Mister Jacks! Mister Jacks!" A woman rang out over all the others and was called upon. "Do you think this may be an alien intelligence? Are we making any attempt to communicate with it and what is your opinion on their hostility?"

Jacks smiled. "I believe I said something about jumping to conclusions before." His comment drew some nervous laughs from the audience. "That's not an assumption we're willing to make right now. When we learn more, I'll be back to tell you. As we approach the object, we'll gather as much data as we can. However, I do need to return to my duties. Thank you."

Dirk turned away from the screen as the various reports shouted, begging for one final question. He looked directly at the camera. "There you have it. The Space Agency has their work cut out for them today, that's for sure." Another set of pages was set on his desk. "I've just been handed some more information, this time about the Space Agency.

"Five years ago, seemingly as a sign of good faith between the countries of the world, the multinational Space Agency was formed. Taking from the top minds of NASA, Roscosmos, the CNSA and others, they set out to explore our solar system with the eventual goal of pressing beyond to other parts of the galaxy.

"They have released a number of photographs to the public as well as some videos. While many have considered them unnecessarily secretive, others have praised their advances. With the resources of the world behind them, they have found success no single organization has been able to achieve.

"I, for one, am confident that their involvement means we will get to the bottom of this event quickly. If anyone on Earth has a chance, it will be them. Now, we would like to show you what we already know and if you're just joining us, we'll bring you the recorded press conference of Wyman Jacks, Space Agency administrator."

***

Doctor Alexander Meyers sat at his terminal, sweat making his shirt cling to his chest and back. He wiped his forehead with a paper towel that long since became too saturated to do much good but it was all he had. Staring down at his personal screen, he watched as the two experimental ships cruised toward the invading object.

God, I hope this is a good idea. Each craft had a crew of fifteen. They were two prototypes, essentially the same type of ship with a few modifications so they could test different defensive scenarios. They were both armed with missiles and guns but also carried decent scanning equipment, the kind Meyers hoped would garner some additional information about the invader.

As they drifted closer, he watched from multiple cameras. One sat on an orbiting satellite, providing a distant view of the situation. Others occupied the hulls of the ships themselves, granting a sort of first-person perspective of the operation. Communications remained steady, uninterrupted by static or interference.

If these were invaders, they weren't bothering to jam their communicators.

Meyers already measured the invading vehicle, putting it at thirty-eight kilometers. Massive, but not devastatingly so. It gave him some mild amount of confidence in the Earth ships on their way to meet the thing. What should they expect? Violence? Or would it ignore them? Once it arrived near the moon, it simply stopped moving, expelling little radiation and no detectible signals.

Maybe it was on an automated course and upon arrival, the crew had to wake up. Meyers wrote several papers on traveling to other star systems, with and without the benefit of faster than light travel. Cryogenic stasis topped the list of his theories, allowing a crew to go vast distances without suffering the effects of age and time.

It stood to reason they may not have heard from their visitors for this very reason. After all, what intelligent life would travel a vast distance just to sit on someone's doorstep and remain quiet? The very idea didn't make any sense to him. The explorer in him found it insulting to imagine Earth's first contact would be hostile.

He hoped an advanced race would've learned from past mistakes, just as he hoped humanity had from their interactions with indigenous life in the early days of European exploration. Of course, a nagging voice in his head reminded him of something many people the world over probably considered. Superior technology did not necessarily equate to a higher sense of morality.

"Ground Control, this is Demeter One." The voice came from Lieutenant Commander Walter Garrit. He'd been helming his particular ship since the first test run. "We are nearing the object now. Still no response to our presence."

Meyers leaned close to his microphone. "Maintain course and heading." He checked their feed from the satellites. No signals left the object. Nothing changed from the moment they detected it to the approach of their two vessels. "Are you picking anything up on your scanners?" Their sensors were minimal, meant for maneuvering more than anything else so he didn't expect much.

"Negative. No radiation or anything else."

Meyers saw it long before they did. He turned his attention to the cameras again, eyes wide. The larger vessel seemed to throb at the center, the globe bulging. It expanded, smaller parts breaking free from the whole. Dozens of them, perhaps a hundred, flew free and began a descent toward Earth. "Demeter One, are you seeing this?"

"Affirmative, Ground Control," Garrit said. "Please advise."

Meyers didn't know what to do, or exactly how to proceed. Attacking them seemed out of place. They didn't know if they were hostile. Then the decision was made for him.

A beam of energy lanced out from the larger vessel, striking Demeter Two. The ship throbbed twice, lights flickering before they went out completely.

"We have been attacked!" Garrit called. "We are engaging."

"Wait!" Meyers shouted, but it was too late. Demeter One opened fire, blasting away at the enemy ship. A translucent, green octagon stuttered into existence. It faded away after the last of the projectiles made contact.

Demeter One veered off, hitting their thrusters to buy some distance. Another energy beam burst from the larger vessel, narrowly missing their target. Meyers shouted for them to hurry, to get away from the alien craft but something must have been wrong with their communicator. Garrit swung the ship around and made another attack run.

Again, the strange octagonal energy appeared and faded but this time, the energy beam fired again. It caught Demeter One dead center. Electricity danced over the hull, crackling like a weather vortex before fading away along with the power on the ship. Communications went down and the two ships began to drift.

"My God …" Meyers stood up, staring at the screen. "Contact Colonel Jacks. Tell him to get in here right away. We have a huge problem."

Chapter 1:

They have to get me up there. Captain Warren Miller struggled to remain calm as he sat in a terrible traffic jam behind countless civilian vehicles. They were all desperate to leave the city but none so hungry for it as he was. If he could get to the Space Agency base, arrive in enough time to make a difference, he had a solution for their current problem.

Dirk Reidel's voice filled the radio, rambling on about what they knew and what they thought they knew. Most of it was bullshit guesses. They read far too much into Colonel Jacks's comments but that was probably the point. It kept them fixating on the larger object that was impossible to hide.

The smaller ones, those were a concern. Space Agency people knew about the object for the better part of a day. It arrived near Saturn and moved directly to the Earth, pausing in its current position by the moon. A research buoy picked up and conveyed a great deal of information back to base.

That's how they knew about the tempered metal, the shape and the fact it was definitely *not* naturally occurring. All attempts to communicate had been met with silence but additional efforts were underway. They called in every department head, putting them to task on finding some way to speak to the object.

If anything caused the power outages, it was likely those smaller things coming down, masking their presence perhaps. Or, it may have been a side effective of them entering the atmosphere. Warren didn't believe that or it would've impacted greater areas. Power dropped in targeted places.

Warren had been on leave and joined the secure conference line after Jacks contacted him. It didn't take long before he got in the truck and floored the gas … then promptly found himself stuck. People threw out theories but the one that concerned Warren the most was the idea that they might be dealing with an unmanned device, a robot sent to observe.

Another person took that theory to the next logical conclusion: that they might be dealing with a hostile device which could cause untold destruction. Had it crashed into the Earth, the sheer size of it would've been enough to cause unimaginable destruction.

Jacks stated early in the call that the men who discovered the item initially believed the Earth was doomed. Considering the speed at which the device approached the planet, there was no time to react, no way to intercept it before it made contact. When it stopped, a collective sigh of relief washed through the Space Agency headquarters.

I have to get our ship up there and confront this thing. Warren didn't want to bring it up on the call. He needed to have a private conversation with Jacks, to bring the point home in person. They had the ship for the job. A battleship that definitely held the punch required to put some hurt on an invading vessel.

It would take time to prep and launch, however. To that end, he contacted Lieutenant Commander Carlos Delgado, his chief engineer and had him go about getting everything online. By the time Warren arrived and spoke to Jacks, they should be about ready to take off. Providing he got the rest of the crew in place ... and clearance.

Jacks terminated the call, bringing everyone into a room at the Agency headquarters. Warren was asked to join them the moment he arrived just before they killed the line. *Damn it, Jacks. You couldn't wait, huh?* The council must've pushed for some heightened security.

The Space Agency hadn't socialized the construction of a battleship to the general population, not yet. They were going to address it during their maiden voyage, turning it into a big spectacle, a celebration of the accomplishment. The citizens of the world needed to see where their money went.

Anonymous polls went out to the world, attempting to gauge their biggest concerns and interests in regard to space. Questions were meant to determine what they cared about most whether it be resource acquisition, exploration, scientific discovery or threats from beyond the solar system.

By far, security topped the charts of what the people wanted. Warren blamed it on television and cinema, creating a culture of paranoia. Horror films of the nineteen-fifties certainly helped breed the mentality then writers built from there. Even novelists dating back to HG Welles fostered fear in the general populace.

The Agency was run by a council of appointed officials from each participating nation. They unanimously voted on the creation of a fleet of defensive vessels, which resulted in several smaller ships capable of launching from the surface. Each of these they focused on a different discipline until they were ready to construct their flagship.

Warren joined the team at that time as Colonel Jacks's first choice as commander of the new vessel. Getting him in early meant he would understand and learn every part of the ship, that he'd be a true expert in how it operated and functioned. Furthermore, he could apply his tactical for weapon placement and system redundancies.

Though if he was being perfectly fair, he spent more time in a fighter cockpit than he did running a large naval type vessel. In order to rectify that, he spent time on their smaller ships, the ones that could essentially make a run to the moon in a matter of hours. Advances in fuel efficiency allowed them to accelerate and decelerate as needed.

Where in the past, astronauts had to account for the weight of fuel and slowing down to land or attain orbit, modern space vessels carried shuttles that could make the trip to the surface. This meant they merely had to get close enough for the smaller ship to get to their destination.

When Warren joined the Agency, they explained the problems they came together to solve. They were, in no particular order, propulsion, gravity and survivability. Once a ship could travel fast enough with artificial gravity and plenty of space to prepare and preserve nourishment, then humanity could truly begin exploring the stars.

The first attempt to generate artificial gravity came from magnetism but it was expensive and impractical from a power perspective. While rooting around for other theories, they discovered a scientist who had developed a crystal capable of withstanding incredible vibrations and through that, he showed he could generate measurable gravitons.

That breakthrough allowed the Agency to build these into the ships, providing an artificial gravity system that was inexpensive and functional. Their smaller shuttles did not benefit from the technology but the larger ships allowed people to operate as normal and with that, the space travel door was open.

Warren's first mission into space involved a trip to the moon. They were there and back in a grand total of twenty-four hours with six of those spent on the actual research mission. Several researchers went to the surface, taking samples and plotting the creation of a lunar colony. They weren't quite to the building phase but plans were in the works.

The experience gave him perspective and allowed him to contribute meaningfully to the project. Warren left the academy with an aeronautics degree which gave him some leg to stand on in discussions with the scientists.

Checking his watch, he felt the pressure of time sitting in that traffic. Warren willed the people to move around him, wished the authorities would get things done. Maybe if he called into the base, he could get a chopper sent to pick him up. Getting stuck in the middle of the city, regardless of his transportation, left him in the same horrible situation as those around him.

Desperate but helpless.

Not all of the Agency missions went off smoothly and they knew they wouldn't. The earliest attempts to send their ships into space met with disasters of varying severity. They lost four entire crews, all volunteers from some of the harsher nations that participated in the project. This meant their deaths could be kept out of the public eye.

Each life lost for the Agency was honored with a star on a particularly large wall. Warren didn't know if the person who built the base had some foresight into how dangerous the work would be or if it was a coincidence but either way, they had plenty of room for a good thousand people without having to bring the marks closer together.

The news started their loop again, playing Jacks's statement and reiterating what they'd already said. No new developments would be released for a while so people would have to be patient. Knowing the general population, that was not happening. Grocery stores were likely swamped and, in less civilized areas, he anticipated looting, even rioting.

At least the people around him seemed content to honk and yell at each other. They hadn't left their cars to start trouble but maybe it was just a matter of time. Though charity was certainly limited with this crew. Frustration became so thick, it could've been cut with a knife. Warren understood, though he believed he experienced it far more profoundly than his other car bound peers.

All the more reason we need to get me up there now to confront this thing. Warren wondered when the media would find out about the smaller objects and if the Agency planned on telling them before it became obvious. Depending on where those things set down or passed over, they'd cause quite the stir.

Some amateur astronomer probably already knows about them, Warren thought. *They're probably trying to get through to their local news network with the information. Luckily, they're all too busy to take such calls right now but soon, they'll be hunting for a new source. I hope Jacks has a plan to contend with that.*

Jacks proved to be a shrewd politician, the kind of man who worked well with the Agency council. He knew how to pick which battles to fight and rarely lost when he put himself out there. Budget concerns tended to top the list of his primary duties but he also had to go toe to toe with their superiors about project direction.

The engineers generally painted compelling pictures of why they should do a certain thing, giving Jacks the ammunition he needed to sell their goals. Early on, they had a lot of trouble with the French representative but he'd been replaced and since then, things moved smoothly.

Many thought the man had been sent to hamper their progress, to gum up the works in an effort to make the alliance fail. They never expected it from the French though, which made intrigue an easier sell after the fact. These theories remained on the down low, between technicians, researchers and military men working there.

A commotion caught Warren's attention. A fight broke out between two guys after one called the other something foul. Other commuters stepped in to quell the violence. The tension of the unknown compelled such behavior, made tempers short and actions hot. Warren imagined the stress they must be under, the sheer terror inherent in facing an alien threat.

Critics of the Agency suggested it was spending a lot of money to do something no one needed. There were problems on Earth that the resources could've been used for. Some asked why look to the stars when our backyard is in such a desperate need of cleaning? The answer seemed obvious to Warren but they had to address it regardless.

Less than a year into operation, the Agency put people on the moon again. They began planning and coordinating the possibility of colonizing other planets. Terraforming research showed how they might oxygenate the atmosphere of Mars. Surveys proved there were much needed resources on the planet.

All we have to do is get there. Those words rang in Warren's head and were the ones Jacks used to sell him on joining up. "No, I'm not asking you to lead a colony but to defend it. Police actions, that sort of thing. Once we start down this path, it's going to happen quickly, Warren. I promise you that."

They had yet to put people on any of the planets but they did have research buoys in place all over the solar system. It allowed them to survey the different satellites orbiting the sun, giving them the kind of information they needed to determine where to go next and how to take advantage of each opportunity.

Mars terraforming would begin within the next six months and the first bio-domes were being built to deploy on the moon. People would follow, researchers and scientists then prospectors and miners, individuals specifically trained to take on the grueling tasks of low gravity work.

The future was happening right before Warren's eyes on a daily basis, right up until the object arrived in their solar system and moved into position to menace them. The timing made him wonder. Had they shown up because of their advances or would they be there either way? Was this thing attracted to the potential of space exploration? Of advanced technology?

That's what I intend to find out.

Screams caught his attention, cries from several people happening behind him. He turned in his seat, eyes widening. A massive shadow fell over the cars, one of the smaller objects flying slowly overhead. "Oh my God ..." he muttered the words but they came unbidden, total instinct. Looking about frantically, he knew there was no escape, not in the car.

Now people poured out of their vehicles, fleeing in stumbling sprints. Another two of the objects joined the first, flying in a formation of three. Warren pushed himself, hurrying past idling cars and trucks. An overpass up ahead provided him some minimal amount of hope, a sense of safety that may not exist but it sure seemed tempting.

And what were these things doing? Why had they instilled such a tremendous amount of urgency to get away? Warren had no idea but those around him seemed to share the fear. Some had flown into a blind panic, throwing people out of the way in their mad dash to escape. Others cowered beside their vehicles, literally losing their minds.

I should've grabbed the sat phone! Damn it! Warren heard engines in the distance, air craft interceptors perhaps. They wouldn't be in time to do anything about these. Thirty more feet to the overpass ...

A person disappeared. He swore it was true but it happened in his peripheral vision, a trick in the corner of his eye. It couldn't have been real. There was no way. Another ... this time, ten feet in front of him. They were just gone. It reminded him of a movie where aliens literally disintegrated people. They were simply popped out of existence. One second there, the next ... gone.

Warren's run became a blind panic. The sound of fighter engines was drowned out by the pounding of blood in his ears. A moment passed ... cool air fell over him. He closed his eyes. *This is it!* The thought didn't make him give up but rather pushed him on, forcing him to exert himself further but it didn't matter.

Not entirely. Not as his vision went dark ... and the world faded ... along with consciousness.

***

Commander Victoria Serling moved through the Agency base, shoving past the technicians and researchers clogging up the halls. Everyone was on high alert, rushing to different stations and meeting rooms to discuss the arrival of the strange object menacing the Earth. While they theorized, she knew what Warren would want to do.

I need to talk to Colonel Jacks before he gets here to smooth things over quickly, to get launch clearance before it's too late.

Victoria joined the Agency straight out of the military, exchanging the rank of Colonel for Commander in the new command structure. She acted as Warren's second and would be his first officer when they went into space. Until then, she worked closely with the crew as they checked and rechecked all systems and functions of the vessel.

The process became tedious and she quickly felt their superiors were merely stalling for time. Some of them were playing a political game, waiting for the right moment to announce their achievement but in so doing, they delayed the project. The sooner they got the ship into space, the sooner exploration could begin.

And had they not wasted so much time in the first place, we might've been in a position to intercept this thing before it became a problem.

Years spent flying combat missions engrained in her a sense of getting things done as efficiently and quickly as possible. Once she transitioned into an administrative role, she cut a lot of fat from response times and helped streamline the processes put in place to acquire equipment as well.

Joining the Agency helped her personal life somewhat as well. Victoria married a marine, a lieutenant in a forced recon unit. He had been on countless combat missions and always came home … until he didn't. It would be wrong to say she blamed the military but part of her heart struggled with continuing to serve.

Her new post was different enough that she was able to walk away from the past, to lose herself in an environment where the primary goal was getting into space. Exploration and the advancement of mankind's efforts to colonize the stars felt like a far nobler ambition than having a sole purpose of sending people to fight.

Her husband, Paul, would've wanted her to find some way to move on, to find some happiness wherever she could. He'd been a selfless man, which ultimately got him killed. During a particularly brutal battle in the middle of enemy territory, he saved ten lives, including a number of civilians.

The final act of bravery earned him a posthumous Medal of Honor. When she received it, she found the piece of metal to be of small comfort. After a lifetime of serving the military, of putting her own life on the line, she couldn't help but be proud of him. Though the war took her husband from her, his final acts distinguished him in a way few epitaphs could have.

Victoria met Warren Miller in the military and they briefly served in the same unit. He handpicked her for his first officer and her record did the rest of the work for her. No one argued about giving her the assignment and a few months after a brief conversation with Jacks, she received her transfer orders.

Since then, she'd developed a positive relationship with the various section heads and many of the researchers. They appreciated how she could dissect a process and help them make it better. It ingratiated her to everyone on the base and it ultimately made the whole Agency look good to the council.

Victoria stepped aside as two technicians nearly ran her down, peering into the reflective glass in front of her. She wore her light brown hair cropped above her shoulders to keep it out of the way. Blue eyes looked exhausted, despite the fact she slept fine. Pale features didn't get out much, especially with how much work there was to do.

How the hell did Miller justify leave? Victoria envied him on one hand but on the other, she didn't really have anywhere to go. Her friends were all deployed and her family was scattered all over the US. Besides, in her mind, the end of the project would provide a bigger reward than any vacation. *What would I do anyway? Drink wine and sleep?*

Jacks stepped out of a conference room just as Victoria arrived and she grabbed his arm before he could storm off. "Colonel," she said, "we really need to talk."

"I'm a little busy right now, Serling," Jacks replied. He looked at her hand. "Meyers said we have a huge problem I need to tend to in control. Make it quick."

Victoria let him go. "I get that. I'd like to have some authorization to be busy as well. I need your permission to prep the Leviathan for launch. We both know that Captain Miller is going to request it the moment he arrives and he'll push too. If I'm already getting her online, then we'll be that much closer to getting out there."

"Demeter One just ran an op to make contact," Jacks said. "I'd have to get permission from the council and I need to gather a lot more information before I meet up with them. I'd rather not be saying *I don't know* to every question they throw at me. You of all people understand protocol. We need to be careful about bucking process. Not sure this is the time to do so."

"Begging your pardon," Victoria replied, "but I'd say this is precisely the time. You know I'm all for sticking to our established protocols. That thing out there doesn't care about our bureaucracy. For all we know, those devices could be coming down here to attack us. I'm not saying let's start shooting but we should take the gun out so it's easier to aim. The Leviathan should be the first responder."

Jacks sighed, staring into her eyes. She could tell he was swayed by her message but he remained silent for a moment. She took the opportunity to drive the point home harder. "Besides, you know the council will ask you if the ship's ready to go or not. They have people to answer to about our defensive capabilities."

"Why do I get the feeling you've already been prepping the ship?" Jacks asked. "And are just asking for permission to cover your ass?"

Victoria smirked. "Pretty sure Captain Miller beat me to it, honestly but I can only say that there are people aboard and they may be doing their jobs." She shrugged. "Beyond that, I can't say specifically what they're all up to until I join them which I'll be doing after this conversation."

"If you're confident the vessel will launch …"

"We all are. We've been ready for months. The stalling came from the council, not technical challenges." Victoria lifted her hand to stave off his annoyed look. "That's the scuttlebutt at least. You know how that can be."

"Yes, very well." Jacks's eyes narrowed. "Rumors flow around this place like shit through a goose."

"Vulgar, but accurate," Victoria said. "I thought you had to be somewhere. Will you give me your authorization?"

"Alright, fine." Jacks shook his head. "But you're *prepping* for launch. Do *not* take that ship up until you have clearance. Is that perfectly understood? I've already got an operation under way and I don't need tower control distracted."

"Absolutely, sir." Victoria grinned in an effort to soften her message. "I'm sure this is the right call."

"I hope so." Jacks turned and strode off. "You'd better hurry, Commander. I might have orders for you to take her up with or without Miller after this meeting."

Victoria turned on her heels and hustled down the hallway, back to the massive hangar where the Leviathan slept in its steel confines, waiting to be unleashed. She once again had to navigate a myriad of people, still clogging the halls as they tried to find their respective focus groups.

Clicking on her communicator, she established a connection with Chief Engineer Carlos Delgado. He answered immediately. "Engineering."

"Serling here," Victoria replied. "I just got clearance to *prep* the ship. Are your people working?"

"Oh yeah," Carlos said. "Captain reached out to me a bit ago. We're running some tests on the engines and the artificial gravity modules right now. I'm sure we'll be done in the next twenty minutes and we can start the ignition process. How long before you come aboard? And what about the captain? Are we waiting for him?"

"We don't have launch clearance so we've got time to let him get here. I'm almost to the hangar now and will ensure the bridge staff has taken their posts. Hopefully, they can finish their preflight check in less than an hour but I won't hold my breath … unless you've already gone through some of the list?"

"*Some*," Carlos said. "Not as much as I'd have liked. Our part of this process will take longer than the bridge so the moment we heard about the object, we came aboard and started working. I had a feeling the council would order us up ASAP. Sounds like we're taking some initiative?"

"I talked Jacks into authorizing your activities." Victoria drew out her security card and scanned it to get through the door leading to the hangar bay. It slid shut the second she stepped through. "It didn't take much though. They're sending some of the smaller ships to check it out, those two test ships with guns, I think. Everyone's worried about what we're dealing with here."

"I am," Carlos admitted. "I don't mind saying it."

"Well, remain calm," Victoria said. "I'll see you in person in a couple minutes. Serling out." She rounded a corner and paused at the clear plastic wall that separated the hallway from the work area. Taking in the massive flagship, it never ceased to give her a sense of awe. Spanning just over twenty-three hundred feet long, it was the largest space vessel ever built by man.

Bristling with weapons and the most advanced technology humanity ever conceived, it was prepared for the perils of space, of visiting other worlds and discovering the secrets waiting for them out there. Victoria never dreamed those things would come to them first, that they would experience them at home.

Somehow, I feel naive about that. Whether they were dealing with something automated, an alien intelligence or something else entirely it felt like fate to encounter it so close to their own launch into the cosmos. They were months, perhaps weeks away from leaving Earth and yet, the unknown came to them.

I suppose it's convenient.

Victoria headed to the docking arm and ran her card twice more to get through to the ship proper. Utilitarian walls were covered with gray metal plating, hiding the various subsystems beneath. There was little in the way of decoration or aesthetic. The people who built the Leviathan were interested in making it work, not pretty.

She headed to the nearest elevator and took it down to the engineering section. Carlos and his team would be hard at work even without the promise of launching the ship in the next few hours. Guards were stationed at the door when she arrived and they offered her a salute which she returned on her way by.

The primary engineering section was a wide-open space with ladders and stairs leading up to catwalks covering five stories. Carlos stood on a ladder, discussing a component with a young man who crouched beside him. The chief engineer sported a nearly shaved head and what little hair he had was black flecked with gray.

He was only forty-one years old but he acted as if he topped sixty. As he finished his conversation, he came back down to the bottom level, barking orders to technicians on the other side of the room. He caught sight of Victoria and approached. "Hello, Commander. Welcome to controlled chaos or, as I prefer to call it, herding cats without incentive."

Victoria looked around. There were enough men rushing about that they nearly bumped into each other. She smirked. "Looks pretty relaxed to me. One would wonder if you guys never did this before."

"One would be right." Carlos ran his hand over his head. "I can tell you, it's pretty intense down here and this crew is getting nervous. Some think we're not ready to launch … which I personally don't understand. We've been checking and rechecking systems for a while now. But fear of change rules, I suppose."

"I guess so." Victoria clasped her hands behind her back. "How long to finish the preflight checks?"

"Our part will be done in an hour. You'll need to speak to Derringer about his part." Carlos was referring to Lieutenant Nicolas Derringer, the primary pilot of the Leviathan. He'd be on the bridge, working through his own set of challenges. "I'm not sure what his process is for launch."

Victoria smiled. "I'm aware. I'll head up there now. If you need anything, let me know right away. I want to be ready as soon as possible. When Captain Miller gets here—"

"Yeah, I know," Carlos interrupted. "He'll be pushing hard to get into space. And I'm with him. This situation's creepy. We need to be up there. If for no other reason than to gather more data on that thing. Close up scans would go a long way toward formulating a good idea of what it is."

"I'm glad we're on the same page." Victoria left his section and boarded the elevator, considering the next steps. The rest of the ships didn't require as much time to prepare for departure. Medical already had what they needed and the tech labs were just battened down computers.

Weapons, on the other hand, needed to be checked. She pulled out her tablet and made a note to ensure she got it on the list. When the elevator stopped and the doors opened, a rush of overlapping conversations assaulted her senses. At least fifteen people were crowding the bridge, a section that was meant for only five.

Panels were off the walls and technicians used wiring diagrams to check and recheck information. Nicolas was at the helm, speaking into his com while tapping away at the console. His black hair looked wet from whatever he used to slick it down. Of all the people around him, he seemed the most at ease, the most at home in the chaos.

Ensign Madeline Blanchard sat at the communications console, looking harried. Her blond hair was in a tight bun but her expression was one of frustration. "I've already explained, we're in a preflight check status. I can't authorize you to offload those terminals." She paused. "Because we're in lockdown! Does that seriously not make sense to you?"

"What's the problem, ensign?" Victoria asked.

Madeline looked up, her expression turning to one of relief. "Commander. I'm dealing with one of the tech lab leads. He's got a bunch of computer equipment that was supposed to be removed from the ship yesterday but it didn't get done. He wants it out of here now but the regulations state that during preflight check, we don't offload equipment."

"In this case, make an exception," Victoria said. "I doubt weight will be a factor but let's err on the side of caution. Tell him he has twenty minutes to get that stuff off the ship and I want a report of why it didn't get done yesterday. I already know the answer but if he's going to push us to be lenient, he can pay for it with some documentation."

"Yes, ma'am," Madeline replied, returning to her work.

Victoria approached Nicolas. "Lieutenant, would you mind telling me what all these people are doing on the bridge?"

Nicolas didn't look up from what he was doing as he replied. "Apparently, they were scheduled to secure the protective panels on the console over there. I told them to be quick about it. I'm not excited about a bunch of exposed wire and conduit. They said it wouldn't take very long."

Victoria raised her voice. "I want those panels installed in the next fifteen minutes and you off the bridge. If that's a problem, explain it right away. Otherwise, hurry up. We're in preflight check status." Once the technicians picked up the pace, she returned her attention to Nicolas. "There. Now, where are you at in the process?"

"So far, all systems are green," Nicolas said. "Power's solid. I've got control of thrusters. Engines are online but I'm still waiting for Carlos to say we can ignite. I'm not sure what all they have to do."

"I was just down there," Victoria replied. "We should be good within the hour. Madeline, check in with all other departments and make sure they're all properly staffed and that all crew is accounted for. If anyone is missing, we need to find out where they're at and how soon they'll be here." She sat in her chair, bringing her computer online.

Alright, Warren, where the hell are you now? I can get us going only so far but they'll never let us take this thing up there without you. Victoria sighed. *Your leave couldn't have come at a less opportune time.*

Chapter 2

Warren opened his eyes and immediately regretted it. Nausea gripped his stomach and his limbs ached with fatigue. Blurred vision slowly cleared, the ground coming into sharp focus. Steel-gray metal, like what they used for the Leviathan, was cool against his bare hands and as he pushed himself up, strong hands grabbed his arms.

He struggled away but one of them spoke, a man with a deep voice. "Whoa there, man. Relax." The guy stepped back and let him go. "It's cool. I think we're in this together." Warren looked up at him, a tall black guy with a bald head and muscular build. He was wearing army fatigues.

Others came up behind him, also in military uniforms. Each of them looked curious, afraid and nervous. Warren understood. They appeared to be in some kind of metal box, one that appeared sealed. The floor vibrated ever so slightly, a notion that was more sensed than felt. As he pushed to his feet, the big guy helped steady him.

Some remained in the back, a number of people in civilian clothes. None of them acknowledged him as he stood. One sat in the corner, rocking back and forth. Another paced, muttering to himself as he did so. Still another tried to make a call with their phone but it was clearly broken. A final person was lying down, possibly asleep.

"You've been out the longest."

"Who are you?" Warren asked.

"Name's Dexter Pollard," the black guy replied. "You can call me Dex. I'm a lieutenant in the marines. The others … well, we all haven't been properly introduced yet but you wanna start?"

"I'm Captain Warren Miller of the Space Agency. I was heading to our base when … this happened."

A blonde woman stepped forward. "I'm Lieutenant Debra Knight."

"Corporal Jake Terrence over here." He was a younger man, maybe twenty-one. He wore his brown hair shaved to stubble and looked exceptionally thin, as if he'd just gotten out of training. "Armor."

"Sergeant Gary Brennan." He stood at just over six feet with clear blue eyes and a black stain on his scalp that must've been the beginnings of hair after it was shaved recently. "I'm a marine with Dex. We're from the same base."

Dex gestured to the others. "The civilians over there haven't been very talkative. I woke them up and calmed them down but they're pretty messed up just now."

Warren nodded. "Now that we're all properly introduced, do any of you know what's going on? Are they going to be okay?"

"We've all been in this room," Dex said. "Abducted by those things. Since you're Agency, maybe you can tell us what's going on. As far as they're concerned." He looked at the civilians. "I figure we'll have them hang back. I don't even know their names. One of them said something about a bad car accident and his wife dying … it's rough."

"Yeah, enough about them." Gary stepped forward. "What're you got, Agency guy? Because I sure didn't buy that bullshit your Colonel was selling. You guys had to know about this in advance. There's no way you didn't. Not with all that money you got flying around. I want more information and I want the truth!"

Warren smirked. "I'm flattered you think I have all the answers. I don't have a clue what's going on right now. I thought I was dead, honestly. When I was on my way to the base, I was stuck in traffic. A shadow fell over me and everyone around me. We started running … people … they …" He paused, rubbing his eyes. "They disappeared. Vanished like … they were disintegrated."

"Exactly!" Dex pointed out. "That's what happened to me too! Hundreds of us!" He looked around. "But where the hell are all the rest? Why are we alone?"

"I don't know." Warren sighed. "The Agency kept the weird smaller space ships secret for as long as possible to avoid panic … and I guess they were right to. People freaked out big time. That was a terror run if ever I've been involved in one. But it was unnatural. Like, I've never been so frightened in my life. It didn't even make sense."

Debra grunted. "I'm glad you guys decided to hide that information. Maybe half the people who got taken wouldn't have been if you would've spoken up."

"So you wanted them going crazy?" Warren asked. "Rioting in the streets? Looting stores and taking to the roads, causing traffic jams and accidents? You guys know what people are like. In the face of a disaster, they lose their collective minds and we end up with all kinds of tragedy. It sucks that we have to keep things from people but that's just how it is."

"They could've stayed home!" Debra shouted. "In their houses, away from the streets!"
"Spare me your indignation and think about what's going on," Warren interrupted. "We have a predicament that goes way beyond what's happening on Earth. If I'm right, we're being taken back to that object right now and God knows what happens when we arrive."

"Notice something?" Gary said. "Everyone in this room … we're all military."

Jake snapped his fingers. "He's right! What's that all about? It must mean something."

Warren narrowed his eyes in thought. "I doubt it means much. Luck, more than anything. Processing? You know, when prisoners are divided up into specific groups. It's probably something like that. Where were you all going when this happened?"

Debra said, "I live in off base housing. I was on my way in to work my shift at the hospital. I'm a nurse."

"Me too," Jake added. "Er … the going to work part, not the nurse thing. I took a back way to avoid traffic."

"Same," Dex replied, "only I got caught in traffic. Hundreds of us got caught at once. Unless Gary was relaxing in bed, we can guess they didn't bother taking people straight out of their homes. Then again … probably would be irresponsible to jump to any conclusions."

"Interesting." Warren rubbed his chin. "I'd love to understand how they divided us up."

"I think a more important question," Dex said, "is where the hell we are right now?"

"Space," Warren replied. "Heading back to the mother ship. Congratulations. You're all officially astronauts. Though I'm guessing none of you are particularly excited about the prospect. Have any of you tried anything? Get through a panel? Look for a door?"

Dex nodded. "Yeah, I walked the room. The walls and floor are smooth. I didn't find any seams or gaps. However they got us in here is obscured. Not saying I'm an engineer or anything, but for now, I think we're trapped."

"Okay," Warren said. "Not the best news but better than if you would've figured something out and cast us all into space."

"You don't think they're going to probe us, do you?" Jake asked, drawing a withering glare from Gary. "What, man? You know what they say about aliens. They're always sticking things in people's asses."

"Always, huh?" Gary asked. "You make it sound like aliens are running a convenience store where folks show up to be tortured by them."

Jake shrugged. "I'm just sayin'. I know you've heard the stories. I sure as hell have and they're horrifying. I mean, creatures like these have no feelings. They're not like us at all. They lack um … that thing … it's like … eulogy? No … that's not it, but it's an 'e' word. Damn it!"

"Empathy?" Debra offered.

Jake nodded. "That's it! Yeah, they lack that!"

"Good to know." Dex turned to Warren. "What do you think, man? What should we do?"

"Well, our young friend might be exaggerating but the spirit of his concern is very real. We don't know what these things want or why they took us. I think it's safe to assume it was hostile and we should definitely prepare accordingly."

"How so?" Gary asked.

"I don't really want to find out the hard way that these things are intending to do something terrible to us." Warren looked around the room but it was simply a metal box. He had no idea which might be the way out. For all he knew, the floor might open up on their arrival and dump them. "I think we need to be ready to fight."

"We're unarmed," Debra said. "And we don't know what we're up against. How can you hope to stand up to something you've never even seen?"

Dex chuckled. "Lady, this is what we do. We've been killing threats we couldn't see for a hundred years."

"Those were *human*," Debra pointed out. "These, you don't have any idea! They might be physically tougher. I shouldn't have to be the one to explain it to you." She gestured to Warren. "The Agency must have studied the possibilities of extraterrestrial life. Surely, you understand the dangers of what you're proposing."

Warren nodded. "I certainly do and I can tell you with complete certainty that if we don't fight, if we don't at least try, we may lose the opportunity to do so. Whatever we encounter when one of these walls opens must be considered an enemy and we have to do anything we can to escape."

Gary raised his hand. "I've got a concern." Dex glared at him. "It's a serious one, LT. What if we succeed at fighting these things off? How do we get back home? Believe me, I'm all about kicking the shit out of some alien bastard that dragged me off of Earth but when we're done, we gotta leave. Right?"

"Yes, that's a problem," Warren said. "I'm not sure how we'll deal with that so we're going to be playing some of this by ear. What is it you boys talk about all the time? Improvising? Overcome? All that stuff?"

"We're in it," Dex said. "And we'll fight to the end. First order of business will be getting our hands on some weapons. Bare hands might get us out of this mess but if we want to keep going, we'll need something harder. Even a pipe would do well."

"Okay." Warren hummed, looking around the room again. "I think we'll know when this thing stops. Do you feel the vibration on the floor? Once that ends, we'll get ready. They could come from any side, even the top. Be prepared for that. Debra, stay out of our way. The rest of you, fight like your lives depend on it. Believe me … it does."

"I attended combat training," Debra said. "I can help."

Warren nodded. "I apologize for the assumption. I thought you were objecting to the plan."

"I did," Debra replied. "But that didn't mean I couldn't participate. I don't want to be here anymore than you guys do. I'll help the team, if that's what you've decided. We're in this together, right?"

"Indeed." Warren frowned. "Does anyone know how long we've been traveling?"

"Thirty minutes," Jake said, "give or take."

"Okay, depending on how fast their propulsion is, we may have another hour or so before we arrive at the larger object. I recommend you take this opportunity to get some rest." Warren sat down and leaned against the wall. "Focus on the vibration. If you feel it stop, let us all know right away."

"Are you people talking about violence?" The civilian with the phone stepped forward, looking desperate. His thin hair was sticking up, sprouting on his head like weeds. He wore a suit that was disheveled, the tie askew. "Because this sounds crazy! What's even happening to us? Why were we taken? What's going on?"

"Settle down," Warren said. "We're doing the best we can. Trust me, we'll do everything in our power to keep you safe and get you home. But right now, you just need to sit down and remain calm. Okay?"

The man muttered something about the situation being unbelievable and stormed away. Dex shrugged and took up his own position, leaving Warren alone. He slid down the wall and stared out ahead of him, thinking of what might be happening on Earth. *I hope you're prepping the ship, Serling. You might have to launch without me.*

***

"This is Dirk Reidel coming back to you with some updated information about the strange object currently orbiting our planet." They'd been looping the information for almost an hour when someone finally brought him something new. Viewers had to be tired of listening to him reiterate the same stuff over and over.

Dirk quickly read over the page and his eyes widened involuntarily, a major faux pas for a newscaster. He cleared his throat and looked up into the camera, adopting his practiced, neutral expression. "We have eye witness reports and video footage of smaller objects entering Earth's atmosphere. Furthermore, it seems the Agency has interacted with the object as well. Please have a look."

He turned to the monitor to see them for himself, squinting to take in the round objects casually floating not even three hundred yards above the ground. "Sources state they measure seven-hundred square feet and are moving at approximately one hundred miles an hour. Dozens appeared over the United States with others in Europe, Australia, Russia and the Middle East."

One of the interns tossed another sheet on his desk and he quickly read the information. "Oh my. We have many reports that state they saw the objects cast beams over vehicles and people on the streets. This might ... I don't want to jump to any conclusions, but they are either taking people somehow or ... or killing them."

It sounds a lot like alien abduction to me, He thought. *Jesus Christ, I've stumbled into a conspiracy theory.*

Dirk was handed more information, showing him additional incidents of the objects casting their beams upon populated areas. No place seemed to be safe and he needed to tell it without breaking down emotionally. Drawing a deep breath, he cleared his throat and spoke. "We have reports of these objects firing this beam on people all over the world, in just about every major city."

He paused, then added, "our thoughts and prayers go out to the families of those impacted and we hope we discover their fates soon enough. Authorities are hard at work, attempting to get to the bottom of these incidents. I am certain there will be a military response to these and we will let you know what they are going to do as soon as we are informed."

That shouldn't get me in too much trouble. Melvin, his producer, didn't look particularly angry so he was either beaten down by the situation or didn't care. Either way, Dirk added another thirty seconds of material to his overall story. He wondered how much mileage they would get out of it before they needed something else.

But alien abduction probably went a long way. If people were even watching anymore, all things considered.

***

Colonel Jacks stepped into the council meeting, fully prepared for them to go at him with both barrels. He anticipated them being in an agitated state as they were pressured by their respective governments for answers. The questions tossed at them would be obvious and the inference they hadn't done enough just as likely.

Just a moment before the politicians arrived, Doctor Meyers moved close and whispered, "did they get a hold of you? I told them to contact you right away to tell you what happened with the Demeter."

"I heard there was a malfunction," Jacks replied. "That the results were inconclusive and that we've got some smaller objects descending on the Earth."

Meyers laughed, but it was clear he was not amused. "Unbelievable. I don't know how they got *that* message. No. That's not it at all. The object *shot* our ships just as the smaller units were leaving. We attacked but it was ineffective. The alien craft has some sort of shield. My people are analyzing it right now ... to the best of our ability."

"There've been hostilities?" Jacks sighed. "That's going to change matters."

"It gets worse. I can't believe they didn't tell you." Meyers rubbed his eyes. "Those smaller objects have either captured or killed people. Most of them are on their way back."

"How many?" Jacks asked.

"We don't know yet. They haven't been tallied."

"Shit." Jacks didn't know what to say. "Okay, thank you, Meyers. We'll figure out why my report was lacking later. Right now, get ready to answer some questions.

Ted Grandy stepped into the light before Meyers even got back to his podium. Grandy was the US representative and a longtime supporter of the Agency, one of the men who pushed for the budget they needed. He proved to be a staunch ally but just then, his expression suggested a lack of patience Jacks hadn't seen before.

"Colonel," Ted began, "it seems we have quite a few problems. Let's start with a quick break down. How long have you known about the object? When did we detect it?"

"Our research buoy picked it up when it entered the solar system near Saturn," Jacks said. "From there, it moved swiftly into its current position. Our people didn't have time to wake me up before it arrived. Since then, we've been studying it from afar with the scanning equipment at our disposal though I have something to report about contact as well.

"We know that it's constructed from an unknown metal type and that it is not naturally occurring. Unfortunately, the list of what we *don't* know dramatically outweighs what we do. The smaller objects are essentially miniature versions of the big one. We're assuming they are designed for entering atmosphere."

"Is that because," Jean Aguillard, the French member, spoke up, "the larger object would cause massive destruction if it tried to enter atmosphere?"

"Yes, sir," Jacks replied. "It's big. We've measured it at just shy of forty-kilometers around. Yes, it would cause a lot of damage if it came down on us but this isn't a world killer by any stretch of the imagination. An asteroid large enough to annihilate the planet would have to be nearly a hundred kilometers."

"When will you know more?" Ted asked. "We have a lot of people to answer to and I'm sure you're not going to be able to give us the details we want right now. I need to give them a time frame and a plan of action."

"That's … something we should discuss." Jack rubbed the back of his neck. "We have made contact with the object with our experimental attack vessels, Demeter One and Demeter Two. They … appear to have been attacked."

This brought gasps from the council.

"Yes, we're attempting to verify the status of the crew. The object itself did not advance or move after the engagement. Now, we are prepping the Leviathan for launch. If this thing becomes hostile, we'll need a lot more firepower in position. And if we decide to attack." Jacks shrugged. "We'll be ready to do so."

"Yes, I have heard this," Jean said. "People all over the world supposedly though the reports are not substantiated yet. Is the ship ready? We were waiting for the opportune time to launch and I believe we have found it."

"Yes, it's been ready," Jacks replied. "We've held off to make a political statement, to show off what we've accomplished with all the money we've spent. I can't think of a better testament to our success than defending the Earth against a potential threat. What about you?"

"I agree," Ted said. "I'm in favor of letting the Leviathan launch when ready. Is Captain Miller prepared?"

Jacks paused. "Captain Miller is on his way back to base and we expect him soon. His first officer, Commander Serling, is preparing the ship as we speak."

The council began muttering amongst themselves. Ted spoke up. "We'd be more comfortable with the captain at the helm."

Jacks nodded. "I agree. But we may not have that option if we want to get the jump on this situation. I assure you, the crew of the Leviathan has been training hard together. Commander Serling is an excellent military officer with an impeccable record. I don't have any cause to think she would be unable to handle this."

"Of course," Ted said. "Still, I would like to ensure you give the captain just a little more time to arrive. You have authorization to launch immediately upon his arrival."

Jacks sighed internally but he kept his face carefully neutral. There was no reason to argue. These men put their faith in Miller a long time ago and he'd been assuring them of his success personally over the past six months. At least they did have the sense to suggest only a little more time. Anything else, and that would've caused an argument.

"May I say," Jacks spoke carefully, trying to clarify, "that if he doesn't arrive soon, we should launch anyway?"

"Yes," Ted replied. "Don't hold out too long. I believe preparation takes a while anyway, does it not?"

Jacks smiled and nodded. "Indeed."

"There you have it. We've got a built-in delay." Ted turned to a pile of paper. "I'd like to go over some of the finer details about what your people have discovered with Doctor Meyers if you can spare him for a while."

Alexander Meyers had been on the project since day one. He started his career as a young NASA genius who rose through the ranks with some solid theories and excellent research. When the Agency came about, he was the top candidate to lead the technical side of the house.

Since then, he'd gone almost completely gray but maintained a youthful look about the face. The contrast made it hard to place his age but the file said forty-eight. He tended to be a good politician but it was always obvious he didn't enjoy it. His world lived in a lab. Even with the possibility of heading into space, he made it quite clear he never intended to board a ship.

"Yes." Jacks gestured to Alex. "He'll take over for me for a few moments while I step out of the room. Thank you." He left the room and established a com connection to the Leviathan bridge.

"Serling here."

Jacks frowned. "I thought you had a com officer on there."

"I've got your signal routed directly to me," Victoria replied. "What news do you have?"

"The council just talked to me about the launch. You've got permission to prep but they want Miller on board before you leave."

"I do too," Victoria said, "but it might not be practical to wait. Did you tell them that?"

"I did and they agreed. They still want us to delay a bit to see if he shows up. Can you try to reach him? I need to get back into this meeting and help Doctor Meyers before he's eaten alive."

"Yes, we'll do what we can to find him." Victoria paused. "Thank you. I know they were probably rough."

"It's my job," Jacks said. "But they haven't even started yet. I'll talk to you when this meeting's over." He clicked off the com and went back into the room, steeling himself for the rest of the interrogation. As he expected, they were drilling the doctor with a myriad of semi-informed questions that he would have a hard time answering.

"Begging your pardon," Jacks interrupted. "There's something we should focus on before we get too deep in the weeds. We've issued only one statement to the public so far and I know for a fact the media will be seeking information anywhere they can get it. I'd like to make sure the press is doling out what we want, rather than what a conspiracy nut can regurgitate. Especially with what happened."

"What do you propose?" Ted asked.

"First off, we need to talk about a response to those objects and what they did to our people."

"Yes," Doctor Meyers said, lifting his hand. "They have already left and returning to orbit. Several fighter planes attempted to engage but couldn't keep up as they departed. Even the US interceptors weren't able to scramble and get to them before they were on their way back up."

"We definitely need to get a head of this," Jacks said. "You know how the media is and worse, the general population. With those things flying around either killing or kidnapping people, we need to find a way to assure them … to prevent the inevitable riots and other carnage that goes along with this type of thing."

"Now is certainly the time," Jean said, "to reveal our warship. Show the people we were prepared but that this happened far quicker than we could've anticipated."

Jacks smiled grimly. "My thoughts exactly."

"Give us a moment," Ted said. The council left the room, returning to their little conference area where they could have some privacy.

"I hope we can spin this well." Jacks rubbed his eyes. "The news outlets are going to crucify us."

"Not when we launch the Leviathan and save the world," Alex pointed out. "That's why we built a battleship, right? To fend off an invading force."

"We don't even know if our weapons will penetrate the metal," Jacks replied, "or those shields you talked about. I wouldn't get too excited about attacking them. We might be in for a real shit storm. And nothing quite backfires like failing to deliver on a promise to the entire world. I want to talk about the Leviathan, give them some hope but I won't tell them we're going to destroy anything."

"Probably wise." Alex looked at his tablet. "The larger object would take quite the force to knock out. Perhaps an internal explosion could do it but I need more data about what's inside. Right now, the exterior is blocking all our scans. We'll run some simulations against our current offensive capabilities to see what the chances are of getting through."

"Perfect." Jacks looked up as the door opened. "Oh boy. Here they come."

Ted returned alone. "I've spoken to the others. Get with the communications team and make sure we word our statement well. You have authorization to go public with something in the next hour but make it quick. Talk about the Leviathan but don't make any promises." Jacks smirked at Alex. "We'll reconvene for the rest of our questions in four hours."

"Thank you," Alex said. "That should give my team a chance to compile some answers to the questions you posed."

Ted nodded. "We'll send them over to you. Thank you, gentlemen. Good luck." He left them alone.

Jacks let out a sigh of relief. "That's good news for us. Do you need anything from me before I start preparing this statement?"

Alex shook his head. "No, I'll be in the main lab if you need me. Good luck talking to all those people. I don't envy you one bit."

"Believe me," Jacks opened the door and let Alex go first. "Of the two of us, you have the harder job. You have to make sense of all this. All I have to do is respond to questions and make sure our ship is in the air. Seems pretty easy by comparison, don't you think?"

"Believe me," Alex said, "science is easier than talking to people. I've spent my whole life proving that fact. Talk to you later, Colonel."

***

Victoria leaned forward, peering at the floor as she considered Warren's location. During the secure call, he claimed to be on his way but he also mentioned some pretty heavy traffic. The civilian population already started flooding the streets, fleeing their homes for the promise of someplace safer. Where, she had no idea.

"Ensign," Victoria turned to Madeline, "reach out to the main gate and see if Captain Miller has arrived. If they say he has not, then try his satellite phone. We need to locate him ASAP."

"Yes, ma'am." Madeline began speaking quietly into her microphone.

Victoria considered how they'd go about a search if something happened. During such an event, the roads likely became hazardous. Other drivers could've caused delays with accidents. Worst case scenarios played through her head, not to mention the news about the smaller objects flying around shooting strange beams at crowds.

If Warren ended up dead on the side of the road, it'll be quite a blow. Victoria scowled. *What an unfair way to go for a man on the verge of making history. I refuse to believe such a thing is possible. He must be out there. Whatever has prevented him from arriving will be a monumental obstacle. It could even be the aliens themselves.*

Victoria turned to one of the monitors. It was tuned into the news network, showing some amateur film footage of the incident involving the alien attack. Beams burst from the small vessels, spreading over the cars and people. Interference made it hard to see but when the lights faded, people were definitely gone.

Dead or taken? God, that's the question.

Madeline interrupted her thoughts. "The main gate has not seen Captain Miller. They state all traffic in and out of the base has been limited and no one has been admitted for over an hour. Also, I received no answer on the satellite phone. It's still ringing right now."

Damn it. Victoria stood up. "Nicolas, give me your assessment. What do you think's going on and what would you suggest?"

"Something had to happen." Nicolas turned in his seat. "It might sound like a fool's errand but I think we need to conduct a search. Get a chopper up to find his car. If that satellite phone is on, we can trace it. Maybe he's hurt"

"I agree." Victoria stepped over to Madeline, leaning on the console. "Put base command on the line for me. Establish a connection to Tiffany Banks."

Madeline complied, tapping at the console and speaking to the attendant on the other end. "This is the Leviathan, we need to speak with Major Tiffany Banks right away." She turned to Victoria. "They put us on hold for a moment."

Victoria rolled her eyes but nodded. Everyone was busy, so it shouldn't have come as a big surprise. She'd encountered Tiffany in the army though only at social functions. The woman rose through the ranks and proved to be a tough marine before joining the Agency. As base command, she headed up security.

If they hoped to search via the air, Tiffany would provide the authorization. Otherwise, they would have to gain authorization to send one of the shuttles inside the Leviathan. Technically, they would require authorization from Banks as well, at least until they left. Once the Leviathan took orbit, authority fell to the commanding officer aboard. For a little while longer, they were beholden to base control.

But Victoria wasn't sure she'd let that stop her if the conversation didn't go as she hoped.

"This is Banks." Tiffany's voice burst through the speakers. "What's going on?"

"Hi Tiffany," Victoria said, "Serling here. We're short one commanding officer and I was hoping you could do a solid by helping the search efforts."

"How so?"

"He should've been here twenty minutes ago," Victoria replied. "We know what happened out there to civilians and the like, but we'd like to send a chopper to check it out. Can you deploy someone? Sooner the better. Launch is delayed until he's on board. He had a sat phone you should be able to track the signal from."

"You know we're a little busy, right?" Tiffany asked. "We're monitoring com traffic from various bases and we have a lot of missing soldiers coming up, not just here. Our people are all tapped out keeping the base secure and finishing our duties. I'm sure you understand, there are a lot of requests coming through hot and heavy."

"And while I respect that," Victoria replied, fighting to maintain her patience, "we take priority. The council would like us to intercept the object that just attacked our people and we can't exactly do that without Captain Miller, at least not until we've proven he isn't coming. So if I have to come down there and take the chopper myself, I will but I'm pretty sure you've got some people who can do it faster."

"I ... will make it happen." Tiffany replied. "Sorry, we're under a lot of stress down here."

"I totally get it," Victoria said. "How soon can you launch?"

"I'll have the bird up in less than ten minutes." Tiffany paused. "Don't ask me to hurry, that's the best I can do."

"Thank you, Tiffany. Have the pilot contact me when they take off so we can help them find the phone signal. Serling out."

Madeline killed the connection, her eyes wide.

"That was pleasant," Nicolas said. "Must be hell down there."

"Very likely," Victoria replied. "At least we're getting what we need. Keep a tight eye on the scans, Madeline. I want to know the moment that helicopter takes off. If you don't see it leave in ten minutes, get her back on the line and I'll deal with it."

"Yes, ma'am." Madeline went back to her duties.

"How's the preflight checking coming?" Victoria asked.

Nicolas looked back at his console. "Engineering says they're roughly ten minutes away from igniting the engines. Otherwise, everything else is done. If we had the captain, we'd start a countdown, I think."

"Hm." Victoria leaned on the arm of her chair, contemplating their options. Part of her thought they should begin the launch countdown. It might even push Tiffany to do her job faster. Would Jacks be annoyed if she didn't tell him first? It didn't matter. She needed to take the initiative. "Let's start a thirty-minute countdown for launch."

"And I'll inform control?" Nicolas asked. "They've got a lot to do on their end."

Victoria nodded. "Inform them right away. Patch any communications from Colonel Jacks straight to me. Be prepared to push the countdown out though. I've got a feeling we're about to raise some pulses in control and God knows they'll be shouting directly at our boss long before they bother us."

Chapter 3

Warren stared into space. One side of him hoped the Agency were preparing for launch and planned on getting the Leviathan up as soon as possible. Everyone had to know what the smaller objects were doing, scooping people up from all over the place. He didn't know how many they took but it must've been thousand. Probably a lot more.

If Jacks and Serling weren't moving, then the people taken might be in for a death sentence when they arrived at the larger object. Of course, if they attacked, how would the captives escape? Warren needed to find a way to get them out of there. He had faith in his new companions but it may have been misguided.

After all, when whatever wall opened up, they had no idea what they would be dealing with. If they encountered things wearing some sort of armored suits, they'd be in a lot of trouble. Furthermore, these aliens might be carrying weapons. Warren doubted their captors invited them to their vessel for tea and conversation.

Unless we *are the tea*.

"The vibration!" Dex's voice startled Warren out of his thoughts. "It's slowed down."

"Excellent." Warren climbed to his feet. "Okay, we have no idea how this will play out. I wish I could offer a better plan. Know that I'm confident we can do what we're about to do. However, if there are dozens of them or it looks like we are in way over our heads, do not engage. We can't escape if we're dead. You get me?"

"We do." Dex spoke for them all but it brought a round of nods. Debra didn't look quite as sure but she moved to the corner, lowering her center of gravity. Each of them poised for action. Something hissed on the other side of the wall to Warren's left. He directed his attention there, wondering if he happened to be standing beside the door.

"This is insane!" The guy with the suit said. "These militant assholes are going to get us killed!"

"Calm down." The guy who was rocking himself spoke up. "They're doing their job. Just sit back and pray, okay? That's what we've got. You aren't going out there."

"They're going to get us killed!"

"Shut up!" Dex rasped. "And get down for God's sake!"

Gary moved to the opposite side of the room, meeting Warren's eyes for a moment just as the wall began to shake. It began to slide down, a slow descent that was little more than a quiet brush of metal on metal. Cool air filtered into the room and it smelled vaguely sweet, like some kind of berry or candy.

Dex crept closer, dropping low to the ground like a football player waiting for the snap. The muscles in his arms pressed at his dark skin, making his tee shirt bulge and his neck look twice as thick. The whites of his eyes were huge as he stared at the door, giving him a frightful look all around. Marines called it their death face.

Warren balled his fists. Tension built in the room. Curiosity and nerves battled for dominance even as adrenaline made his limbs shake. He became a horse, ready for the run, wondering why the gate hadn't opened so he could dash onto the track. The wall reached the half way point, enough that he could see outside.

A twenty by twenty antechamber connected to their object with a more obvious door on the other side. Two humanoid figures stood before the door, each wearing black shiny suits and round, opaque helmets. Both held what looked like pistols in their right hands though they kept them aimed at the floor.

Even as the wall came down, they seemed to be looking at one another, gesturing as if in some kind of conversation. They weren't paying attention to the room they were about to enter. Some part of it caught Warren as comical. What could possibly have taken their attention away from their captives?

I doubt we're going to find out, Warren thought. *God knows how these things communicate.*

Dex and Gary sprung from their positions, throwing themselves at the aliens. They connected with their targets, taking them to the ground in an instant. The helmets made a metallic clang as they bounced off the floor but as the marines began to pummel their targets in the bodies, the familiar thump of fist to flesh echoed off the walls.

A third alien came from around the corner, stepping back when it caught sight of the marines pummeling its friends. It started to lift its weapon when Warren lashed out, throwing a kick that connected with the thing's wrist. The pistol buzzed as a blue light burst from the tip. The blast splashed against the ceiling, leaving a black mark on the metal.

The weapon sailed through the air and slid across the ground just as Warren followed up with a punch to the chest.

His opponent stumbled backward against the wall, bouncing off. It tried to retaliate, throwing a wild haymaker that Warren ducked. The captain fell back, dodging another punch aimed at his face. A third attack he blocked and followed up with a blow to the alien's gut. A huff within the helmet showed it at least felt pain but it fell back, arms raised defensively.

Warren tested his opponent's defenses, tossing a couple jabs. The alien blocked the first two then dodged backward, hurling a kick that connected with Warren's upper thigh. He moved with the blow, absorbing the impact.

"Let's go!" The shout came from the suit guy as he and the other civilians darted out the door, even the one who tried to calm him down earlier. Warren started to shout after them but they were really moving, sprinting into the hallway and beyond.

Warren started to shout after them but the alien used the distraction to rush forward, slamming his shoulder into Warren's gut. It lifted him an inch off the ground before they both hit the floor. The helmet clattered against the metal before the thing came up, drawing its fist back. Warren deflected the first attack, took the second to the cheek then bucked his attacker off.

They crawled back to their feet. The alien swayed. Warren took advantage of the momentary weakness, kicking the thing between the legs. It did the trick. It bent at the waist, an instinctive motion before its head jerked to the left.

Warren followed its gaze to one of the discarded weapons. The alien dove for it. Warren tried to catch him but narrowly missed grabbing him.

Debra got their first, picking the gun up and pointing it down at the approaching alien. Dex and Gary approached and grabbed the thing's feet, dragging it backward away from her. It scratched at the floor but the marines moved it with ease, bringing it back toward the room they were stuck in moments before.

"What now?" Dex asked. "Those two are done."

Warren collected one of their weapons and examined it. It looked a lot like one of their own pistols only with rounded edges and a point instead of a barrel. He aimed it away and pulled the trigger. The weapon vibrated subtly in his hand, releasing a blue beam of light that once again stained the wall black.

Simple enough. Warren turned to the others. "Let's see what we're up against."

Jake crouched over one of the unconscious bodies, examining the helmet. "I'm not sure how to get this thing off. I don't see any latches or levers. No buttons … it's smooth all around as far as I can tell." He looked up at them. "Maybe it can only be removed from the inside. That would be a smart safety feature, don't you think?"

Warren nodded. "It would." He turned to the conscious one. "Try to pull it off that one. And we have to make this quick. They might have communications in those helmets and that would mean they've requested reinforcements."

Dex grabbed it from behind, hoisting it up to its knees. Gary approached from the front, pressing his knee into the alien's chest. He grabbed the helmet and pulled on it, straining until his whole body seemed to tremble and he finally gave up, stumbling off. "That thing's really on there good. There's no prying it off with bare hands."

"Okay." Warren stepped in front of the alien and aimed his weapon at its head. It immediately started to struggle, wiggling its hands and gesturing to the helmet. "Let up on it, Dex."

Dex complied though his expression suggested he did so reluctantly. The alien gripped both sides of the helmet, twisted to the left and took it off. A perfectly human face looked up at Warren with brown eyes and dark hair, pale skin and regular lips. It was definitely male and could've been from Ohio. Though, upon closer inspection, there were minor differences.

The eyes were a bit too angular, the ears a touch pointed, the pigment of the skin too light. Tiny as those distinctions may have been, Warren caught them now as if they were obvious and slapping him in the face. The alien's jaw was pointy, his hair too silky. They might've looked similar but they were not the same.

"What the hell?" Jake muttered. "Are you kidding? How is this possible?"

"Your world isn't unique, human." The alien's voice made Warren jump. He spoke English without an accent. "Nor is the evolution of your species."

"You'll see the difference," Warren said. "Just give yourself a moment."

"I don't care about how they look," Dex said. "How do you know our language?"

"We studied it long before we came here. In order to interpret your words and understand the best method of interacting with your kind." It looked between them all. "We miscalculated a few things."

"Like what?" Warren asked. "Our natural inclination to live?"

"Your endurance. None of you should've been awake when that door opened."

"Sorry to disappoint." Warren crouched in front of him. "Why did you come to Earth? What were you going to do with us?"

"I'm just a technician," the alien replied. "I don't have that information. My colleagues and I collect those things we recover. That's it."

"That's it, huh?" Warren scowled, examining the creature's face for any signs of lying. If the thing had pantomimes, they weren't obvious. "How many others are there like us? How many of you are there on this thing? And how the hell do we get out of here?"

Sounds from the other side of the door attracted Warren's attention. Dex cursed. "Sounds like the reinforcements you were worrying about."

"Did you call them?" Warren asked the alien.

"Of course I did. You should simply surrender. It will go much easier on you."

"Not going to happen." Warren cracked the thing on the head, knocking it unconscious. "Grab some guns, gentlemen."

"What about the civilians?" Debra asked. "They ran for it."

"I know," Warren replied, "and I'm not going to risk any of us running after them blindly. We're going to have ourselves a little brawl but it'll be on our terms, not chasing after maniacs. Hopefully, they make it okay and we catch up to them. However, until we have our bearings, we need to be cautious. Those that aren't armed, stay behind us and to the sides."

Dex added, "if you see an opportunity to grab a weapon, do so and jump in."

"He's right," Warren said. "We need numbers if we want to get out of here. Remain calm and alive. We'll try to save those guys as we can but right now, rule one is survival. Let's get to it."

***

Dirk Reidel went upstairs to the roof, peeking around the door before stepping into the light. He drew a deep breath while casting a wary gaze about the area, scanning the sky for any more of the small objects. They knew they were on their way back to space but there could still be stragglers out there, looking for lone people to steal.

Nothing appeared on the horizon as far as the eye could see. Oddly enough, one of the smaller objects did pass by seven blocks away but the power remained on in that district. That was inconsistent with what they knew of the aliens so far, of how they attacked the planet. Most of the areas they visited, they killed the lights.

Perhaps those areas they missed had their generators situated in a way not so easy to tamper with.

He moved to the edge and gazed down on the roof across from his. The door burst open and a woman ran out onto the roof, sprinting toward the edge. Dirk's eyes widened and he shouted for her to be careful just as a couple men came out after her. They moved swiftly, legs pumping as they kicked up gravel on the roof.

She turned and tried to fend them off but she'd already reached the edge. One of the men grabbed her but she threw herself backwards. Toppling over the side, her attacker went with her and they plunged down to the street below. Dirk looked away before they hit the ground and when he looked up, the other man was running back toward the door.

What the hell did I just witness? Thoroughly shaken, he went back inside where an intern grabbed him by the arm.

"You're needed back on the set right away!"

"I'm … I'll be there." Dirk followed the young man in a daze and when he arrived, he could barely read the paper on his desk. He felt like he should tell someone what he saw, to relate the horror but there was nothing anyone could do. Instead, he tried to collect himself and merely looked into the camera. It comforted him, even as he had to swallow hard past the bile rising in his throat.

"We're back from our short break, providing you with live coverage of the event happening over our planet at this very moment." Dirk didn't recognize his calm voice, the smooth demeanor allowing him to work through what he'd just witnessed. He downed a glass of water while the various networks offered some local news.

The recorded information played again, explaining the arrival of the large object and the discovery of the smaller ones. He watched the screen to his right with the sort of earnest expression he learned in school, the one that said he was absolutely enthralled. An intern dropped a page on his desk, distracting him.

Glancing down, he his eyes widened. *The Agency wants to offer another statement. They'll be ready in a few minutes. Read below to the camera to prepare the audience.*

Before Dirk could act on it, breaking news appeared on the screen from South Africa. Their military caught up to one of the objects and were about to engage. An insane media helicopter risked their lives to gather the footage, showing the battle as it unfolded, an attempt by humanity to deal with the threat before it escaped into space.

Two fighter planes blurred by, banking hard toward the object. Another two came at it from another angle. Streams erupted from rockets as they hurtled toward the alien craft. Their explosions burst into orange and gold flames, smoke rising from a strange green aura that appeared around the sphere.

Planes flipped about, seeming to setup for a second attack run. Some kind of energy beam shot from the alien, dead center. It connected with one of the air planes, obliterating the tail. Dirk winced as the pilot ejected, the remains of his vehicle tumbling to the ground below.

The others fired again, more missiles barreling toward their target. This time, the beam shot down two of the incoming rockets before blasting another airplane. A straight shot to the nose obliterated the entire craft, likely killing the pilot instantly.

The others attempted to disengage, two fighters flying off. The object seemed to ignore them, climbing steadily toward orbit

Dirk cleared his throat as the feed went silent. "Ladies and gentlemen, I'm sure I echo your thoughts when I say that was a terrible thing to behold. I'm sorry to interrupt that tragic event but I've just received word that the Space Agency would like to provide another update. This press conference will begin momentarily. Thank you."

He pursed his lips and finished off with, "later, we'll have astrologer Ruben Lydell on the show to discuss these events and what they could mean for Earth."

"It's *astronomer*." A voice whispered harshly from off camera.

"Forgive that mistake," Dirk said. "Astronomer Ruben Lydell in one hour. Please stay tuned for the press conference. We're cutting back to the summary." When the camera pulled away from him, he glared at the person who whispered to him. They shrugged and got back to work.

More news hit Dirk's desk, the kind he dreaded having to impart. "We're receiving reports of rioting all over the world. Extremist groups are claiming we have reached the end times. Another suggested we are on the verge of some type of ascension and these beings have arrived to show us the way.

"Please stay in your homes. The authorities are urgently pressing people to remain calm." Dirk struggled not to tremble. He understood the concern. After seeing the attack on the object, and the military failure to bring the thing down, he knew it would only compound the fear coursing through every single person out there.

They cut to other footage.

The course of the human race, of every single life, had been dramatically altered for all time. The possibility of aliens always existed. The advent of the Space Agency partially was meant to prove out an alien encounter. Many countries were willing to dump stupendous amounts of money into projects to explore the galaxy.

Fate had a funny way of stepping up the time table. Humanity planned on plunging into the unknown but before they could even pull back the curtain, the unknown arrived on their doorstep. As the scientists of the Agency worked to unravel the mystery of these objects, the rest of the world held their breath and wondered how much will this affect me? Then the attacks happened and they knew.

Most people likely underestimated the impact of discovering alien life. Sure, they knew things would change but so many conventions stood to be tested. The notion of divinity, of God and mythology, may well be thought of differently by these newcomers. They might even have proof, one way or another, of the existence of the Almighty.

Science might've been turned on its ear. What sort of technology did it take to get across the cosmos? How did they do it? Were these beings like humans or did they have some other form entirely? Hopefully, the Agency planned on answering some of those questions in their press conference but no one cared about such high-minded ideals just then.

People wanted to know if they were safe and if the worse was over.

Dirk knew there were other profound notions which would fall under scrutiny but he wasn't clever enough to come up with them. Needless to say, much would be unraveled in the days to come. If they could find diplomacy, somehow get in contact with the beings to discuss what they had done, everyone might eventually benefit from their arrival.

"Pst!" An intern caught Dirk's attention and he looked over at them. "The conference is starting in twenty seconds! Announce it quick!"

"Ladies and gentlemen," Dirk spoke as he turned to the camera. "I've just been informed that the press conference with the Space Agency is about to begin. Let's see what they have discovered."

The screen to his right cut to the podium where Wyman Jacks once again took the stage. The colonel looked tired but resolute. As he set down several pieces of paper, he cleared his throat and turned his attention to the crowd.

"Thank you all for your patience as we've worked on this mystery," Jacks said. "As you know, several smaller objects descended from the larger one, entering Earth's atmosphere and seemingly, they attacked us. At this time, the majority have already broken orbit and are returning to what we've labeled *the mothership*. Some of them have already arrived.

"We've all seen the damage they've caused and know they may well have killed many people. Scientists at first thought it might've been a recon mission. They were wrong. Many military units around the world responded to this attack with varying degrees of failure. What I mean by that is that some lost their pilots and some did not."

"Our first response to the mothership was not successful but those were prototype vessels that were merely to test the first iteration of our weapons. We have a far more profound response on the verge of launching. For the past several years, we have been building a flagship for our young fleet. This vessel, named *Leviathan*, is a fully armed battlecruiser, capable of sustaining human life for months at a time.

"We wanted to use this vessel to explore the galaxy, to defend ourselves should the need arise. It has. We wanted to make contact, we wanted to talk but it is quite clear that these visitors had another plan entirely. This does not mean we will rule out discussion should they reach out. Especially if they have not killed our people, we will negotiate to find a peaceful resolution.

"However, this is considered a dire situation. They were the aggressors. We are prepared and will meet them with every ounce of might we possess."

"Colonel Jacks!" One of the reporters shouted. "Reports around the world show our weapons are not harming the objects and your own attempt proved fruitless. Do you know whether your battlecruiser's weapons can even harm this thing?"

"We are hoping to gather some better scan data shortly," Jacks replied. "We'll then be able to determine that but we may not have time. The goal is to confront it before it has a chance to leave."

"Can you comment on the missing people? Do you have any idea what might have happened to them?"

"No, we are still working through the data to determine what those beams did. Were they harmful or something else? That's what we're working on."

A woman shouted his name twice before being called on. "Can you confirm that your own Captain Warren Miller is missing?"

"I cannot." Jacks stepped back from the podium. "No further questions."

The room erupted as the colonel left the room and Dirk took back over. "There you have it, folks. The Agency has divulged the existence of a battlecruiser of human design which they intend to field soon. I hope this means they have a plan to save those people, if indeed they can be saved. We will keep you informed of any other developments as they present themselves."

***

Jacks closed the door behind him, seething about the last question. The Agency managed to keep things quiet for years without hardly any leaks. Something getting out in the middle of a real event grated on his nerves. Who in the organization would possibly have spoken about Miller? Why would they have even brought him up? He didn't say who commanded the Leviathan.

He stepped into the conference room where technicians and administrative staff alike chatted loudly. His presence silenced them all. Jacks closed the door behind him and leaned against it, turning a glare to each of them in turn. When he finally spoke, he kept his voice low so he wouldn't shout.

"Someone gave information to the press," Jacks said. "They asked about Captain Miller and whether or not he was missing. I want to know who. I'm *guessing* they're working in the command center but they could be on the Leviathan, I suppose. Root them out at all costs."

"Sir," Madison Timmons lifted his hand. He served under Jacks as a major in the army. "Don't you think we have bigger things to worry about than someone talking to the press? It's a pretty minor offense in the grand scheme of things."

"If the person we're dealing with can talk to them," Jacks gestured over his shoulder, "then they're not to be trusted. They could just as easily turn spy. I don't trust anyone that's willing to break their oath and reveal classified information. Yes, I believe this takes priority for at least a couple investigators. Get on it. Now."

"Yes, sir." Madison nodded.

"Next, get with tech and find out what's going on with our simulations. I'll contact the Leviathan and talk to them about Miller. Everyone else, you should already have an assignment so get to work. If you need anything, I'll be the man running around on fire. Thank you."

Jacks stepped into the hall and pulled out his com unit. He ensured it was set to a secure connection and contacted the Leviathan, hoping they had more information about Miller. People were either dead or abducted and that changed things considerably. The Agency no longer looked toward diplomacy, regardless of what he said.

They were pretty much at war but no one was willing to admit it. Not yet at least.

***

Warren pressed himself against the wall just half a moment before the door opened. Several of the aliens burst into the room, each wearing the same uniform as those they'd dealt with. Dex and Gary opened fire, the blue beams connecting with their targets who were tossed off their feet before slamming into the ground, unmoving.

The aliens shot back, causing the two marines to scatter. Warren took aim and popped one in the head, the helmet glowing briefly before the creature screamed and hit the floor. He had to throw himself out of the way as another blast seared the wall right behind him, charring the dull metal.

Jake engaged an enemy who came close to him. They struggled for a brief moment before the thing's weapon went off. Jake's eyes widened and blood poured from his mouth as he collapsed to the floor.

Warren climbed to his feet and dashed for the door. "Get out of the room!" He shouted. "Get into the hall! Hurry!"

Dex and Gary burst out after him. Debra came after them, making it through the door way just as one of the energy beams caught her in the shoulder. She spun in place and collapsed to the floor, on her back, gasping like a fish out of water. Gary grabbed the collar of her shirt and dragged her away, firing blindly into the door.

Dex shouted out, "we're down two, Captain! What now?"

"Seems like they kidnapped a lot of people," Warren replied, aiming at the door. "We'll pad our numbers soon enough but it won't help if we don't know what to do or where to go. I guess right now, our only hope is to figure out how to take the ship from them." He shot one of the aliens as they came through the door. "We have to get out of here."

"Can you walk?" Gary shouted at Debra. "Are you able to walk, ma'am?"

"Yes!" Debra nodded. "Just … help me up, please."

Gary checked her over, firing again at the door as he did. "The wound isn't bleeding. It's a bad burn, basically."

"Small favor," Debra muttered. "I didn't get a weapon."

Warren noted they were in a hallway that stretched off into darkness in both directions. The walls were the same type of metal as the last with no seams or gaps. There were other doors impressed into the walls every thirty feet or so. *We're in some kind of prison area. How the hell do we open these doors?*

"Let's move out," Warren said. "This direction." He gestured to his left. "Keep an eye on that door and if anyone comes out while we're moving, shoot them. I'll take point."

More buzzes from the weapons sounded behind him as the marines held their back. Warren hustled toward the darkness. Blue beams suddenly erupted before him, lighting up the hallway and revealing three enemies. He fired at them, causing one to dive for cover. He scored a hit, catching one in the chest.

The other fired again. Debra cried out and hit the ground. Warren blew him away and got his friend. He turned to his fallen comrade, noting she'd been hit in the face. Most of the skin melted away, making her completely unrecognizable. Gary slapped his arm, dragging him out of the moment.

"Hurry it up, sir! We don't have time!"

"She's gone!" Dex shouted. "Come on!"

Warren picked up the pace, pausing by one of the dead aliens to grab his weapon. The marines followed suit. *We'll need these if we get some help and boy do we need some*. They came upon a T intersection and turned, pausing there. Gary and Dex kept an eye on the passage way, weapons aimed.

Footsteps echoed off the metal but it was hard to gauge distance in the vast structure. Warren moved closer to one of the doors and examined it. The indentation had an obvious frame. Leaning in to really study the wall, he saw a discoloration from the rest, barely visible in the odd lighting around them.

Pressing his hand against it, the door opened and he found another twenty by twenty room like where they emerged from their object. "I got in here!" Warren called to the marines. "There might be people on the other side of that wall over there. More humans, I mean … if we can figure out how to open it up."

"No time to try!" Dex shouted. "Come on, move! Head down this hall again! They're coming!"

They broke into a run, sprinting away from the incoming attackers. Warren cursed the situation. A little breathing room might afford them some allies but without time to study the technology, to get through the doors and walls, there was nothing they could do but keep running.

Three men held little chance of survival alone on the alien vessel. Worse, the fact they killed several of their captors probably meant they weren't going to be taken alive. As a credible threat, capable of murder, the aliens had no reason to capture them anymore. Especially with plenty of victims in other cages.

Warren continued to lead the way, taking a hard right when he was able to. The doors on either side made him slow down. These weren't the metal panels they saw before but actual bars, revealing the insides. Most sat empty but as they got to the middle, a woman threw herself against the bars.

Jet black hair was wild, hanging to her shoulders and she peered at him with wide, jade green eyes. High cheek bones and a blade of a nose gave her a noble look and her clothes, though disheveled, held exquisite details. Her long black coat held subtle embroidery along the button bands and the sleeves were wide, ending midway over her forearm.

A white shirt underneath was smudged with something dark and her black trousers ended in tall boots just below the knees.

The suddenness of her appearance started Warren and he lifted his weapon toward her. She held her hands up defensively and took a step back. "Slow down," she spoke in excellent English with only a subtle accent that reminded him of Welsh though not exactly. "I'm in a cell. There's no reason to shoot me."

"What the hell?" Dex stepped forward. "What is this place? Who are you?"

She peered at Dex through narrow eyes for a moment before replying. "Are you the one in charge of this ... whatever you are?"

"I am," Warren said. "But the questions still stand."

"My name is Avania Nika Dilanth Keth of the Royal House of Keth." She stood up straighter as she spoke. "I do not know what you mean when you ask *what is this place*. If you're referring to this section of the vessel specifically, you can call it the prison. If, on the other hand you mean generally, then this is a collection ship."

"Collection?" Warren shook his head. "What do you mean? Collecting what?"

"Prisoners," Avania replied. "Of all sorts it seems. Wait …" She leaned close, lowering her voice. "You are … human? Is that right?"

"Yeah, we're human," Gary said. "What's that make you, lady?"

"I am an alanta." Avania replied in a way that made the statement obvious. "I should have known the way you're acting after my introduction. Few of the cultures these animals collect wouldn't know me or my royal house and since you are not dressed as guards, I can only assume they have finally broken royal decree and arrived at Earth."

"Yeah, they're at Earth," Dex said. "And they're stealing people. We have to get out of here."

Avania smirked. "And the three of you think you can do it alone, is that it? That you will successfully escape this ship? I suppose it is possible. You've gotten this far." Her expression hardened. "If you help me, I will help you."

"Captain," Dex turned to Warren, "we don't know why these assholes locked her up. There could be a good reason."

"There's always a good reason to the captor," Avania pointed out. "I represent opposition to the rule of the sitting nobility, to the way they treat others and kidnap them. For that, they put me in a cell and intend to have me executed when I'm returned home. Standing up for the rights of others does not win you friends in this place, I'm afraid."

Warren looked her over, puzzling through what to do. There wasn't time to think too much. Release her or continue on alone? He didn't like either option but then again, she had something on common with him and his people in one important way. The aliens that ran the ship locked her up too. That meant something.

"Pretty sure the enemy of my enemy is my friend," Warren replied. "Do you know this ship? Do you know how to get us to a shuttle or something to escape with?"

"I do." Avania nodded. "Let me out and I'll lead you where you need to go."

"What about the other prisoners?" Gary asked. "How're we going to save them?"

"I'm sure they have plenty by now," Avania replied. "Which means if the four of us leave, they will likely not bother to follow. We can escape without incident, or at least, without them pursuing us."

"We're not leaving human beings with these people," Warren said. "If that's your offer of help, then we'll take our chances without you. Our objective is to save as many of ours as possible, get off this thing and confront the alien ship by whatever means are necessary to ensure the safety of Earth."

Avania sighed, her shoulders slumping. "Very well. I will help you with that too." Her mood changed as she grabbed the bars in tight fists and shook them. "Know we are going to have to deal with more than rescuing them though. If we take the prisoners with us, then they will certainly follow."

"Definitely worth the risk," Warren said.

"Alright." Avania gestured to the bars. "Get me out of the cage and we'll be on our way then."

"Um ..." Warren shrugged. "How do you propose I do that?"

"For the love of ..." Avania extended her hand. "Give me one of the weapons. I know precisely where to shoot."

"Captain ..." Dex grabbed Warren's arm. "Is that a good idea?"

"Did you think I wasn't going to arm her?" Warren asked. "We need numbers, Dex. Whoever we release has to be able to contribute to the fight."

"We don't have time to debate," Gary pointed out. "I hear more coming ... from somewhere."

"Why aren't there guards?" Dex asked. "Where is everyone?"

"Collecting." Avania tilted her head. "It's a busy task. How many crew do you think they have? Anyway, the sounds you hear are two hallways away at least. This is not to say we have a lot of time to waste in conversation but at least you won't have to shoot anyone for a few moments. Of course, I'd prefer if you'd hurry."

Warren took the extra weapon from his belt and offered it to her handle first. Gary lifted his weapon and aimed it at her, stepping to the side of the cage. Dex did the same. She took the gun and stood off to the side of the bars, aiming at the wall to her left. "Stand a bit further to the sides, if you don't mind. I'd rather not hurt any of you."

The men complied though Gary and Dex didn't lower their guns. Warren figured they'd be paranoid but took it to an excessive place. They desperately needed allies, especially one that understood the environment and where they were. Additional humans would be just as confused as they were.

If Avania proved to be telling the truth, then they hit the jackpot.

The weapon buzzed and the wall sparked, causing a bright flash that dazzled Warren enough to look sharply away. The bars rattled and when he blinked off the glimmer in his eyes, she was stepping out. Slapping at her jacket as if to dust it off, she frowned at her outfit before directing her gaze at Warren.

"What do I call the three of you?" Avania asked. "Captain, was it?"

"I'm Warren. That's Dex and the other one's Gary."

"I see. No wonder you thought my name was long when you go by so little." Avania admired her gun for a moment. "I hope you are prepared to use those weapons. You will certainly need them. Follow my lead and stay close. We'll start with freeing your comrades … the ones which can be saved at least."

"What's that mean?" Dex asked. "What do you mean *can* be saved?"

"I believe you'll have the misfortune of finding out."

Chapter 4

"The helicopter has left," Madeline announced to the bridge. "It is heading toward Captain Miller's last known location. I'm putting them on the open com now but it's going to take them some time to get into position."

"Perfect," Victoria said. "Patch them through to my station and I'll coordinate." She waited until her microphone was live before speaking to the crew. "This is Commander Serling. Thank you for getting out there. We appreciate the help. Who am I speaking with?"

"This is Warrant Officer Scott Duran. We've cleared the main gate now. ETA to search area … fifteen minutes."

"Can you patch your camera feed through this channel?" Victoria asked.

"Affirmative. We'll save it for when we get over the area."

Victoria busied herself with reports, looking over information from engineering while the helicopter was in transit. When they drew close to the city, her tiny monitor came to life and she saw what amounted to total chaos. Cars were all askew, some smoking and others outright on fire. People milled about, waving at the helicopter while screaming.

"I'm calling the satellite phone," Madeline said. "Hopefully, it's still in the area so we can track it."

Warren represented one of five key members of the Agency outside the base when the object arrived. The other four were in Europe attending a conference and were unable to get back in time to participate in person. Victoria spoke to Warren personally before he left his apartment and knew he was on the way.

The way that man drives, if there hadn't been traffic, he would've been here a long time ago.

"We're picking up the signal," Scott said. "Moving down a block."

The people on the screen continued shouting and when it became clear the helicopter wasn't going to stop for them, they started throwing things. They couldn't get high enough, not remotely but they kept at it anyway. Victoria switched the visual to the large screen in front of them and she leaned forward, scanning the vehicles as they passed by.

"There!" Victoria pointed, as if Scott could see. "The maroon truck there in the middle! Can you see it?"

"Signal isn't coming from there," Scott replied. "But we see it."

"That is Warren's vehicle." Victoria hummed. "Maybe he brought the phone with him. Follow the signal. Let's see where he went."

I hope to God we're not following some ridiculous thief who stole it.

"I'm throwing two body cam signals your way," Scott said. "We'll send in two soldiers to investigate when we arrive at the destination."

"So he's on the move," Nicolas said. "That's not a good sign."

"Not with all that's going on." Victoria thought of the people throwing rocks and other debris. "We'll gather more. I'm switching to the body cams."

The screen changed, showing a bobbing view out the doors of the helicopter. As it approached the roof of a building, the vehicle slowed and began to hover. "Deploy," Scott said. "Signal's definitely coming from this building. It's close by so likely near the top. Clear and get back up here with the package."

Victoria squinted at the screen as the view changed to them rapidly sliding down a couple ropes to the roof. They dashed toward the nearby door, each taking a side so they were looking at one another. Both men were dressed in full body armor and helmets. They carried assault rifles with scopes and suppressors.

If anyone was prepared to contend with the type of trouble happening out there, it was them.

"Opening door," one of the two soldiers stated before testing the handle. It came open and they poured into the dark space, their cameras switching to the filmy green of night vision. They went down a short flight of stairs and entered a hallway with doors on either side. It was some kind of high-rise apartment building.

What would Warren be doing there? Victoria thought but she wasn't naïve enough to think it wasn't his satellite phone alone that they were about to locate. *Some fool stole it from his car and we're about to find him.*

One of the doors burst open. "Contact!" The two soldiers shouted in unison. A figure came out into the night vision, little more than a lime blob. "Gun!" Assault rifles whisper-thumped as they discharged into the target, tossing him back onto the ground.

The attack turned the situation into chaos. Shots erupted in the hall, cracking noisily as the violence intensified. The soldiers burst through one of the doors and took cover. Lights burst overhead as if someone cranked on the power suddenly. Night vision settled to regular color. Blood on the walls came into sharp contrast, old and dried from some previous atrocity.

Victoria forced herself to lean back. A grim feeling fell over here. If Miller *was* in the building, he might've been dead.

An armed individual charged into the room, discharging a pistol several times. One of the soldiers cut him down, blasting him in the neck and face. They moved back to the door, trying to reclaim the initiative. There were at least a dozen combatants outside, armed men who had been civilians not long before.

One of the soldiers dropped into a crouch, leaning out to open fire. He fired fully automatic, spraying into the gathered crowd. The victims had nowhere to go. Bodies danced before dropping to the ground in heaps. A couple made it to cover but few of them came out unscathed. Whatever they hoped to achieve in entering the hall failed.

Victoria's eyes darted to the second camera, trying to watch the man's back. She opened her mouth to call out a warning but knew it was too late. Another armed man, this one creeping out of a door they'd already passed, leaned out and took a shot with a pistol. It struck the crouching soldier in the back, slapping his body armor.

His partner blew the guy away, dropping a round in the man's forehead. Blood splattered the wall and the two soldiers hustled out of their position and continued their search. They had to step over a pile of bodies, some gone, a few gasping out their final breaths. The walls were saturated in gore, gleaming wetly in the low light.

Those are some tough bastards, Victoria thought. *I hope they're planning on coming with us when we leave the planet*.

"You're right on top of the signal," Scott said. "You should see it at any moment."

The soldiers went into the room where two surviving attackers took refuge. They found them, lying on their backs panting like road kill. Wounds on their legs and sides showed they had a short time left to live. One of the two soldiers disarmed them and rooted through the room.

They found the satellite phone on a table with a pile of other things, devices and other stolen objects. One of them grabbed it and secured it to his belt before they cleared the rest of the residence. There were no other people, alive or otherwise. These looters didn't bring people back, only their belongings.

That's that. Victoria looked down.

"Ma'am," Scott spoke into the microphone, "it appears we've only found the phone."

"I saw," Victoria said. "Thank you for your efforts. You should return to base as soon as possible." She turned to Madeline. "Can you get into those traffic cams? Maybe we can see what happened … catch sight of the incident. Perhaps confirm our fears."

Madeline went to work just as Victoria's com buzzed. Jacks's face appeared on the screen and she clicked it on. "Yes, sir?"

"Any update on Miller?"

Victoria hesitated for a moment before replying. "Search and rescue located his sat phone. We're patching into the traffic cams in the area to see what specifically happened but I'm pretty sure this is where one of the smaller objects swept through. If that's the case … we need to find out what those things did to people. Captain Miller …" She didn't want to say it. "Well … you know."

"I see you started a countdown."

"Considering the situation, I stand by it."

"Me too." Jacks remained quiet for several moments. "Push your countdown to forty minutes so we ensure we do everything right but I'm authorizing you to launch. We can't risk losing the ship in our haste to get up there so … do it right. Good luck, Serling." He killed the connection.

Victoria stood up and stepped over to Nicolas. She rested her hand on his shoulder. "Set the countdown to forty minutes and inform ground control. Madeline, after you've got those camera feeds up, send a ship wide message informing all departments of our authorization. It's time to make history, folks. Pray that it's the positive kind."

***

Warren remained close to their guide as a tinge of doubt entered his mind on whether or not he made a mistake in trusting her. He didn't have time to vet her, to make a decision based on anything besides blind desperation. Part of him sided with the marines but paranoia would not get them off that ship.

Putting some trust into this woman might've been their only chance. Regardless of her species, the circumstances of their meeting made it clear she was *not* on the side of the aliens who abducted them. He wanted to somehow confirm the reason she said she was in the cell in the first place but he had no idea how to do so.

Avania could've been more dangerous than their adversaries.

Warren put a theory into motion. The aliens kidnapped humans for some nefarious purpose but rationally thinking, it didn't make them inherently wicked or evil. They might be filling out a zoo, a menagerie of creatures from around the galaxy to study. Depending on how clinical they felt about humanity, it might all boil down to cold science.

Their culture may have considered Avania to be a dangerous criminal, a murderer or worse. He needed to get to the bottom of her involvement in the situation, in what it was she was doing there. Unfortunately, as with their attempt to rescue their people from the other rooms, there simply wasn't time.

Not if they didn't want to enter a risky firefight that already claimed multiple lives.

"We're going the wrong way," Dex said. "Our people are back there, lady."

"There are degrees of jeopardy," Avania replied. "Those behind are not in danger yet. If I'm correct, and I pretty much guarantee I am, then we need to intervene in a part of the collection process."

"And what is that?" Warren asked.

They approached a blank wall and Avania tapped part of it. A section slid to the side and the sound of machinery clanking away filled the room. Unconscious people were held aloft by the shoulders, strapped up like cattle. They were carried along toward a bright light and disappeared behind a wall.

"See for yourself," Avania said as she stepped inside. "This is the true part of collection where they rip the essence from the body."

"You mean the blood?" Gary asked.

"No, I mean—"

"Who the fuck cares?" Dex interrupted. "We have to stop that shit! They're killing our people, regardless of what you want to call it! Let's go!"

"Slow down," Avania said. "We will save as many as we can but we cannot run toward the danger in this case. No, we need to come upon the operators with some stealth. Once they are killed, I can turn this off and you can collect those who are still alive." She gestured and led them to the right.

Warren couldn't take his eyes off the people being carried nearby. They seemed to be unconscious, their heads slumped so their chins touched their chests. Arms and legs hung limply from their trunks. They looked dead already and he wondered how many were. The fact she used the term *essence* stuck in his mind.

Blood definitely counted as part of that but she meant something more. Did these people believe in the soul? Or were they merely referring to the energy that sparked through the body to generate motion and thought? More questions to stow in the back of his head for later, especially as they moved into a dangerous situation.

There were no frills on the alien ship, just plenty of space and rooms. This *collection* run must've been for dozens if not hundreds of subjects. The place they found Avania could've housed over fifty prisoners right there. Those smaller vessels, like the one that abducted Warren from his car, could've held more too.

They had to have. There's no way all these people would be in here if they didn't pack those things up like cargo cars.

The notion wasn't lost on Dex. The marine gave warren a grim look before returning his gaze to the countless human beings being dragged by in the strange chamber. *At least they're not conscious. What a small favor for whatever they're going through. These creatures intended to put* us *in there too.*

Up ahead, they saw a control station with two more of the suited aliens working at it. Another attached straps to more unconscious humans that came in on a conveyer belt. The casual way these beings acted toward the bodies made Warren sick. They exhibited the empathy of butchers.

Warren lifted the pistol but Avania put her hand on his forearm. "We must get closer. Their prisoners are extremely valuable to them but if they think they might lose, they could terminate everyone inside this thing. We'll soon be in optimum range. Missing isn't really an option here."

"I'm a good shot," Dex said. He aimed his weapon, drawing an irritable sigh from Avania.

"Very well. If you're so determined to go now, just be sure you kill the one working the controls first." Avania nodded to him. "Please do the honors of starting the fight."

Dex finally looked back at Warren. "Can I go?"

"Oh, you're asking permission now?" The comment made the marine glower. "Sorry, just wondering if you remembered who's in charge. I'm glad you do. We'll take these alien pricks out and save our people. I'm ready."

Gary beat them all to the punch, firing his weapon and catching the guy at the controls directly in the chest. The others reacted immediately, diving for cover behind the conveyer belt. This effectively gave them cover behind more humans and they started shooting back. Blue beams filled the air as Warren and his team moved closer to the wall, out of the line of fire.

"They were quick to respond," Dex muttered.

"And we have to move," Avania replied. "Or your people will die. I'm not suggesting we charge but haste is of the essence. Shall we?"

"It's not your fight." Warren put his hand on her forearm. "We've got this."

Avania yanked away from him. "You don't get to tell me what my fight is or is not. I'm going with you. Now follow me." She moved swiftly along the wall, pausing just before a corner. Moving any further put them in the line of sight of their opponents. She cleared her throat and shouted something in another language.

A like response came back, though guttural and seemingly full of rage. It reminded Warren of Japanese. The hard syllables gave it a commanding, frightening edge. Whatever the guy said made Avania smirk. She looked back at Warren and chuckled. "You look quite confused. My apologies for addressing them in our tongue."

"What the hell did you say?" Gary asked.

"I told them to surrender. That we wouldn't kill them."

Dex jumped in, "what did *they* say?"

"They asked who let me out, called me a not very nice name and stated they would skin us all alive if *we* didn't surrender." Avania shrugged. "They're calling reinforcements so I think we have to be daring to conclude this standoff. What do you say? Have you any lust for glory in you?"

Gary groaned. "They're using human shields over there. It's not like we can just jump out and start shooting."

"What's the lives of one for hundreds?" Avania asked. "They can only use two at a time."

"That's not okay!" Dex shouted.

Their alien opponents issued another lengthy commentary in their language, carrying on for quite a while this time. Warren used the time to think of another solution. He looked all around but there was nothing they could use. The area was wide open. Avania might be right but he hated that she even suggested it.

"This time," Avania said, "they are suggesting we're all criminals and should give up before the reinforcements arrive. They are not going to be as kind as these two. According to our targets, at least. They must be hoping to distract us for a while which means the others are busy elsewhere."

"You said there aren't many," Gary said, "so what're the numbers we're looking at?"

"This vessel has many floors but that doesn't concern us now." Avania leaned against the wall. "I don't mean to be harsh, but those are your people out there and the longer we wait, the more the converter kills."

"Fine, I've got this." Gary dashed out of cover before Warren could even lift his hand. The marine fired his weapon, throwing himself sideways so he hit the ground after four shots. Dex leaned out to cover him, cursing the whole time.

Warren crouched, trying to get a line of fire but a blue beam nearly seared his face off. He leaned back with a wince.

Gary got to his feet and started moving, crying out. If he was hit, he didn't slow down before he reached the control panel, leaning against it for cover. He couldn't have been more than ten feet from his opponents. The buzzing vibrations of the guns filled the air as the two aliens laid down continual suppressive fire but Warren didn't see blue beams anymore.

"Dex!" Warren shouted. "What're they doing?"

"Focusing on Gary." Dex took some shots. "This God damn piece of shit is hard to aim!"

"I've got it!" Gary yelled back. Warren risked leaning around again, noting the two aliens were blasting away at the control panel. Gary rolled from his cover then leaped over the conveyer belt. A continuous sound of buzzing lasted for ten seconds. Dex charged and Warren followed, weapons at the ready.

By the time they got there, the fight was over. The two aliens were dead, lying in heaps nearby. Gary leaned against the conveyer assembly, holding a nasty black wound on his shoulder. It wasn't the only damage he suffered. He'd been hit in the stomach and leg. Some of his left hand was missing, burnt off from the middle of his palm down.

"Jesus Christ!" Dex knelt beside him, practically twitching. Warren had seen the helpless look on a man before several times and he knew there was nothing to be done for Gary. The man was on his way out. "You didn't have to do that! There was another option! We would've found it, you impulsive maniac!"

"People were dying …" Gary coughed up blood. Gore made his chin glisten. "Had to act … had to … make something happen … quick."

"Oh, Gary …" Dex examined his wounds, his head moving frantically between each. "I … I don't know … this … you're … God damn it."

"I know …" Gary winced, closing his eyes tightly. "There's nothing you can do. I get it. But … Help those people."

"I'm on it." Avania was on the control panel, tapping away at the console. The device stopped and silence fell over them. "As they come back out of this thing, I'll need your help to get them down."

"I'll help." Warren turned away from the two marines, giving them a moment together. The first five people they unstrapped wore uniforms. A couple were already dead. A grand total of nine survived their predicament going into the machine. Avania wouldn't bring any others out. "We can't give up on them!"

"Look at their vitals." Avania gestured to the screen. Warren didn't know what he was looking at. "They're already dead … and not likely in any recognizable form." She sighed. "They killed over ten-thousand in this machine alone."

"Ten *thousand*?" Warren felt ill trying to fathom the number. "How do you know?"

Avania pointed to the screen. "I'm looking at their completion rate at this point. But we can't focus on that right now. We need to save the ones who are okay … wake up those on the conveyer belt and get the hell out of here. That's the plan, right?"

"Yes." Warren glared at her. Frustration hit him hard. Having escaped their captors and fighting their way through the ship, they were far from helpless but it didn't feel that way. There were too many unknowns. Even as they bolstered their ranks, he had too many questions and needed some answers soon to feel any control over the situation.

But ten thousand lost? That was insane. And how many more at other stations? How many people did they take? How could so many be dead already? He felt lucky that Dex didn't catch on to that. He would've lost his mind. Not that he wasn't already in a bad spot as his friend passed away. These aliens had certainly declared war on the human race.

"No!" Dex shouted. "Oh, Gary. I'm sorry, man … I'm so sorry."

Warren stepped over to check but he already knew what he'd see. Gary was gone. "Hey." He put his hand on Dex's shoulder. "We might have more assholes coming in. Let's try to wake these people up and get out of here before it's too late. God knows we don't want to lose anyone else."

Dex nodded and climbed to his feet, stepping away from the body of his friend. They turned to the prone people lying on the conveyer belt and began to examine them.

The first two seemed to be in a deep sleep though when Warren shook one, he didn't wake up. He wore military fatigues and had a US Army patch on his shoulder. No rank or insignia decorated the uniform. A youthful face put him at no older than nineteen, twenty at the absolute most.

"What's wrong with them?" Warren turned to Avania. "What did they do?"

"Before I can answer that, I need to know how you escaped." Avania looked over one of the victims as well. "You should've been unconscious."

"We weren't," Dex said. "Captain Miller was but he woke up en route. When we docked, the vibration in the hull stopped and we jumped the assholes who came for us."

"They did seem distracted though," Warren added. "Like they didn't expect us to be awake. In fact, they weren't even paying attention when we initially attacked, remember? The third guy we interrogated stumbled back when he saw you guys take his buddies down and he only barely got his weapon ready before I got him."

"Ah, so something malfunctioned," Avania replied. "Or they merely made a mistake. Typically, they run the oxygen light in the collection pods. Those creatures who are inside do not have enough to stay awake. They fall asleep so that they can be easily removed and put into the converter. Plus, they tend to cram them full. It seems they may not have had as many in your chamber either. Fortunate."

"So how do we wake these people up?" Warren gestured to them. "They seem to just be asleep but … do they give them a drug or something?"

"No." Avania slapped the person closest to her and the person stirred. She did it again and they lifted their arms defensively.

"I'm awake … I'm awake!" The man muttered. "Stop hitting me."

"And there you have it." Avania gestured. "A slight bit of force seems to do the trick."

"Okay, we'd better hurry." Warren gestured to Dex. "You start at the front of the line over there and I'll work toward you. Avania, watch our backs … if you can manage that. I'd rather not get shot from reinforcements. Consider that we are on a major time crunch here and any delay could mean our lives. Move it."

***

Victoria peered at their countdown, which broke the thirty-minute mark. They had twenty-eight minutes before they would take the Leviathan into space for the first time. The monumental event was supposed to have been full of fanfare. Public relations planned a festival for it, inviting prominent members of the world to observe in person.

Necessity did away with all that and instead, they would be rushing out to meet a threat. Victoria didn't know how to feel about it. She wished they could've given the technicians their glory, let them bask in the adoration of the people who barely understood the accomplishment. They deserved a moment in the spotlight, free from the stress of a catastrophe.

However, necessity pushed up the timeline, one they had been dancing around for months. Victoria and Miller had discussed the launch many times. They privately agreed the waiting was ridiculous. The council wanted *the perfect moment* to make it happen but none of them could agree on when that would be.

The Americans looked to Independence Day. They wanted to coincide the first launch of the battleship on their glorious day. France argued they had such a celebration to consider as well. Others said it should be a neutral time of the year but considering the sheer number of countries involved, it was hard to find one that was also weather friendly.

Alien interaction made it so the day didn't matter. Attacking cities, killing the power, murdering or abducting citizens … all of it pushed the human race toward a war with an unknown threat. They refused to communicate, acting in an automated manner. It was as if they didn't feel humans were worth talking to, that they could do whatever they wanted.

"Commander," Madeline's voice broke her train of thought, "Chief Delgado's on the line. He says it's urgent."

"Patch him through."

"We've got a problem," Delgado launched right into it. "We've got a fuel balance problem that we're working out and it'll likely take longer than twenty minutes."

Victoria lifted a brow. The news didn't entirely surprise her but the delay wouldn't go over well with anyone. News agencies expected the Agency to respond. More importantly, if the smaller objects had been full of abducted people, time was not on their side. Especially not for malfunctions that should've been caught during all the tests they'd conducted.

"I see. And what happens if we don't delay launch?"

"Possible explosion during the ignition process," Delgado replied. "I'm running a simulation now. It seems that we inadvertently damaged the fuel regulation module during our last test. We have an extra and we're testing it now. Once that's finished, we can swap it out, run the fuel test again and we should be ready."

"How long will all that take?"

"Test is almost done now. Ten minutes to remove the old one, fifteen for the new, five for the quick test and ten to get the fuel regulated." Halfway through the comment, Delgado started to sound sheepish. "Forty minutes. I'll ... I'll try to make it thirty."

"Do," Victoria said. "Ensure you take whatever precautions are necessary. We can't afford more damage. Let me know if you run into any more delays. Serling out." She killed the connection and fought hard not to show her irritation visibly. "Nicolas, make sure there are no other surprises with ground control or other departments."

"Yes, ma'am." Nicolas got on his com.

Victoria reached out to Jacks to give him the news. He might use it as a talking point later about how they weren't ready after all. Everyone knew the complexities of the Leviathan meant risk of some part failing. Stress tests were meant to work out the bugs, to ensure they caught broken parts.

Their diagnostics needed improvement more than anything. The broken regulator should've been discovered after the last test, not minutes before launch. Engineers would be debating the problem for weeks. If the aliens left without further incident. Providing the ship could take flight, they may just make such a thing happen.

But just then, Victoria couldn't help but feel doubtful of their chances.

Madeline brought the video feed up from the traffic cameras and they watched it in silence on the big screen. Shadows fell over the vehicles. People poured out of their cars, fleeing as beams of light blasted them. They watched the attack several times, trying desperately to see whether or not they could tell if the people were killed.

Did the energy leave dust behind? Or were they gone? Was it a form of teleportation? Maybe the technicians were figuring it out. Even with the tools on the Leviathan, they didn't have what they needed for answers. They knew Captain Miller had been caught up in the chaos but as to his actual fate, no one had a clue.

I hope they figure it out soon, Victoria thought. *If they come back, we need an answer for it*.

***

Jacks got off the line with Victoria and slapped his desk. Madison jumped when he did so, making the colonel frown. If the ship couldn't do its job, they needed to do *something* else in the meantime. There were other ships available but none of them were combat ready. They were meant for research and exploration.

None of them even had any real weapons installed.

However, we might still be able to gather some data that way. Jacks didn't like the idea. They would be sitting ducks near that object. If it took any aggressive action, they would be dead. Was it worth the risk of men and equipment? They might have no other choice. Earth remained in jeopardy until that thing left.

"We need more data. We have to take action." Jacks rubbed his eyes. "And I think you know what I mean when I say that. We're in a sticky position with the Leviathan. It can't launch until they fix that regulator. I'm thinking we need to put our other ships in play. Get the close up scans we need of the object."

Madison leaned forward. "Sir, I strongly advise against that. Those ships …"

"I know," Jacks interrupted. "They're not meant to intercept. But if we use them in a research capacity, we might do pretty well."

"Do you really think so?" Madison shook his head. "The device already shot down two of our ships."

"It might happen again but we have no choice," Jacks pointed out. "If we don't gather data, we can't find out what happened to those smaller objects. No, we have to step up and show we're willing to try things, even if they're dangerous. At this point, we're floundering. The world needs to see we can handle this."

"It's not going to stop the rioters," Madison said, "or the crazy cults coming to talk about the end of the world."

"I get it," Jacks said. "Assurance will be limited. But if we get *anything* about those shields, we'll be in a good place. Look, I'm not thrilled about this. We're in a shitty situation, trying to shovel our way out. Go out there and give the order. I'll talk to Doctor Meyers about what happened to the Leviathan. Hopefully, his people are already writing better diagnostic programs."

"Yes, sir."

"Wait." Jacks stepped over to the door. "What's the deal with our investigation into the information leak?"

"Ongoing," Madison replied. "I'll check in with the investigators when I'm done here."

Jacks nodded. "Good. Thank you."

Jacks turned to his tablet as Madison left him alone again. The news report was going, still showing the same data from earlier in the day. They incorporated some of the strange events happening around the world as many people lost their minds. He understood the worry. After all the violence, attempted military action and the attack, the chaos seemed mild.

Authorities in every city had their hands full and they were all turning to the Agency to respond. That's why Jacks didn't have a choice but to send those research vessels to get some data. He needed something to feed the council and the public. Hopefully, a positive message that would calm them down for a while.

In the absence of fact, people invented their own and those with the loudest voices incited wild behavior. Jacks knew his teams were in the best position to quell all the noise and help understand the situation they were in. If they could only get over the hurdle of technical glitches and problems, he could send an effective message to the entire planet.

Until then, Jacks had to suffer through the worst tension of his career, accepting the fact there was no hurrying their progress, no pushing to get things done quicker. They were bound to fate and he prayed it fell on their side. If not, a lot more might fall than the Agency and their various employees.

The Earth itself was potentially on the line.

***

Chapter 5

Warren understood pressure. He'd fought in wars, flew in the most dangerous of circumstances and gambled with his life on hundreds of occasions. Soldiers put their faith in him, trusting his judgement and leadership. Never before had he struggled with nerves so much as while trying to wake up the people they saved from the converter.

Maybe if I knew what the hell it was, I might not be so concerned about it. Oh, what am I saying, of course *I'd be concerned. This thing is terrifying.* They ended up with fifteen able bodied individuals with five injured past the point of participating in any sort of real conflict. Dex filled them in and let them know what was at stake.

None of their recent recruits had any idea what happened. Snippets of their stories all sounded the same. Stuck in traffic … running with a large group of individuals in a parking … trying to get into a building, to safety. They were abducted like the rest were. In droves, they were attacked by the aliens and brought to the mothership … to be rendered down to … whatever.

Seven of the pistols still worked and they distributed them to the men and women most suitable to use them. Though they took less than five minutes to rouse their people, it felt much longer. Warren couldn't believe reinforcements hadn't descended upon them. He turned to Avania. She'd made it clear this was one of several such devices.

"Where are the other stations?"

Avania sighed. "We don't really have the time—"

"We'll make the time," Warren interrupted. "Lead us to the next one. You haven't told us what these things do but it's bad enough that you wouldn't let us pull the rest of the people out. Assume we're not leaving any of our comrades to die in them than we have to."

"I understand your loyalty," Avania replied, "I really do but we've been lucky so far."

"Tell that to Gary!" Dex blurted out.

"Yes, not him …" Avania closed her eyes for a moment. "We'll fetch more of your people. We'll need to really pack in a shuttle …" She looked at the group, frowning. "Follow me and be quick about it. The next one probably won't be as easy."

"Why?" Dex asked.

"Because if they didn't send people here, they believed it was lost. They'll reinforce the others and hope we come for them." Avania shrugged. "At least, that's their normal protocol. I've seen groups raid these vessels before and that's how they were repelled. The converters are the most valuable pieces of equipment on board."

They were on the move when Warren got closer to her. "I'd love to know what they're doing. What you meant by *essence* when you said they're collecting it off of people."

"Essence meaning the life force that makes you human. It includes the blood, the energy, all that animates us. The spark of survival and personality. All of it, collected through a painstaking process that leaves the shell little more than dust." Avania shook her head. "It was … a somewhat frowned upon exercise."

"And what for? Why bother? What's the benefit?"

Avania looked him over, examining his face for several moments. When she finally responded, she looked away, staring straight ahead while still walking. "Simply put?" Her eyes narrowed. "Life extension. Prolonging the spark, both physical and mental, in a certain caste of my people."

Warren's mouth went dry. Her matter-of-fact description of the converter stunned him to the core. It took him a good half a minute to grasp what she said and when he did, anger replaced the confusion. Before he understood what they were doing, he merely wanted to escape the ship. Killing them was self-defense.

Now, he felt an instinctual desire to destroy their vessel and prevent them from ever doing anything like ... *conversion* again.

"You're okay with this?" Warren asked. "'Cause you don't sound too broken up."

Avania shook her head. "Not at all. It's one of the reasons I was in that cell. We can discuss this at greater length soon but right now, we really need to focus on the task at hand. There will be time and I understand your indignation, I truly do." She seemed to notice his expression did not soften. "You will simply have to trust me."

"I'll work on that." Warren moved ahead of her, clenching the handle of his pistol tighter. He couldn't wait for another crack at these aliens. During this next encounter, he would not be so gentle with his attack or how he directed the others in the assault. Understanding their purpose gave him a newfound drive to wipe them out.

Whatever the cost.

***

Avania worried about the endurance of the humans. Their planet had been off limits for generations, allowing them to thrive, grow and kill each other completely on their own. After the initial visits in the distant past, once certain elements of their culture were put in motion, the alanta culture decided they no longer needed help.

Humans began looking toward the stars early in their development. Their hearts full of adventure, they even managed to make it as far as the moon with primitive equipment and raw desire. That courage served them well but it also made them a target for her cousin, Sorna, the man who forced Avania to go on the run.

Alanta technology advanced quickly when they developed faster than light travel through the creation of stable wormholes. Biology in particular thrived until scientists uncovered a method to extend life indefinitely through a process called transference. It required purified life essence pulled from other creatures, but it proved highly effective.

Many of the alanta people considered the act blasphemous, even referring to it as vampirism but a certain portion of the ruling caste saw opportunity. They began to imagine ruling for generations, never growing old, maintaining their vigor while others faded. The concept was far too tempting to turn down.

Early tests proved certain races simply weren't suitable for life extension but held other benefits. Human beings provided the best results but Earth was an out of the way planet. So the alanta people made a special visit after the fall of one of their greatest empires. Back then, the plan was to take a sizable enough portion of the population and seed a different planet.

That became the great experiment. Ten million Earthlings were taken. Their historical records called the event *The Black Death*, a convenient disguise for the disappearance of so many human beings. Indeed, many did die from a virulent disease but not the numbers they reported later. That merely covered up the shocking loss of so many.

So they were moved to a new planet where they were allowed to live in relative comfort though all had to give themselves up at a certain age. Avania remembered her history classes, each of them granting almost divine importance on the planet in question. Unfortunately, after several hundred years, the breeding of those humans ceased to be effective.

The last of them died off.

Avania could only imagine the reaction from the humans when the massive ship arrived in their system this time. When the smaller vessels descended upon them, they likely panicked and rightfully so. Standard procedure involved radio silence. Swoop in, take the resources and get back out.

Chances were good the ship's captain already plotted a course for the next system on their route. Most of the collectors kept their schedules tight, with little room for error or delay. When they set out on their run, they needed to maintain strict timing to meet delivery promises from their employers. They peddled in the lesser essences but this one, must've been greedy.

It's a big business. The most valuable commodity in the universe these days. Which was why they immediately began rendering their finds down the moment they got them on board. They didn't have time to waste so that meant putting the humans, and whatever other creatures they captured, straight into converters.

Furthermore, they needed to get out there before the alanta government made the move. Human essence had been stored up so they weren't in danger of running out *too* soon, but they would want to know the flow had been picked up again. That meant another mass abduction. It would've been far more peaceful than the collectors but these humans wouldn't have chalked up the loss to a disease.

They would've known the truth.

Warren seemed particularly moved by the situation and she didn't blame him. However, thinking she had anything to do with it was ridiculous. She refused to accept guilt by association, by having been born part of a royal house. After all, her family had been all but wiped out for their views on transference.

We tried to stop it and in return, we were exiled, murdered or fled for our lives. The collection crew hadn't been looking for Avania. They just got lucky on one of their runs and planned on collecting the reward on her head. Those in her family who didn't die were hunted. Her cousin didn't make a concerted effort to find them but his money sat on the table.

Bounty hunters were not uncommon but Avania swore she'd gone far enough to avoid them. Few wanted to venture into the less civilized systems, let alone a religious commune. One of the monasteries for the old gods took her in, providing her sanctuary. The lack of luxury bothered her but it had been safe, a place to plan what to do next.

The collector's owner lacked scruples if he sent a ship out to that particular planet. Unless the captain proved to be enterprising. No one bothered the place or the people so it was possible he simply wanted to get at a location with a viable population for transference. Great fortune for them, terrible luck for Avania.

On top of the money they would make from all the essence they collected, the bounty would certainly pad their pockets to a tremendous degree. It might be the most lucrative run those bastards ever made. Depending on how they spent their money, some of them could probably retire.

But I've escaped, Avania thought. *And these humans aren't going to let them get home with all this essence. No, if I read them correctly, my allies are planning on destroying this ship for good. That won't bode well for them in the long run but it will protect their planet for today. They'll need a plan for the future, though.*

Their primary concern rested firmly on what would happen in the next encounter, the next hour not a week or month down the line. The people around Avania fell into survival mode and they fully intended to remain that way until they were out of danger. She believed that's where their abrasiveness came from and tried to give them a pass.

I'm feeling the same way right now, if I'm to be honest. The difference between her and them came down to understanding the situation. She knew what she was facing and fully grasped what it meant to be trapped by the collectors. Prior to the humans releasing her, she mentally prepared herself for eventual execution. *They've given me another chance to live.*

More importantly, they provided her an opportunity to get even with her cousin, to take back her kingdom. Every day she drew breath was another spit in that bastard's eye and another moment she could spend attempting to bring the traitors to justice. Sitting in the collector's cell nearly extinguished her hope but now, it burned as bright as ever.

Avania peered up ahead, noting a mild yellow glow covering the floor. They were approaching the next collector. This one would be better protected than the last, the men ready for a fight. She doubted they counted on the sheer number of humans they rescued. The fact so many of them proved to be ready for a fight shocked her.

I give these humans credit. They are a tough breed. Far more enduring than I anticipated. In another time, when Avania's family ruled over the alanta people, they would've eventually reached out to humanity, extending a hand of friendship. Those creatures who aspired and achieved enjoyed lucrative treaties with them.

The current ruling body looked at other races as little more than exploitable resources. Slave labor, essence for transference or even toys for their perversions. While in the monastery, Avania received word they had opened the old arenas again, forcing captives to fight to the death. Their barbarity knew no limits, no bounds.

"We're approaching the next converter," Avania announced. She pointed to the ground. "You can see the glow from the process there."

"I got it," Warren replied. He turned to the others. "Listen up, these animals were going to kill all of us. They've already taken many lives in their sick, perverse process. If you want to get off this thing, if you want to be able to look yourselves in the mirror for the rest of your days, then you're going to fight like you never thought possible.

"We know they've reinforced this area. We also know they are desperate to hold on to their commodities. Don't forget that *you* are what they consider a resource! Our deaths, our bodies, give them what they need and if we let them, they'll do this again. So when I give the word, those of us who are armed will charge.

"The rest of you wait until we're engaged before you move. Save as many of our people as you can. Get them off the conveyer belt and the hanging devices. We'll need every able-bodied person to make this work." Warren held his weapon up. "Are you with me?"

The humans shouted in unison, an inarticulate sound which Avania assumed compliance.

"Then let's go!" Warren darted off down the hall with his zealous people running behind. Avania hesitated for half a moment, wondering if she should risk her own life the same way. They likely had the situation under control. There was no reason to assume otherwise with their numbers. Even if the collection crew mustered everyone, they couldn't stand up to that assault.

Not while guarding the other stations at the same time.

Damn it, I have to aid them. Avania sighed and charged along with them. *I might not survive the day, but at least I'll have helped someone with a cause. If it can't be my own, then I'll settle for theirs.*

***

Jacks entered the control room just as two of their research vessels began an approach to the object. One was the Seeker with Commander Avery Harden in command. The other was the Probity, helmed by Demetrius Singer. Both men were solid, experienced officers but this situation would test them for sure.

Jacks sat beside one of the operators, a young man who stiffened at his presence and looked terribly nervous. As the lead administrator, he knew he cut an imposing figure but just then, he wasn't worried about making one of the operators nervous. He'd be involved in many more such missions in the future so they would all have to get used to his presence.

The job put to the two ships up there had to be the scariest of any mission performed by an astronaut crew. Two vessels had already been attacked. They hoped these two unarmed ships would not bring upon such a response, but instead, allow them to gather data. Providing they were ignored, the research vessels carried the very best of sensor equipment.

Data. Jacks reminded himself why they were risking so much. *They have to collect something for us to analyze, to give to the people while the Leviathan resolves their glitch.*

"This is Commander Singer." The voice came through the speakers, echoing in the room. "We are approaching the object now. Piping our cameras through to you but my God, this thing is enormous. Magnification is allowing us to gather extensive textural detail of the surface. We're ready to scan, over."

Jacks hit the button at his console, leaning toward the microphone. "Commence when ready and immediately send the data our way. We need anything you've got. Keep an eye out for any sort of power surges or odd signals. Prepare to back off if you have to. Do you read, over?"

"We read you," Singer replied. "Please stand by, over."

Jacks leaned back, staring up at the blank screen. It flickered and suddenly the object came into view. The surface was displayed in high definition detail, down to tiny lines upon the metal like circuitry running in all directions. Light glanced off of it, making it clear the embellishment must've been a different color of metal on the smooth surface.

"Anyone have a thought about what those are for?" Jacks asked. "Theories? Guesses?"

"Conduits for energy," one voice tossed out.

Another said, "venting systems for faster than light travel."

"How about decoration?"

Jacks appreciated the break in the silence. Throwing out the question got them thinking, tore them away from the tension of the mission and allowed them to focus on the task at hand. He wanted to make sure his people were still using their brains, not giving in to panic and fear.

Agency headquarters had to remain stable, without discord. His people were in the best position to handle the situation but truth be told, they weren't exactly trained for an invasion. The battlecruiser had been intended to protect the fleet as they advanced outward, not defend the planet as their maiden voyage.

Off to the left of the screen, he knew the Demeter ships were floating, devastated from their run on the alien vessel. Thirty men and women, dead. Jacks shook his head at the senseless loss of life, the total waste because of these creatures who invaded Earth space. He would have to write letters to their families. The thought made his heart sick.

"Scans are coming in now," Singer said. "It has not moved nor done anything in particular in regard to our presence. Permission to close in."

"Granted," Jacks replied. "Do as you see fit, commander. Mission is yours."

"Thank you, sir. Surface composition is … not in any of our records. We're sending the data to you now but this doesn't make sense. The computer keeps finding unknown elements. We're running a diagnostic to ensure accuracy but I don't doubt the message. Part of the interference from the surface is an energy field of some kind. The shield we saw when the Demeter fired on it."

Jacks nodded. "Do you have any additional information about it now?"

"The closest thing we have is our environmental repulsion shields to avoid contact with space debris," Singer explained. "But theirs is much more concentrated. Like a true energy defense. Doctor Wilson suggests that the odd markings on the hull are emitters which reinforce the barrier. It must be constantly engaged but only visible when we attacked it."

"Can you tell how powerful it is? Can we penetrate it?"

Singer sighed. "*We* don't have anything on board that could. Maybe a physical probe but short of that? No. It's definitely capable of keeping anything out."

Doctor Meyers spoke up, "how'd those smaller objects get in? Did these shields lower when they arrived or were they able to move through? It's an important question we need to answer."

Singer replied, "we weren't observing when they returned to the larger vessel so I'm afraid I can't answer that."

"But we were recording it at the time." Meyers moved to another station and tapped away. "I'm bringing the feed up down here." One of the objects approached the vessel and when it drew close to the mothership, something flashed and it entered through a rounded hole. That hole sealed immediately, leaving the smooth surface behind. "Did we get readings then?"

"We did," one of the techs said. "Looks like there was a *minor* power surge but it barely registered on our meters. It was so small, I'm surprised anyone bothered to take note. This could've been anything, including one of our own people turning on a row of servers downstairs."

Meyers stood up and addressed the room. "We can surmise that these aliens have incredible power regulation. They are able to create a shield around their vessel which requires only a minor surge when they want to open it up. Furthermore, it barely registers when they make adjustments. That's an important factor to keep in mind. And … we know the smaller ones have the shields too."

"What's it tell us?" Jacks asked. "What do we know about it from your theory?"

"It explains their beam weapons," Meyers said. "And their seemingly reactionless propulsion. Concentrated, destructive energy could be possible as well. So far, we've seen what amounts to a non-lethal variety I'd say."

Another one of the engineers snapped his fingers. "If getting here required *them* to use that much power, then faster than light travel must require a ridiculous amount of energy. Especially if they have such a firm grasp of regulation. What sort of reactors do you think they have on that thing?"

Meyers shrugged. "I don't want to speculate but I can say this, we've encountered a giant here. Their technology *vastly* exceeds our own and while that might've been something we were taking for granted, proof of it is pretty intimidating." He took a moment to look at some readings and shook his head. "Wow. That's … incredible."

"Don't leave us in the dark," Jacks said. "What's wrong?"

"Those power outages were targeted," Meyers replied. "Just as when they hit the Demeter vessels. Singer's ship just picked up small bursts from the surface of the shields. Doctor Wilson thought they were random but if you check their trajectory, they are aimed specifically at the different places that are currently without power."

"Meaning the people trying to restore electricity are wasting their time," Jacks said.

"Exactly but more importantly, they're intentionally performing this action." Meyers brought a map up on the big screen. "They targeted specific locations, possibly those they thought presented the biggest threat. Unfortunately, they do *not* coincide with the missing people so we can't make that jump. It does mean they were worried about *something* in those locations."

"Isn't that us?" A technician asked, gesturing to the map.

"Yes," Meyers confirmed. "They tried to bring our power down but the base is shielded."

"Wait, they tried to take us out too?" Jacks narrowed his eyes. "When they attacked?"

"Yes, right away. They're all gone now though, so why are they still keeping us in the dark?"

"To buy themselves time to leave," Jacks replied. "Maybe they don't know whether we have the ability to retaliate or not, so they're playing it safe. That's what I would do."

"Sir," Singer spoke again, "we're picking up a large energy reading now, much bigger than before. We're pulling away and buying some distance."

"Do that," Jacks said. "And get well out of the way."

"The energy surge is picking up …" Singer's voice took on a tension Jacks had heard plenty of times before in his military career. The man was afraid and the stress came out as he chewed his syllables. "We're moving at full speed but whatever's about to happen will … in less than forty seconds."

Jacks forced himself to remain calm, drawing a deep breath before he spoke. "Get out of there, Singer! Just move. Put everything into the engines and get out of there."

"Thirty seconds." The connection dropped.

"What happened?" Jacks asked.

"Singer has cut communications," Meyers replied. "The surge he's talking about is coming from the alien shields, I think. It seems to be directed at the Probity specifically. The Seeker is pulling away. They're parting."

"Smart ploy." Jacks nodded. "Avery doesn't want to be caught in whatever happens there. God damn it, what's that surge going to do, Meyers?"

"I really can't say, sir." Meyers shrugged. "If I had to guess, I'd say that it would do the same thing to the ship as it did to Demeters One and Two. Hopefully, these ships have enough shielding to keep the crew alive this time if so. We're probably talking about some kind of EMP."

"Good God." Jacks rubbed his eyes. "Get the Probity back on the radio!"

Alarms went off throughout the area and Jacks looked about frantically. Everyone flew into overdrive, their hands flurrying over the controls. He refrained from demanding information or a report. He knew they needed to do their jobs but his curiosity and controlling nature battled with his need to keep quiet.

"The surge has gone off," Meyers said. "I was … right, unfortunately. The Probity has no power. It's drifting."

"Christ, can they get it back up?" Jacks asked. "What about the Seeker?"

"So far, it's fine." Meyers tapped the console before continuing. "They should be able to restart the engines if they weren't damaged in the surge. But they're in zero G right now and they'll need to get environmental suits on soon. I'll have Commander Harden start a rescue operation to help them out."

"Wait." Jacks held up his hand. "We might be leading them into the same situation. Have them continue to withdraw."

"Sir," Meyers glared at him, "Commander Singer's team needs help."

"And right now *only* Commander Singer needs it. We can't afford to have four ships down. I'm sure you agree with that." Jacks scowled. "No, until further notice, Singer's on his own. Those people are trained and I have faith in them. Start analyzing the scan data you received and get me more information on these aliens."

"Yes, sir." Meyers turned away, clearly disgusted. Jacks understood. He wanted to send people to help as well but practicality demanded they preserve the resources they had. He hated to assume Singer's team was lost but he knew in his heart, it was more than likely. They knew the risks and unfortunately, they were bitten.

I only hope it proves to be worth it. I've got information for the council and the world now. The operation wasn't a complete loss. Now, I just have to tell everyone what we found so they can start worrying about a different set of problems, instead of the ones they all made up on their own.

***

Doubt hovered at the back of Warren's mind moments before he called for the charge but by then, it was too late. The hallway was wide open. Their enemy knew they were coming. Any attempt at stealth would be a waste of time. Every second meant more people died in the terrible machine. Life and death hung in the balance.

The men and women under his command understood the situation better than any five soldiers ever would. Having nearly been rendered to nothing themselves, they had a special interest in saving the others. Even as they picked up the pace and ran toward danger and potential death, not one of them faltered.

Some of his people were not even military. Those civilians they rescued remained in the back, unarmed, dazed but determined to survive, to fight. The most zealous of them seemed prepared to put themselves at risk for it but Dex held them back. There was no reason to sacrifice them, not when perfectly capable soldiers stood ready to lead the battle.

A yellow glow lit their way, an indication they were closing on the machine. Blue beams flew past them, attacks from their opponents as they tried to suppress the attack. Warren pulled the trigger, the first to return fire. It was as if he flipped a switch. The armed ones on his side opened up, making the air vibrate with all the buzzing.

None of them knew the extent of the weapons they used. Whether they had ammunition or might overheat. It didn't matter. Desperation drove them on, a type of zeal that overwhelmed self-preservation. They knew the score. Surrender or capture meant death. Victory was the only option.

More people fell around him. Warren instinctively flinched to the left, the heat from the beam searing his skin as it passed by. Their opponents were apparent from the flashes of their weapons, each one illuminating a target for a split second. He took advantage of the visibility, taking aim before pulling the trigger multiple times.

Screams competed with the buzzing. Human and alien alike cried out as casualties rose. Warren felt utterly shocked that he had yet to be injured, that he'd made it so far in the front of the charge. He sensed his fellows around him. None of them faltered, even as the injuries continued to rise.

The aliens began to fall back, moving toward their conveyer belt. Warren knew their ploy. They wanted to use the humans as shields again, to put some doubt into their attackers while they could continue to shoot without worrying about what they hit. He couldn't count them but the bodies of their dead created an obstacle in the hallway.

Two marines pulled ahead, jumping over the corpses and firing their weapons wildly. One of them cried out and Warren swore the man must've been shot but he kept moving, tossing his pistol off to the side. A moment before it bounced on the ground, Warren noticed it was steaming from the handle and barrel.

Now I know. These things do have limits. Leave it to a marine to find them.

Dex grabbed him and dragged him to the ground, narrowly saving him from another shot. They landed on something soft, a couple of bodies of the aliens. Something wet soaked through Warren's shirt, making him sneer as he considered what it had to be. Shouts around them echoed off the walls.

The word *surrender* got tossed around. More buzzing happened. Warren pushed up on his elbows and aimed ahead. A target stood … he nearly pulled the trigger, his finger twitching half a second before the alien threw his arms up in the air, his weapon tapping the floor. *Did that just happen?*

Dex stood as their companions secured the prisoners, three in all. Warren counted the dead. Seven of his own people and more than eight aliens. They lost nearly half their force in the conflict but now all of those standing were armed. A grim pall fell over the group as they tended to the people they came down to save.

"How many humans could they possibly have taken?" Warren asked aloud. "And how many have already died?"

Avania stood at the control panel and when she looked up, her brow furrowed. "I …" She cleared her throat. "I … the number is … high."

"How many?" Warren insisted. "Tell me!"

"Two-hundred … thousand." Avania winced as the others started shouting. "They have processed well over three quarters of those."

Warren felt as if someone punched him in the gut. The number was unfathomable. So many. "How could they possibly churn through them so quickly?" He asked. "How is this possible?" Debra, Gary and Jake added to the list. He counted the survivors they just preserved and found himself surrounded by nearly a hundred people.

But that was not even a drop in the bucket compared to the sheer number of individuals who had been brought aboard. *This is an atrocity*.

"Where's the next converter?" Warren asked. "Where do we have to go?"

"Further along," Avania replied. "However … the number of dead …" She paused. "It may be prudent to take one of the shuttles you arrived in and escape with those we have saved."

"We have to try," Warren said.

Avania approached, lowering her voice as she spoke to him. "I've seen the numbers. We will not get there in time to save a significant number. There are two more converters on board and they've been going this whole time. By the time we get to the last one, at this rate, we will barely scrape another fifty or so. And that is being optimistic. How many will we lose in the attempt?"

"So we should hurry." Warren's conviction faltered. He felt terrible for what he intended to do, what he felt was *the right thing*. Human beings were being slaughtered down the hallway and he genuinely considered leaving them there. She was right though, and he hated her for conveying the message. "Must be a nice luxury to cast off lives so easily."

"I think there's more honor in saving lives than risking them for a lost cause." Avania's eyes blazed as she peered into his face. "I believed you to be the leader here but if you can't make this type of decision, you may not be fit."

"Don't presume to understand me."

"Then behave in an appropriate manner." Avania took a step back and swept her hand over the people around them. "Look into their faces and decide what we'll do. I'm prepared to follow you regardless. I will help in whatever way I must to get us off this ship and to safety. We are in a dire place. Act accordingly."

Warren gestured for Dex to join them. "We need secure a shuttle and get out of here."

"What about our other people?"

"Think about it." Warren scowled. "They're already dead. We need to save the ones we can. Once we're back on Earth, we've got a surprise for these pricks and will take them down. Providing I get there in time to launch it." He looked at Avania. "Mind leading the way? Seems like it's time to go."

Chapter 6

Jacks sat in his office, watching real time collaboration between the scientists and the technicians over the data collected on the object. He was hoping they'd have some reasonable information soon, something he could take to the council but so far, they were in theory mode. That wouldn't help.

Hard facts! Jacks felt frustrated. *I need hard facts. Without them, we're all just spinning our wheels and the world knows it.*

A knock at the door ended when Doctor Meyers stepped inside. "Simulations are done. Our weapons would certainly damage the metal but those shields are another matter entirely. That technology …" He shook his head, eyes wide. "I'm having a hard time explaining … it's potent. Repulsion on a level that we've only talked about."

"Break it down," Jacks said. "You think it can stop our weapons?"

"My initial calculations suggest it could shrug off decent side asteroids." Meyers sat down with a sigh. "We're going to have to find another way to crack it if we intend to destroy the thing. If that's what you intend to do with the Leviathan. Somehow, we'll have to deal with that defense."

"What about their blast that knocked out the Probity's power? Can the Leviathan defend against it?"

"The good news is we've done an analysis and determined that they basically hit the ship with a concentrated EMP blast. Luckily, the Leviathan had the problem that kept them grounded so we can put something in place to protect the core systems. Essentially, if they are hit, the reactor will not go offline. They'll just have to reboot effected systems and move on."

"What's that mean for the Probity's crew? Or the Demeter ships?"

"We haven't been able to raise them on communications," Meyers replied, "however, if the Probity crew got their environmental suits on, there's a good chance they're alive. Once the situation's under control, we can help them. They might need to abandon ship but I'm hoping it's just a matter of a few repairs."

"How's that ship different than the Leviathan?"

"Technology on the battleship is the most advanced we've got. Everything is shielded for combat. While that doesn't necessarily help against the EMP, it is reinforced. It shouldn't overload the way our first ship did. Plus, we're ready for it. Forewarned is forearmed in this case, especially when it comes to toys. To put it simply, they tipped their hand."

Jacks rubbed eyes, leaning back in his chair. The Leviathan hadn't reported readiness yet. They were still in the testing phase of putting in that damn regulator. *At least I have information.* He looked up just as Madison burst into the room, eyes wide. Sweat soaked his hair and he'd gone totally white.

Horrors filled his mind as he considered the alien attack. They'd done it once, why not again? The next time, it might be far worse. Everything that might happen played out in Jacks's mind. He drew a deep breath to relax. Blind speculation put him in the exact state he wanted to keep his people out of, a state where thinking became difficult.

"What the hell, Madison?" Jacks didn't bother to hide his irritation. Panic was one thing but anger, that worked. "What's wrong?"

"Sir … we've got a huge problem." Madison swallowed hard. "The media … they want a comment on video footage from some private astronomy lab? They witnessed the incident between our ships and the object and now, they want to know if we'd like to talk about it. They're demanding answers and would like to know if they witnessed our battleship failing."

The news could've been far worse. Jacks sighed. "Of course someone saw it. Why wouldn't they?" He stood up. "I'll make a statement right away. Let them know to expect me. Meyers, talk to the Leviathan and find out what's going on. I want that ship up there soon so we can get some better news than what they've drummed up for themselves."

"I will." Meyers nodded. "What're you going to say?"

"Something like the truth," Jacks replied. "Only with some positive spin on it. Don't worry, I think I've got this … unless one of those astronomers turns out to be our leak." He scowled at Madison. "Speaking of which, any luck?"

"No, sir," Madison grunted. "You understand, I've been a little busy. Too busy to worry about that!"

"I told you, two investigators can be pulled." Jacks put his jacket on. "Are they not working on it?"

"I honestly didn't get around to it."

"Get around to it. Now." Jacks moved to the door. "I won't ask you again and I expect you to fulfill requests. Go and I'll see you both later. Hopefully, we can spin this our way and if not … well, public opinion might not matter much if we end up going to war with the first aliens we come across. Wish me luck either way."

***

Victoria fought hard not to tap her foot. Delgado hadn't reported in for a while and everyone sat on pins and needles waiting for action. The vast majority of crew members aboard the Leviathan were soldiers, fighting people who had been in conflict before. While they might've been accustomed to waiting, they weren't particularly good at it.

The world outside raged against the situation. Victoria knew where it came from. History proved it out. A technologically superior force arrived and the lesser civilization suffered as a result. Those who survived the attack tended toward panic, insular fighting and all manner of other horrors. Sometimes, they banded together but not before they suffered a great deal first.

"Doctor Meyers is on the line," Madeline announced. "He'd like to speak directly to you, ma'am."

"Put him through, please." Victoria watched her console and when the light turned green, she spoke up, "what can I do for you?"

"Colonel Jacks is about to meet with the press," Meyers replied. "He'd like an update on your status. How soon can you launch?"

"I'm afraid we're still working out the problem," Victoria said. She wanted to express frustration about it but kept her tone all business. "It's a delicate procedure, as I'm sure you know. A mistake could lead to a catastrophic result. We'd like to avoid blowing up before we even get into space."

"Understood. I've sent technicians over to install a device that will help defend against EMP attack. We've seen the aliens use that now."

Victoria's brows rose. "Explain that last part. What do you mean?"

"We … approached the object with some of our other vessels. One of them was attacked and disabled. Our studies indicate that they've found a way to use directed EMP attacks, not only at our ship but key areas around the planet. Even our facility was hit. When we finish installing the shield in your reactor room, you *should* be able to weather such a blow."

"Should?" Victoria sighed. "That doesn't instill me with much confidence, doctor. If I have to lead this ship in an offensive, I need to know I can withstand the enemy's counter assault. Consider this, it may not even matter if we can get the ship up there if they can simply shut us off the second we move into attack range."

"That's why you're getting the upgrade." Meyers paused. "I don't mean to be the bearer of bad news. I wish I had something more positive to report but that's what we're dealing with right now. Please inform me when you hear from Chief Delgado. We want to authorize a launch the moment you're ready to go."

"And Captain Miller?" Victoria asked. "Have we given up on him?"

Meyers paused for a long moment and she started to wonder if he dropped the line. When he finally spoke again, he did so hesitantly. "At the risk of sounding fatalistic, yes. We have. You'll be taking effective command of the Leviathan."

"Did Colonel Jacks tell you that?" Victoria asked. "Because I'll need to hear it from him to make a change in the roster."

"I'm sure he'll tell you when he's out of his meeting, ma'am. I ... I'm obviously not authorized to give you an order." Meyers cleared his throat. "I have to go now. Um ... Meyers out."

Victoria crossed her legs and leaned back in her chair, staring at the screen. She admitted, she'd written off getting Warren on board but she couldn't quite place the moment she allowed herself to believe he wouldn't arrive. Launching the Leviathan had always been a privilege she hoped to *share* with him, not take it in such a paltry way.

We'll be going up there to avenge his capture and possible death. The thought didn't really give her any solace. *I suppose I should be thankful that I'll have the opportunity to be part of that instrument, to give these 'visitors' a taste of what they deserve. They certainly have cost us enough*.

Victoria stood, pacing down to Nicolas's station. "I'm going to see what's keeping Delgado. They're also installing a new piece of technology on board and I want to know how long that will take. You've got the bridge until I get back. If anyone contacts us, Colonel Jacks or Doctor Meyers, patch it through to my private com."

"Yes, ma'am."

"With any luck, we'll be up there soon but until then, hold things together." Victoria left the room, clenching her fist as the door closed behind her.

A concern crept in the back of her mind, about the facility they were on the verge of attacking. If the humans they abducted were alive, if they somehow survived their capture, then launching an assault very well might've meant killing them all. Somehow, there had to be a way find out for sure.

But if the technicians couldn't figure it out with their scans, the Leviathan would not likely do a better job. Could they get someone on board? A shuttle might be able to land and save people but would it be swift enough to avoid the EMP attack Meyers talked about? She needed to put some plans together and offer them up to Jacks.

Before they got into space, they needed some tactics to win a conflict. They'd been so worried about interception, they didn't talk about specifically what that looked like. Now was the time to put some strategy in motion. When she finished talking to Delgado, she'd put together a proposal.

Until then, the ability to launch would be nice.

***

Avania began to worry about stealing one of the collector's shuttles. She knew how to operate them, but they weren't designed to transport people about comfortably. As long as the occupants survived the trip, they did their jobs. Most suffered severe damage while traveling in them, especially with the lower oxygen levels.

Life support was kept to a bare minimum and Avania wasn't sure she could regulate it to do any better. Environmental suits were out of the question as well. They were kept in crew quarters and in the upper decks, neither of which they would be visiting. This meant they'd have to take their chances.

She figured out what must've happened with Warren's craft. They didn't collect enough people to use the majority of the oxygen. Those people began to wake up and when they did, they rested through the trip, ensuring they would be fit to attack their captors and ultimately overpower them.

Then they began their crusade to disrupt collection activities, a cause Avania had no problem getting behind. The humans didn't prove to be as practical as she would've liked but they had spirit and compassion, two things the majority of her caste seemed to lack. Especially her cousin and his sycophantic regime.

This chance meeting with these people is a gift from fate. I cannot hide in the shadows any longer. Would the humans help? Probably. They were passionate about the people they lost, the incursion into their space offended them and they definitely seemed like the type of race to hold a grudge.

I'll need to understand them better if I'm to make them allies.

Captain Miller seemed to be an overly emotional, head strong type. He commanded his people well enough, compelling them toward dangerous action to save their fellows. But he seemed so abrasive. When he and his friends first released her from the cell, he'd seemed confused, but genial.

After explaining the converter, transference and what it was for, he became distant and harsh. Perhaps it wasn't directed specifically at her. The situation was stressful, particularly to the humans. They were stuck in a terrifying situation without a full understanding of who they were up against.

It would try anyone's patience.

"You," Warren said, nudging her with his elbow. "Avania. I need a better understanding of this ship if we're going to stop it. Furthermore, how can we communicate with Earth? We need to let them know what's going on."

Avania glared at him for the nudge. "When we're on the smaller pod, we'll be able to communicate with your people. As far as an understanding, I can tell you they have powerful shields but mostly defensive weapons. This is not a vessel built for combat. They disable their enemies and flee. That's the tactic."

"How?"

"They can directly target parts of a planet or other ships, shutting their power down in the process."

"That seems bad," Dex said. "Is that bad?"

Warren nodded. "It's bad. We'll have to find some way around it."

"Yes, well … we'll have some time when we leave since you've deprived them of their prize." Avania looked around, ensuring they were still going the right way. If they followed the protocol she was familiar with, they would be securing the other converters and plotting their next move.

Meaning the collection crew wouldn't bother with an attack until they felt more confident about a victory. *They'll probably hit us when we try to take the shuttle. The confined space will make for a nightmarish battle, but one they will have the equipment for. And we can't simply depart. I have to override their remote controls.*

"What is it?" Warren asked. "You look concerned."

"We're captives on a massive space vessel designed to murder people," Avania said. "They planned on taking me back for execution all for profit. What's not to be concerned with?"

Warren scowled. "What should we expect when we get to the shuttle?"

"Opposition. Though not right away. I will need to do some work on the computer before we can launch. I'm afraid it will take several minutes."

"Meaning we have to hold it down." Warren sighed.

"It's not all bad," Dex said. "If it's basically the place we woke up in, then we'll have a narrow door way they have to get through to take us on. That will limit their numbers and they can't possibly overwhelm us. Four shooters could hold that room and we've got more than that. I'm feeling good about our chances."

"There you have it," Avania replied. "The challenge will be on me to set manual control."

Warren put his hand on her shoulder, drawing a withering glare. He moved it away quickly but didn't seem as bothered as he should've been. "I had another thought. What's to stop them from blasting the shuttle and shutting down the power? We'd immediately be captured again."

"Their crafts are immune to the attack," Avania explained, "they often hit places on a planet *while* their shuttles are in action. The metal compounds are, essentially, shielded. On the surface, you'd see lines riding all over them. Those are one part emitter, one part insulation against their own attack. Believe me, we will escape."

"But?" Warren asked. "I sense there's a second part to that."

"Chances are good they'll be making a second run. So far, nothing's stopped them. Why not dip again? They're going to make a fortune. May as well push."

Warren started to respond but hesitated. He smiled. "Okay then. How much further to the shuttle?"

"We're almost to one of them now." Avania gestured ahead of them. "We'll be in the hallway with all the hangar bays. Then, we pick one, I crawl into a horrifyingly confined space and you kill any collectors who try to stop us. I'd like to say it will be as simple as I made it sound but ... well ... you'll see."

***

Jacks finished the press conference, feeling like he'd just been kicked in the face repeatedly. The reporters were like wolves nipping at his heels throughout his report and no matter what he said, he didn't seem capable of satiating them. By the time it was done, he wanted a drink but there was still plenty of work to do.

They discussed the mission seen by anyone still in front of a screen. He let them know that the crew of the Probity was likely alive and that they were planning a rescue mission. People wanted to know why the Leviathan hadn't performed the mission. One of them even called out the technical glitch, another tidbit thrown out by the leak.

He distracted them by explaining that they'd learned the enemy's strengths and would soon be attacking it. This seemed to get them back on track before he cut the meeting short and headed to the control center. The moment the door closed behind him, irritation was replaced by rage and he had a hard time keeping his voice down.

Jacks approached Meyers and leaned against his console. "Did you speak to the Leviathan?"

"They're almost done with their problem," Meyers replied. "Our EMP shielding is also installed and should be working. Oh. Commander Serling needs an official order to place herself in command of the ship. Her words, not mine."

"I don't think that's a problem right now." Jacks rubbed his eyes. "If Miller somehow *magically* shows up, he can take over but she's in charge anyway so … it doesn't matter. Will your shield thing work? Will it stop the enemy attack harming the Leviathan?"

"In theory, yes."

"I'm sick of everything being a theory, Meyers."

"You think I'm in love with it? You think I want to have so much unknown? Science is about making an educated guess then using a set process to prove whether it was right or wrong. I can't simply *tell* you something will work when I have no ability to test it under the proper circumstances."

"Understood. I'm sorry." Jacks rubbed his temples as fatigue set in hard on his shoulders. "The reporters were on a serious roll. They knew some of our problems. I guess we'll wait for Serling. That seems to be our only choice right now. Do we have any idea about the state of Singer?"

"No, sir. I'm afraid our scans aren't much good with that thing so close to us."

"Damn it! We'll prioritize them for the Leviathan mission." Jacks arrived at the control room. "I'll talk to you soon, Doctor. Jacks out."

***

Victoria arrived in engineering, nearly colliding with a young technician dashing through the door. She stepped aside, looking over the chaos in every section of the room. Delgado stood at the center of it all, shouting commands and pointing at people as he went. Somehow, he managed to conduct the people, keeping them moving in a semi-orderly fashion.

"Delgado!" Victoria shouted. She didn't dare step onto the floor for fear she'd disrupt the careful choreography of their repairs. "I need a report! What's going on down here? Why haven't you finished the installation of that regulator?"

"Because some asshole thought it would be a good idea to throw on this EMP shielding thing!" Delgado said. "We've had to take some precise measurements to ensure that it covered the reactor and all the generators as well. Otherwise, the thing would be a pointless waste of space. Believe me, I'm not happy about it!"

"How long?" Victoria asked.

"For what?"

Victoria sighed. "Seriously? Until we can launch!"

"Oh." Delgado looked around and shrugged. "Soon? Start the countdown again."

"You couldn't have reported that sooner?" Victoria bit her tongue from saying anything else. She simply nodded. "We need to talk but we'll start the countdown up again. You let me know if anything comes up. Don't go radio silent again. We've got too much going on to be running all over the place."

"Sure thing!" Delgado went back to his routine of guiding his people as if she'd never shown up. Heading back to the elevator, she contacted Nicolas while waiting. The situation made her fume. None of them had worked together during truly stressful situations. Now that the pressure was on, they had the opportunity to see how each of them responded.

So far, Victoria wasn't impressed.

"This is Nicolas."

"Start the countdown again. The regulator's in place."

"Just now?"

Victoria scowled. "Probably a while ago. I don't know. Just … start the countdown. I'll be back up in a moment."

She barely boarded the elevator when her com chimed again, this time from Jacks. Either he had more bad news or he just wanted to follow up on the challenges they were facing getting the ship launched. Regardless, Victoria didn't really want to have the conversation. She clicked it on.

"Serling."

"I just spoke with Meyers. He said you were still in a holding pattern with that regulator." Jacks drew a deep breath before continuing. "I'm assuming you've checked into that by now and have an update."

"You assumed correctly. We're starting the countdown again. The shielding device Meyers had installed should be done momentarily. The regulator's ready to go. Nicolas is reaching out to ground control as we speak to initiate the sequence. We should be good."

"One last thing," Jacks said. "We've got someone leaking information to the press. Madison's supposed to have put investigators on it but they might be on the Leviathan. Lock down coms from the ship. Authorized connections only, understood?"

Victoria lifted a brow. "What kind of information have they leaked? Anything classified?"

"They mentioned the glitch on your ship," Jacks replied. "And we both know what that does to our credibility. Right now, this was the worst time to air our dirty laundry and yet someone did it. I want to know who, why and what they got out of the deal but that's not your problem. You're on containment."

"Yes, sir." Victoria didn't think it was as big of a deal as Jacks made it sound but it also wasn't a battle worth fighting. He was obviously passionate about it and wouldn't let go. The best thing to do was just comply and move on. She had enough happening that she didn't want to deal with his foul mood. "I'll make sure it happens right away."

The line disconnected just as the elevator opened. Victoria took her seat, wondering how Warren would've responded to the various challenges she faced in his absence. He certainly didn't have more patience than she did but he knew Jacks longer. They might've even been friends, though she had a hard time believing the Colonel had any.

"Did ground control respond?" Victoria asked.

"Yes, ma'am. They are on board and the countdown is back on. We're looking at fifteen minutes." Nicolas paused. "Yes, fifteen minutes as of now."

"Alright, I'll cross my fingers and hope we don't encounter any other issues." Victoria crossed her legs and tried to relax. It wasn't likely to happen but she gave it a shot anyway. The next couple of hours would be the most tense of her life and would make the challenges getting into space look like a vacation.

Chapter 7

Warren ushered everyone into the antechamber between the shuttle and the main craft, ensuring they were all inside. Those who needed help were taken to the back of the room with the hope they'd be safe when the aliens attacked them. He kept an eye out for any of the civilians that had been in the shuttle with him and he was relieved to see the guy who had been rocking in the corner.

"What happened to the others?" Warren asked him. The man shook his head, wearing a haunted expression. "I see. Go ahead, get to the back of the room."

Dex joined him. "I think everyone's secure."

"We'll need a lookout," Warren said. "Someone who's got some nerve. It's dark out there and God knows they won't see much before they get attacked."

"I'll do it myself," Dex replied. "Just make sure that alien lady gets her part of this handled, okay?"

"Will do." Warren scanned the crowd, finally locating Avania amidst the crowd of people milling about. The room seemed a lot smaller with all of them in it and he had to shove his way through to get to her. With so many stuffed into the dense chamber, he realized the aliens wouldn't have to try hard to shoot people.

They're going to have to stay down, practically lying on the floor. That's going to go over like a fart in church.

"Hey." Warren decided on talking rather than touching the woman. She had quite the attitude about her, which surprised him since they effectively saved her life. "What's the deal? What do you need to do?"

Avania stared at the wall then pressed her hands against two different sections. "I'm about to breach into the shuttle itself. There's a panel within that I'll need to access. That's where the real work begins. I'll be in position to launch so you might want to have someone near me to relay our readiness."

"So we can fall back into the shuttle."

"Exactly." Avania stepped back as the wall dropped, revealing the familiar chamber Warren woke up in earlier. Even though it was a different cell, he still shivered at the memory and backed away. "Good luck. We will both likely need some fortune over the next several minutes."

"Don't take too long," Warren said.

"Only as long as I need." Avania hurried in. "Don't forget to send someone in here!"

Warren called for everyone to get down. Many crouched but those closest to the walls went prone. He joined Dex at the door, peeking out. The hallway seemed entirely too quiet. The enemy had to be gathering somewhere. They couldn't possibly allow so much profit to waltz off the ship without a fight.

Which means they need to capture *their targets. Dead people won't have any value.* The grim thought was one he decided not to share. The cruelty and casual disregard of these aliens disgusted him, to the point that he looked forward to their attack. He wanted to put as many of them down as he could. *They'll hopefully learn not to come back.*

Of course, that wasn't the likely outcome of their current actions. Truth be told, if they blew up that ship, they needed to prepare for a counter attack. It may not come for a while but it would certainly happen. And if they weren't ready, the Earth would not stand up to a real assault.

Warren only saw a fraction of their technology and knew they were up against giants. The beam weapons alone spoke of that. Their transference process added another piece to the puzzle. Arriving as they did. Intergalactic travel. Every fact pointed to an intimidating enemy that made their intentions quite clear.

They were there to harvest human beings and if Earth didn't push back, there'd be nothing to stop them.

"I think I heard something," Dex said. "Just down that way."

Warren risked another glance before pulling back into the room. "I didn't see anything."

"It was there," Dex insisted. "I guarantee it. Here. Watch." Warren complied as Dex fired his weapon. The blue beam illuminated the hallway, revealing a gathering of aliens marching on their position. They both fell back into the room. "I told you! They're practically right there and did you see how many there were?"

"I couldn't count them all," Warren turned to the other armed survivors. "We've got incoming folks! You!" He gestured to one of the unarmed individuals. "Get to the back and wait for Avania's call. You're there to relay her success to us so we can get aboard the shuttle and get out of here. The rest of you, get ready! They're coming."

Warren and Dex each took a side of the door, moving diagonally away. Footsteps pounded the metal outside as the aliens approached. They didn't dash in, didn't throw themselves into the fray but rather paused, probably stacking on the door and preparing for a breach.

If they have grenades, we're in real trouble. The thought made Warren frown. *These guys aren't soldiers. They're like ... game hunters more than anything. Heavier weapons aren't likely to be in their repertoire. Their goal is to bring targets in alive and whole. The process probably doesn't get as much from a crippled subject.*

The more he thought about their converter device, the angrier he became. Warren took a deep breath and allowed himself to let it all go. The next few minutes needed to be about survival, getting his people home in one piece. He couldn't do that in a rage filled state of mind. Maintaining a clear head would save their lives.

A weapon peeked inside the room, firing a random shot that splashed off the wall. Dex's weapon buzzed and the enemy pistol hit the ground, part of the smoldering hand clinging to the handle. A scream echoed in the hall, a mix of pain and fury. It acted as a horn of war as several of the aliens poured through the doorway, igniting a wild battle.

Dex popped the first one in the chest and another in the shoulder. His fellows filled the doorway, laying down an impressive amount of fire but there were simply too many of the enemy to kill them all. Human screams filled the air. Warren was forced to dive to the side, hitting the ground hard enough to jar his shoulder.

He kept shooting, unwilling to give up. They'd die to the last man before giving up to the alien scum. Regardless of who won, the collectors would walk away with a small haul after that fight. Even as the bodies littered the area and cries of pain became louder than the humming weapons, Warren still felt the drive to push on.

We don't have a choice. Hurry up, Avania! We need to get the hell out of here.

***

Avania crawled into the tiny pilot section of the shuttle and had to take several deep breaths to remain calm. She hated tight spaces, especially when she could barely move. Thought slight, she still had to wiggle to turn. The cockpit, if indeed the cramped area could be called that, was only for emergency use.

They counted on remotely controlling them. *If only I had a tablet, I wouldn't have had to crawl around in here.* She popped a panel off to her right, catching her bearings in the electric system. Several modules were plugged into a main board. One of them provided remote access to the shuttle but she couldn't recall which.

And I have no way to scan through these. Avania frowned, looking about for inspiration when her eyes fell on the back of the panel. Someone attached a diagram to it, showing the purpose of each module. *Smart … convenient for me, but smart. I doubt anyone could remember what all of these things do*.

As she examined the chart, violence erupted behind her. Muffled buzzes barely made it to her but she knew what was happening. The collectors launched their assault and if she didn't hurry, they just might win the fight. *And I'll be back in that cell*. She found the module she needed but had a hard time figuring out which was which, mostly due to two empty spaces.

Please don't tell me we picked one that happened to be in maintenance mode. The thought made her heart sink. *Wait. I think it's this one*. Avania gripped it firmly and started wiggling. The thing was securely in place and as she pulled, her sweat soaked fingers slipped, making her nearly smack herself in the face.

Wiping her hand on her pants, she tried again, pinching so hard her fingers ached and went numb. Shaking from exertion, she felt the tiniest amount of give. It was coming loose! Another couple gentle motions left and right and it came free with a tiny pop. A spark made her wince and she held her hand in front of her face, waiting to see if it might happen again.

Avania turned to the controls and clicked a red button to her left. The engines came online and the whole craft began to rumble. Turning in her seat, she shouted at the person behind her. "Tell them we're ready to go! They should get on board now! We can leave in less than twenty seconds!"

"Got it!" The voice replied. Avania took the moment to familiarize herself with the setup. She hadn't flown such a vehicle in years but hoped it would come back to her. There wasn't much to it, at least until they broke atmosphere. At that point, she'd need to remember how to land but hopefully, it had some pre-programmed maneuvers.

Of course, it wasn't *meant* to set down on the surface of planets so there was that small problem …

All this pessimism is going to drive me insane. Avania shook her head. *Hurry up, humans. I'd like to get out of here before I think of more reasons none of this is going to work.*

***

"We're ready!"

The shout gave Warren hope again. He fired his weapon as he climbed to his feet and started back toward the shuttle. Carnage reigned in the area with bodies from both sides covering the floor. Dex charged after him, leaping over corpse obstacles on the way to what promised to be their escape.

As his allies fled, the door began to close. Some of them had to leap over it and others were gunned down before they arrived. Dex and Warren pulled a couple through but not everyone made it. At least six were unable to cover the distance before the shuttle sealed up, stranding them on the other side.

"God damn it!" Warren shouted. "We've got people out there! What the hell happened? Why'd that door close?"

Dex grabbed his arm. "Because we couldn't help everyone! Look around, there's a lot of wounded in here. Those guys weren't slowing down and if we would've waited any longer, we might all be dead."

Warren knew he was right, even as he struggled with the horror losing yet more people to the bastards out there. Would they surrender and be executed with the converter or die fighting? He hated himself for having to leave people behind, alive or dead. Those bodies deserved to be buried at home, not left to rot on some alien spaceship.

"Are we leaving then?" Warren turned and saw an open panel. *That must be where she is.* He approached, leaning in to shout, "hey! When are we going?"

"Just as soon as I leave them a little present," Avania replied. "I assume you still want a chance to take this thing out."

"You're damn right!"

"I'm certain they'll come down but ... just in case, I think I can make them pause." A tremor shook the ship and Warren leaned against the wall to remain standing. "There we go! Time to leave!" The floor began to vibrate, just as before.

We're free. We made it. Warren turned to look at the others. Those with medical skills helped the wounded. Dex made people as comfortable as he could. They walked out of there with twenty people. *Such a small number compared to what those assholes took. What a monumental loss.*

Warren called to Avania, "can we talk to Earth yet?"

"Yes, we can," Avania replied. "We're outside the range of interference. I'll ... toss you back a com unit. There's barely enough room for one person in this thing, let alone two. Here." A black orb bounced onto the floor and Warren collected it. It felt plastic and was perfectly round without any holes or protrusions.

"Um ... what do I do with this thing?"

"Press it against your ear and talk when I tell you it's live." Avania paused. "I'm going to blast the signal because I do not know how to target it. You might get anyone down there so be prepared."

"Let's just hope you don't get someone's house," Warren muttered. He pressed the orb to his ear and waited for it to connect.

***

Dirk finished an interview with one of the astronomers, a man who explained how devastating it would be if the large object crashed into Earth. Revelations in the bible had nothing on that guy. He went on about boiling oceans, rising tides, massive devastation, dust blotting out the sun and a whole bunch of other catastrophes.

Pretty much the opposite of what people needed to hear just then. No one wanted horrors. They wanted to know they were going to be okay. Assurance. But would they get it? The safety he felt in the newsroom suddenly didn't hold much value. Especially after Doctor Catastrophe finished his tale of terror.

Even when the Doctor made it clear that the object overhead wasn't large enough to destroy the planet, the damage had already been done. People were afraid. *Good job, jerk.*

He looked at his tablet while they replayed a segment from earlier. Breaking news from around the world involved additional riots, mass suicides, and protests. Radicals used the opportunity to air their agendas, sometimes fatally. Others simply chose to die and still others used their time to loot stores and other homes.

Better to die surrounded by things I suppose. Dirk wondered if their building would fall under siege, if anyone would drum up the courage to get all the way through the building and into their area. He knew they tightened up security, putting men with guns in the lobby but what he didn't know how loyal they would be.

After all, they had families and friends. Wouldn't they rather be protecting them? What would they do with the money they received if civilization as they knew it ended? Chances were good that anyone who stood by as a mercenary wouldn't likely stick around when the chips were down.

Dirk's tablet began to flicker just a moment before an incoming signal reached him. *Who the hell would be calling me right now?* He didn't have family to worry about him, no significant other waiting at home. His friends all worked with him and they were all present. Someone must've reached the wrong line.

Still, he figured he might as well answer it. He wasn't on the air at that particular moment.

"Um … hello?" Dirk hoped there would be a video connection but the screen remained blank.

"This is Captain Warren Miller of the Space Agency." The voice made Dirk smile. *Now I get it. Someone's pranking me.* "I need a direct connection to Colonel Wyman Jacks. This is an absolute emergency. I can give you a number to call but we need to make this quick. I've got a lot to tell him."

"Captain Miller, is it?" Dirk chuckled. "Space Agency? Next you'll tell me you were one of the people who were kidnapped by the aliens. This is a private line, sir, and I don't appreciate being pranked during such a dark time. We all have our problems, but they won't be solved by harassing people."

"Who is this?"

"I'm sure you already know," Dirk replied. "I'm hanging up."

"Don't you dare! This is *dire*, you idiot! Take down this number, I'm dead serious! We don't have a lot of time."

Dirk started to say something flippant but the man's tone made him hold his tongue. *It can't be possible.* "Listen, I don't know why I should trust you," he said. "How do I know you're on the level?"

"When you call the number I give you and Jacks answers, you'll know!" Miller shouted at him. "Here, take it down and reach out. I swear to God, we do not have time for twenty questions. Do it. Now!"

Dirk wrote down the number and pulled out his mobile phone. He dialed it in and leaned back in his chair, feeling uneasy. He assumed it would ring through to some silly voice mail or just never end but after a few moments, a gruff voice answered the line. "This is Jacks. Who is this? How'd you get this number?"

Oh my God! Dirk's mouth dropped open. He looked around, wondering if anyone else saw his predicament. They all seemed to be busy. *This really is happening!* "Hello, sir. This is Dirk Reidel ... I'm calling on behalf of Captain Warren Miller."

"What?" Jacks shouted, making Dirk wince away from the phone. "How? It doesn't matter. Get him on my line! Transfer him over."

"Um ... he's on my tablet." Dirk scratched his head. "I ... oh! I know how to do this. I have to hang up. Bye bye now." He disconnected the phone and went back to the tablet. "Mister Miller, I got a hold of him and he wants to talk to you. Give me a moment to make that connection."

"About God damn time!" Warren grunted.

Dirk frowned, dialing the number again on the tablet and creating a conference line. Jacks answered right away, "what the hell are you doing, man? Don't you know how to connect a line?"

"Not between two devices," Dirk replied. "You guys should be able to hear each other now."

"Warren?" Jacks asked. "Is that really you? What the hell happened? Where have you been?"

"It's me," Warren replied. "I was on the alien vessel but we've just escaped and are heading back to Earth. Is everyone alright? Have you launched the Leviathan yet?"

"No, there were some problems with the fuel regulators but it's fixed now. We've got launch countdown going. Should be up in ten minutes. How are you getting back here?"

"We stole one of those smaller objects that entered the Earth's atmosphere recently. Please be sure we don't get shot down. I've … I've got some survivors with me." Warren paused. "We'll need medical attention when we land. We'll put down as near to the Agency as we can."

"Understood. We'll delay launch until you get here. Just hurry if you can! I assume you've got a lot to report."

"More than you know," Warren said. "Get ready for us, sir. We'll be there soon."

"Thank God. We were beginning to lose hope. See you soon. Jacks out."

Dirk sat there with two deadlines and realized he should've been recording the conversation. *Damn it! I could've really been a hero with that one! People would've loved to hear it! Survivors! An escape from the alien space ship! And I have no proof of any of it! Damn it all to hell!*

Another set of breaking news stories crossed his desk, more tragedy and misery. He wished he could offer some hope from what he'd just heard but he couldn't corroborate the story. Instead, he sulked and prepared to offer up more of the same. Riots … looting … suicides … and death.

***

Warren pulled the orb away from his head. It made his ear ring but the sensation passed quickly enough. Hearing Jacks's voice was great. The world was still intact, still kicking and ready to defy their potential oppressors. Until the moment he made contact with home, he'd worried it might not be there anymore.

A rational fear considering the circumstances. Warren cleared his throat and addressed the soldiers around him. "Attention everyone, please quiet down for a moment. I just spoke with my superior at the Space Agency. I don't have any specific news but I was first connected with a civilian. He wasn't in a state of panic so I'm taking that as good news.

"I'm going to give our pilot the coordinates for Agency headquarters. There's a medical facility there and they're on standby to receive us. We'll be home soon and I assure you, that everyone here will be taken care of." He softened, brows lifting. "You've all been incredibly brave and I want to commend you for your efforts. We wouldn't be here without each of you."

"We left a lot of people behind!" A man shouted. "Good men!"

Warren nodded. "I agree. It kills me inside but we wouldn't have done anyone any good if we would've thrown our lives away. We need to get back to Earth, to tell people what we saw and prepare for more of this type of thing because no one here's naive enough to think this is the only ship in the universe.

"Others will certainly come and if we're not ready for them, then we'll be right back where we started. Victims to an alien race bent on harvesting us like a common resource." Warren shook his head. "I intend to stand in their way and any of you who have an inclination, and the training, are invited to do so too. We'll find a place for you.

"But know that there's no shame in turning down that offer. Believe me, I get it. But think about it while you're recovering from this ordeal and decide where you want to stand in this building conflict." Warren backed away. "Thank you again ... rest now. We'll talk soon. I promise."

Dex patted him on the shoulder. "Good speech."

"Thanks," Warren replied. "Offer goes to you too, Dex. We could use a marine like you on the Leviathan."

"Go into space intentionally?" Dex shrugged. "Honestly, I'd love the opportunity to dish out some more payback for what happened to Gary. If I get that chance, I'm in." He chuckled. "Besides, I'm not sure I can let you go wandering around without me nearby. I saved your life like ... five times back there."

"I only counted twice," Warren replied, "but I'll give that to you for now. Anyway, I gotta climb up there and give that woman our coordinates."

"You really don't like her much."

"What's to like? She's abrasive and cold." Warren shook his head. "If all the aliens we encounter are like her, then we're in for a rude time in this universe. I'll talk to you soon." He crawled into the passage and dragged himself up until he saw the soles of her boots. *She wasn't kidding!* He could barely move. *This* is *a tight space!*

"What're you doing down there?" Avania asked. "I told you there isn't room for more than one person in here!"

"I needed to tell you where we're going," Warren said. "And I think I might be stuck."

"That means we're both stuck then so you'd better wriggle yourself out." Avania paused. "So tell me where we're going then."

"Um ... I'm not sure how. What figures would you know?"

"Do you make the zero point the middle of your world? Around the center?"

"Yes, we call it the *equator*." Warren sighed. "This won't work. What do you see up there?"

"I've got a computer, a view screen and some basic controls," Avania replied. "Hold on, I might be able to make some space if I shove ... myself ..." She grunted and moved until she was on her side. "Okay, come up here but we're going to have to be quite close. My rear end is inside the maintenance hatch."

Warren turned to his side and pulled us way up, scraping his chest against her boots. She pulled them back against the wall, which made it a little easier but he really had to squirm to get up there. The light of a screen glowed above his head and he found himself facing her stomach ... then her breasts ... and finally her scowling eyes.

"Hi there," Warren muttered. "Sorry about this."

"It's fine. Just ... hurry, please. If you think you're uncomfortable, you should try what I'm doing to give you extra room."

"Understood." Warren craned his neck, looking up at the screen. It was a highly detailed, topographical map of the Earth. "How's this thing work?"

"You can tap the screen ... if you can reach it."

Warren squeezed his arm between them, brushing against her breasts. She tilted her head while glaring at him. "Sorry … I mean … this is … and you're … kind of … hard to … miss …"

"Just get on with it, already!" Avania closed her eyes. "Please."

Warren touched the screen and the map increased in size, flattening until he could see all the continents. "So do I just … tap where we're going?" He asked, trying it before she could answer. The screen zoomed again, enhancing North America. Each tap brought more detail until buildings showed up and roads.

Wow, this is incredible. Warren found the base and tapped nearby, just to the east of the complex. The smaller object could be moved later but putting it down outside seemed the most prudent. Only one part of the Agency was large enough to hold the thing and the Leviathan happened to be there.

"I've tapped where we should go. There's a red circle there. Does that mean we're landing or attacking?"

"Um …" Avania looked up. "Yes, that's where we land. ETA ten minutes at current speed. Now, can you get out of here? I already dislike tight spaces but this has taken a ridiculous turn. It's all I can do to keep myself from screaming like some horrified child."

"I get it," Warren shoved hard against the console, rubbing against her body the whole way down. She winced, her body stiffening. "Sorry …"

"Something just stabbed me in the rear." Avania winced again. "Gah! That really hurts. Kindly make this quick so I can move!"

"Hey, I'm doing what I can here!" Warren found a grip on the wall and shoved again, bumping his head on her foot. Another shove and he was away from her. She immediately flopped back on her stomach, letting out a sigh of relief. Another couple pushes and he'd be out of the chamber.

"I'm almost free," Warren said.

"Fabulous. I'm still in pain."

"I said I was sorry!"

"Noted!"

Warren shook his head as he slipped out and slumped on the floor. He rubbed his forehead where he'd been knocked by the toe of her boot and leaned against the wall. Sweat made his clothes cling to his back and chest. Turned out to be hot as hell up there, especially with a second person so close.

"Did you have fun up there?" Dex chuckled. "Sounded like more than a course correction."

"Stow it, Dex." Warren grumbled. "You should take a look. Coming out was like being born."

"Yeah, I bet you had a real religious experience brushing up against that alien broad."

"I said stow it, man." Warren shook his head. "Marines ... you guys are seriously out of control."

"You know it, buddy." Dex leaned over to pat him on the shoulder. "You know it."

Chapter 8

Victoria received a direct com call from ground control. *That's odd. Why didn't they go through Madeline?* She tentatively connected the line, wondering what new horror they discovered. "This is Serling."

"Commander, this is Doctor Meyers. I have excellent news!"

"Now there's a change of pace," Victoria replied. "What's going on, Doctor?"

"We've received word from Captain Miller!"

Victoria sat forward in her seat. "What? When? Where is he? Is he okay?"

"He seems to be fine. Turns out he was captured by the aliens! He and several other survivors have stolen a shuttle and are on their way here even as we speak. We're delaying launch until he arrives. I … hope you understand." Meyers cleared his throat. "It's not that there was a lack of faith …"

"I perfectly understand and I appreciate it." Victoria felt the tension in her muscles release and she slumped in relief. Much as she prepared herself for the act of going into war without him, she dreaded taking the Leviathan up without the captain. "What's the ETA to his arrival?"

"They're moving quickly, we estimate less than ten minutes. We'll be getting him on board as soon as possible ... with a quick debrief on the ship. We've got a lot to discuss and probably no time to do it. I hope you're all prepared. Things are about to move in fast forward for a while."

"Better than the snail's pace we've been dealing with," Victoria replied. "Thank you for the news, Doctor. Serling out." She heaved a sigh. "Well, Nicolas. What do you think? Feel better?"

"I fly the ship regardless of who's in the command chair."

Victoria smirked. "Now you're just kissing ass. Anyway, countdown's changed again. Captain should be here soon. I'm going to prep the briefing room. Madeline, inform key department heads to report there immediately. The way Doctor Meyers was talking, it sounds like everything's going to happen pretty fast when the captain arrives."

She left the bridge, unable to keep from smiling. All the worry she felt for Warren faded, really letting her know just how concerned she was. She'd lost enough friends to war, losing one to humanity's first contact with aliens seemed flat out wrong. The thought of it killed her. Had it not been for the job, she may have had a hard time holding it together.

Discipline keeps one focused, I suppose. Victoria didn't cry when she received news of her husband's death. She was on duty at the time, working with her people. Keeping her emotions in check then had been the hardest thing she'd ever done. *It's probably not entirely healthy to be able to bottle things up like this.*

Leadership came with some sacrifices. They involved putting aside personal feelings, acting brave in the face of adversity, containing impulses and always maintaining control. She learned the principles through a long career, watching others and correcting her own behavior when she caught herself slipping.

The brief time that she was fully in charge of the Leviathan gave her confidence in all that she'd learned. It showed Jacks and Warren rightfully put their faith in her and she was definitely in the right place. Things were on track for their departure and they wouldn't have long before they finally set out on their maiden voyage.

Hopefully, Warren has some good news about our opponent. Victoria thought. The elevator opened and she headed to the briefing room. *Or at least news about what we're up against. I think the world would love to hear what he has to say … if we'll even be able to talk about it.*

Some of the events couldn't be hidden from the public. Others undoubtedly would become classified. The council liked to keep a tight lid on Agency operations in general. There was no reason to assume they wouldn't be just as intense about the invaders. Whatever could be covered up, would be.

The NDA Agency employees had to sign would be sent out as a reminder and that person leaking information to the press would probably do some prison time. Jacks definitely wanted to know their number. Victoria had seen the insane things people got up to, including riots and looting. Keeping them informed might've slowed them down.

The longer people lived in the unknown, the worse their behavior would become. Victoria figured full disclosure was the best option. Keep everyone informed about the situation and get them behind the chance to defend their planet. The Agency might well turn the event into something out of World War Two, complete with enlistment posters.

All depending on how much power they retained and accumulated based on their performance. Regardless of why the organization was founded, they now had a definitive purpose not written in any charter. Defenders of Earth. While it sounded good to say out loud, the Agency only *just* found themselves in a position to enter combat.

And how the invading vessel was dealt with would ultimately justify the Agency's existence or condemn it.

***

"We're entering your atmosphere!" Avania shouted to Warren. He felt like he should duck or sit down. Re-entry should've been accompanied by rattling, shaking walls or trembling plate floors. He looked at the others, each of their faces etched in some type of fear or worry.

"It's okay, everyone," Warren said. "These things came down before and didn't crash."

"They weren't trying to land," Dex muttered nearby, earning him a withering glare from Warren.

"No one needs to hear that reminder right now, man." Warren turned to address Avania. "Do you have any idea how long it'll take to make landfall?"

"Minutes! Maybe!"

"As in it could be quicker?"

"Oh yes," Avania replied. "Very much so!"

Great. We're going to make a damn crater. Maybe I should've set the course for further away though I doubt any distance outside of five miles would've been safe enough to keep the base intact. Damn it!

"Can you slow us down?" Warren asked.

"I'm working on it … this isn't exactly maneuverable! Just … remain still!"

The vibration in the floor changed, taking on a much more defined shake. He wondered if it happened when the thing abducted him. *Why did I pass out anyway?* The thought was a welcome distraction but when the ship shook violently for a moment, the question was gone. He looked around for something to hold on to but the walls were smooth.

The area began to warm up as the temperature skyrocketed into the high eighties. Sweat already soaked Warren's clothes and now it threatened to dry. It kept getting hotter, like someone cranking up the dial on an oven. People around him started panicking, complaining about the discomfort.

"Um … Landfall in twenty seconds!" Avania's words made Warren's stomach do a flip. He closed his eyes and counted them out, going backward. Nineteen … eighteen … seventeen …

All manner of things bounced through his mind. Flight school … flying in a battle over Sydney, Australia … a football game in high school … a friend's wedding. Fourteen … thirteen … twelve … His parent's funeral flashed before his eyes then hiking in the hills just before he received word of the strange object approaching Earth.

Ten … nine … eight … Colonel Jacks visited him while he was stationed in Germany. They talked about the space program. Warren signed the papers that day for the transfer and never looked back. Five … four … three. He wondered if that had been a good idea. Two seconds before Avania's estimated time to impact, he thought he might've made a mistake joining up.

The floor stopped vibrating. The temperature began to drop, albeit slowly. Dex looked around, tentatively getting to his feet. Others joined him, their faces contorted with confused expressions. Avania slipped through the hole, landing in a crouch before bounding to her feet. She smiled, placing her hands on her hips.

"There you have it. Not my absolute best landing but nothing to scoff at, surely."

"Wait, we … landed?" Dex asked. "But I didn't hear any sound. Didn't feel impact."

"I didn't say I crashed," Avania replied. "Why? Did you expect to? I tried to keep it as smooth as possible. Plus, the coordinates he entered were quite close to a facility. I assumed you didn't want it to be damaged so I had to really finesse this thing during approach. I personally think I did very well."

"You did," Dex agreed. "Thank you for not killing us."

"My pleasure." Avania pulled a small box from her pocket. "Here." She tossed it to Warren. "That's a download of everything this thing had on the computer. It should help us when this is all over. We'll need the data if we hope to make any sort of upgrades or … well … do anything beyond what your technological limitations are."

"Thanks …" Warren examined it but it didn't look like anything he'd seen before. Just a perfect black box. "We'll have to figure out how to access this data. But for now, how the hell do we get out of this thing?"

"Leave that to me," Avania replied. She moved over to the wall they entered from and pressed her hands against two different sections. It began to lower. "I recommend we make haste to speak with whoever is in charge, however. If you want to retaliate, we're going to need to be swift."

"Why?" Dex asked.

"Because it's very likely they will send the shuttles to collect more specimens. And when that happens, we're going to need to be ready to stop them." Avania clasped her hands behind her back. "And after that, the real war begins."

"What's that mean?" Dex looked at Warren. "Do you have any idea what she's talking about?"

Warren nodded. "If we blow that thing up, someone's coming for us. If we let it go, then we're easy pickings and will invite another one. Regardless of how we respond, we're entering a long-term engagement … one I'm not entirely sure we're ready for. That's what I was talking about earlier when I made my recruitment call."

"I get it, but you guys are making it sound like this will happen fast."

"Fast is relative," Avania said. "These fools planned a long cruise. They will not be missed for a while. That gives us time. I hope your people are not the kind to waste such a precious commodity because we will need every minute if we're to prepare. Now … shall we disembark? Medical attention and what I hope will be nourishment await."

Warren looked outside at the field that surrounded the Agency base. The golden grass swayed in the wind. He took a deep breath of the fresh air and let it out. He'd never been so happy to see a place in his entire life and that said a lot considering some of the wars he'd fought in.

The sound of motors reached them as multiple trucks pulled up to the craft. Men disembarked, taking cover behind their vehicles while aiming their rifles up at the opening. "Attention!" A man's voice crackled over a loud speaker. "All inhabitants of this object must raise their hands and depart in an orderly fashion! Now!"

Warren lifted his hands and stepped forward into the light. "Lower your weapons, please! I'm Captain Warren Miller and these are our people."

"Slow down!" The voice shouted back. "Identify yourself again!"

"Captain Warren Miller! I'm one of the leads on the Leviathan project! Now please tell me you brought some medics with you! We've got a lot of wounded who need some attention and no time to screw around with this nonsense!" He stepped fully out onto the grass and several of the men lifted their weapons. "That's a good start."

"Stand down!" Colonel Jacks stepped out of a jeep, rushing over to Warren. He pulled him into a hug. "We thought we lost you, man! We thought you were gone!"

"No sir," Warren returned the embrace, "some of us made it … but not all. God, I've got a horror story to tell you but we don't have time. If we want to take care of that ship, we need to act fast. I've got us the best help possible and a few ideas. Let's get back to base and figure this out. We've got a bit of a score to settle."

***

Jacks sat through the briefing with wide eyes, unable to hide his revulsion and shock. Warren kept it quick and to the point with Lieutenant Dexter Pollard backing him up. The two men had been through a great deal, saw a lot of their own people die and lived to talk about it. He admired the fact they were up for more without some downtime.

What choice do they have? The grim thought made him consider the difficulty of their situation. They needed to disable or destroy the enemy ship. If they escaped, they'd report back what happened and cause more trouble. Once it was gone, Earth would have some time but it would be short.

Conflict, regardless of their decision, was inevitable.

Once Jacks found out they had an alien in their midst, he had her locked up on the Leviathan. The private quarters were put under guard. Warren didn't protest and that seemed to cause some friction between the two. Dex, on the other hand, advocated for her. He made it quite clear they were only alive because she helped.

Chief Delgado and Doctor Morgan Tillinghast sat in on the meeting as well. The former was there to hear about the new technology while the latter planned to give a briefing on the medical needs of those they rescued. Her report showed promise for all of them but her evaluation of the wounds inflicted by the weapons did not sound good.

With the story of their activities on the ship concluded, Jacks turned his attention to Avania and her fate.

"Dex has said you owe your lives to this alien. Tell me more about her. Why was she locked up?"

"She says she's part of a royal family," Warren explained. "Her side doesn't believe in this ... collection process and they were deposed. She was in hiding when these bastards showed up at the planet she was on and took her captive, hoping to take advantage of a bounty. If she returns, they'll execute her."

"Truth," Dex said. "At least, that's what she told us and none of the other aliens really talked after the first one. After that, there was a lot of shooting and very little conversation. But hey, we wouldn't have been able to pilot that ship or stop it from just going right back even if we did."

"She wanted out as much as we did," Warren added, "but I should point out that she didn't help us because she was feeling altruistic. She did it to survive."

"There's always more than one reason to do a thing," Victoria pointed out. "I think you told me that once."

Warren scowled at her and she shrugged.

"Okay, so we know she's at least *partially* on our side," Jacks said. "And she might be able to help us with the next part of our dilemma. Doctor Meyers can attest to you all that taking this ship out isn't going to be easy. We've been looking at the data we gathered and it's tough. The shields alone … we can't penetrate them."

"Something can," Warren said. "That shuttle we stole … I'm sure it could get back on board. If so, we could send it up with enough explosives to put a hole in the world. Once it docks, we detonate and *boom*. No more enemy ship. It's not exactly subtle, but I'm pretty sure it'll work."

"Maybe," Doctor Meyers replied. "The shield interferes with scans and com signals. If we go with your plan, we may have to use a timed detonation. However, I'd like to protest this idea. If we reverse engineer that craft out there, we can learn a great deal about this culture and their technology. Destroying it would be a waste."

Jacks nodded. "He has a point there. That's an invaluable asset you brought to us."

"I'm sure you'll learn a great deal from the weapons," Warren said. "You'll have some time while we pull things together. Scan the hell out of it, take hull samples, do whatever you need to but we need to use that thing as a Trojan horse. Unless our weapons can bring those shields down, this is our best bet."

"We're fairly certain the weapons will work on the hull," Jacks replied, "but the shields are tough. They're also how they attacked our ship up there and shut it down … along with several bases and a few cities. To be honest, I'm shocked they haven't retaliated for your little escape. If you were worth so much to them, that is."

Dex lifted his hand, "begging your pardon, but I really think Avania should be in on this conversation. She understands these people far better than we do and can offer insights we'll need for any tactical engagement. If you consider what's at stake, we should be using every resource at our disposal."

Jacks turned to Warren. "Do you agree with that?"

Warren hesitated for a long moment and finally nodded. "Yes, he's right." He turned to one of the guards at the door. "Bring our guest in here right away."

Dex smirked as the man left. "She's not going to be happy about being locked away again."

"No, I imagine not," Warren said. "I'm sure she'll understand. At least it was a suite instead of a jail cell."

"Gilded cages and all that?" Dex offered.

Warren waved his hand at him. "That's enough. Just … let's focus."

A moment later, the guard opened the door and Avania stepped inside. She held her head high, hands clasped behind her back as she scrutinized the people sitting around the table. Jacks stood up and offered his hand to her as he approached, putting on a smile in hopes that he might sway her from his earlier command of isolating her.

"My name is Colonel Wyman Jacks of the Space Agency. I apologize for having to lock you up but I'm sure you understand the situation is tense right now. We didn't have time to vet you properly."

"But you need my help now," Avania replied. She regarded his hand for a moment before looking him in the eyes. "And so I'm suddenly vetted … or at least deemed safe enough to have a conversation with. Is that basically the story?"

"Basically." Jacks gestured to a chair. "Please, sit down. We have a lot of questions."

"I'm sure you do." Avania sat but remained on the edge of the seat, her posture ramrod straight.

"Are you concerned about the germs here?" Doctor Tillinghast asked. "Disease? Any of that?"

Avania's brows went up. "No, we have a sort of inoculation for interstellar travel. Before we dive into fundamentals of that nature, I'm assuming the immediate threat of the collector ship is far more important. Is that correct?"

"It is," Warren said. "We were thinking about putting a bunch of bombs in the shuttle we stole and sending it back up there."

"An admirable idea," Avania replied, "but not entirely practical, based on your earlier proclivities and qualms."

"What do you mean?" Dex asked. "What're you talking about? You said the people we left behind were … were dead."

"They are," Avania confirmed. "But there will be more. Soon. I'm surprised you haven't already detected the shuttles descending on this planet again. They'll collect quite a few more because they have time now. When I caused that little disruption in their power relays on our way out, I bought you the opportunity to destroy them but now they have no excuse not to collect more resources."

"Damn it!" Warren clenched his fist. "We can't let that happen. We have to save those people. Believe me, I've seen what happened to them and there's no way they should be left to that fate."

"Agreed," Jacks said. "But how? What do we do?"

"I can muster a force," Dex replied. "If you have some marines on hand, I can get them ready and we can go up there with our own weapons. Save the people and get out."

"How's that going to work?" Delgado asked. "We can't penetrate the shields without their shuttle. And if you guys get up there with one of our own shuttles, it'll be turned off like our other ships."

"We go back in the orb thing," Dex said. "Load it with the explosives Warren talked about. We'll put them inside the large ship, get our people and escape the way we came in if we have to. Bombs will detonate after we're out and boom. We've saved the planet and all their prisoners. It'll have to be quick though because we'll want to get aboard sneakily."

"Will they know which shuttle is which?" Warren asked. "Will they realize the one we stole is on its way back?"

Avania frowned, looking away. "I believe I can do something with the computer to scramble that part. If you're willing to take some shots at the ones that are going back to the ship, they may chalk up a computer malfunction to damage. Plus, I think you could distract them with this battlecruiser."

"Get up there and attack," Victoria said. "They'll be intimidated at first, or at least focus on us for a time. That could give them a chance to get on board and do their work."

"I like it." Jacks tapped the table. "It has a lot of risk but I think it's reasonable. Anyone have any problems with what we're talking about so far?"

Doctor Meyers lifted his hand. "We don't want to take out those shuttles. How likely is it that our weapons will cause severe damage? Those are our people inside and if they get hurt or killed trying to make this ruse work … I don't think anyone wants that."

"That is a possibility," Avania said. "I don't know how potent your weapons are. Ours would knock them out of the sky easily. Do you use beams?"

"Projectiles," Warren replied.

"Then we are fine. Concussion will nudge them but the shields should deflect the majority of the damage." Avania shrugged. "You'll have to take the chance, regardless. They have technical superiority but they're not military men. Listening to Dex there, I think that gives you the advantage."

"That's good to hear." Jacks hummed, staring at the table with narrow eyes. "We need to time this well. Get the ship launched, attack those pods … when they come … and have the team ready. How much time do you think we have?"

Avania looked around. "Assuming they have not sent the shuttles yet, we need to muster ourselves now. Get your boarding team, find the air craft to attack and ignite the engines on this ship. You must be prepared to counter their move, the one we know they're about to make."

Jacks said, "I'll organize the air attack. Dex, we have plenty of solid marines available to call upon for this. I'm thinking environmental suits should offset the potential lack of oxygen in that shuttle. Pick your roster quickly. Meyers, talk to Madison to procure the explosives we need to take that thing down."

Warren added, "we'll get the Leviathan up and ready. When the small shuttles are on their way down, we'll head up and meet the mothership. I hope that EMP thing you talked about works, Meyers. But even if it doesn't, I want all crew members to have their environmental suits on and ready."

"I'll make sure that happens," Victoria said. "I would like to point out that we're ready for launch now. The countdown was delayed a couple of times but we can ignite the engines right away. Once we have the word, we'll open the hangar and leave. Nicolas has been fidgeting at his station all morning waiting for this."

Avania stood. "I would like to stay aboard this vessel and assist with the attack. I assume we will be coordinating events from your bridge. If we need to be nimble and make a change, you'll want me on hand. As an advisor, of course."

Jacks nodded. "Totally agree. Warren, get cleaned up and throw on a uniform. I think you've got the ten minutes for that. Everyone else, we've got our work cut out for us. I'll be in the control room the whole time. Keep the tactical com net open and we'll take down this invading bastard. Good luck, people. Get to it."

***

Victoria followed Warren as he left the room, catching up when he was halfway down the hall. "Hey, stranger," she said. "I'm glad you made it back. This thing would've been hell to fly without you and I'm not sure I could've handled talking to Jacks all the time. It's nice to have a buffer."

Warren chuckled. "I'm sure. Thanks for everything you did. Jacks told me about it on the way back into the base ... that you were a real pistol about ensuring we were ready to launch. I was going to push for it if I would've made it in. I'm glad we were on the same page but then ..."

"When we've got a minute, and you're ready to talk about it, I'll be here," Victoria said. "I can't really imagine what that place was like."

"What they were doing was far worse than being there." Warren shook his head. "Believe me, if that's what we have to look forward to, then war's the only option. They basically think we're just harvestable material … they had no empathy, despite the fact we speak their language and even *look* like they do."

"So what's the deal with the woman?"

"Avania?" Warren shook his head. "She's complicated. Don't get me started. Her name alone. Something like Avania Nika Dilanth … House of Keth. I don't know. It was a mouthful when we first met her and I haven't had a chance to learn more about the 'royal' thing yet. I can tell you this, it isn't England style figurehead nonsense."

"I'm sure you remember what it was like fighting monarchy run countries," Victoria pointed out. "The soldiers weren't exactly committed to the cause. Couldn't wait to surrender when we put it to them hard."

"That's because our opponents were starving. They didn't have our luxuries, our conveniences and much as their leaders wanted to keep it from them, they knew what they were missing." Warren patted her on the shoulder. "No, this won't be the same. These people have plenty and I'm worried about their zeal."

"What do you mean?"

"The people we faced on that ship threw their lives away to keep us," Warren said. "Zeal for money, zeal for country … I have a bad feeling that's what we're about to encounter. If that's the case, we'll have quite the force to reckon with. Worse … I don't know that we're going to be able to handle this alone."

"Who's going to help us?"

Warren shrugged. "I don't know but look at it this way. We know the collectors had a route. That means other planets, other people have been kidnapped and stolen. You think they liked it? No, those people are potential allies out there. But … we're getting ahead of ourselves. We need to contend with our own problem before moving on."

"Agreed." They stopped before his quarters. Victoria shook his hand. "I'll see you on the bridge, Captain."

"Hope the water's hot," Warren replied. "Be up there soon."

***

Jacks got Ted on the line, bringing him swiftly up to speed. The politician had a hundred questions, but he held his tongue. He seemed particularly interested in Avania, though they didn't dive into what specifically she was nor her involvement in the upcoming operation. Only that they had a plan to deal with the alien vessel.

"The problem is we're damned if we do, damned if we don't," Jacks explained. "Once that thing is destroyed, we'll be on borrowed time to prepare for a full-scale war … if not invasion. They've made their intentions clear by kidnapping our people and turning them into … essence."

"Understood." Ted sighed. "I'll do what I have to do from this end. Will you have trouble getting the fighters you need to intercept the alien shuttles?"

"No, I've already got them ready to scramble. We're just waiting for the inevitable launch of those things to come down here."

"Very well. Keep us informed and do what you have to do, Colonel. We brought you all together on this project because you're the ones who know. This situation is definitely one we're going to follow your lead on. Captain Miller's escape from that … that mothership will go a long way toward showing we have the right people for the job, too."

"Heroics, I get it." Jacks smirked. "Maybe we should tell the press about it."

"When you have everything in motion, that wouldn't be a bad idea. Look at what's happening all over the planet. We need people to see this isn't the end of the world but the start of a new one. Humanity isn't alone and everyone knows it. Now we have to show them that we can carve a place for ourselves in this universe one way or another."

"Understood. Talk to you soon, sir." Jacks killed the com and turned to Doctor Meyers. "Report on the mothership. Have we seen any activity?"

"Nothing yet," Meyers replied. "Maybe we're wrong and they're not going to attack after all. They might leave. Our people did give them a serious run on their ship. It wouldn't be surprising if they cut their losses. Don't you think?"

"You underestimate the mercenary spirit," Jacks said. "These creatures need their victory, they need the money. More importantly, our people escaped because they made a mistake, one they won't make again. Our people were conscious when they arrived and their escape caused all this. When they grab another batch … well … they'll be more careful."

"That sounds ominous." Meyers turned away, peering at his scanner.

"More than you know." Jacks got on the line to ensure the fighters were on ready status. He needed to coordinate with units all over the world. His contacts in Germany and Australia committed their people and multiple aircraft carriers were ready as well. When those things came down, they'd be prepared for them.

And we'll begin the first offensive against an alien threat. God help us. This is a new kind of war.

Chapter 9

Dexter didn't have time to go through any sort of dossiers so he had to go with what he had. Of the thirty marines available, he picked the ten with the most combat experience. A couple were fresh out of boot and he passed them over. All of them wanted to go. He didn't doubt their hearts but he'd seen enough unqualified men die in battle for one day.

"Environmental suits, rifles and grenades," Dex said. "Keep it reasonable. The shuttle's going to be full of explosives on the way up and, potentially, hostages on the way back. Once you're geared up, I'll give you a briefing. I'm hoping for a reasonable schematic before we leave and we'll go over it. Break and meet back here in half an hour."

Operation Broadsword was fully staffed.

He broke off and headed into the barracks to prepare himself. A quick run through a shower and change of clothes helped him recover sufficiently from his ordeal and he rushed out to find someone who could get him in touch with Avania. She was on board the Leviathan and he didn't have time to get to that hangar and back on the ship.

Dex grabbed a technician in the hallway. "Hey, how do I contact the Leviathan? What channel should I use?"

"Oh, um … try twelve."

"Thanks." Dex stepped into a room with several computers and interrupted some men chatting over them. "Excuse me, I need to contact the Leviathan on Channel Twelve. Can you help me? It's urgent."

"Sure, just use the com unit on the wall there."

"I … have no idea how." Dex shrugged. "Sorry, man. I'm new to all this. Give me a hand?"

"Yeah, no problem." The tech came over and tapped the screen. "Hit this, type in the channel and tap *connect*. They'll answer in a few moments."

"Thanks, man." Dex complied, leaning against the wall.

"Leviathan Control, this is Madeline."

"Hi Madeline, this is Lieutenant Dexter Pollard. I need to speak with Captain Miller or Avania. Whichever one you can muster. It's a bit urgent. I'm the one leading the invasion of the mothership and I have some questions."

"Hold one moment please."

The speaker clicked twice before someone picked up again. "This is Miller."

"Hey, Warren, it's Dex. I've got the men assembling but I was hoping we could get some kind of schematic or … something … of that place. Do you think Avania can provide it or should I go by memory? Might not really have time for her to give us anything of value but it doesn't hurt to ask."

"If you're just there to save the people and get the hell out," Warren said, "then you already know where to go. Hit the shuttles first, expand out to the converters and place the bombs. I noticed you're taking five nukes with you. I'd spread them out if at all possible. Put them near those converters. Should cause quite the bang. How many people are with you?"

"Ten. All of them are battle hardened marines so I know they've got my back on this one and they're all pretty invested too." Dex chuckled. "These guys thought they had their hands full when you and I were there, wait until they get a load of these bad asses. And we're going in better armed. Those alien pricks are about to have a bad day."

"Or at least a worse one," Warren replied. "I need to get to the bridge. You'll get a com unit with your environmental suit. You'll want to link up with us so we can keep in touch throughout the operation. We'll be on exfiltration duty so you'll definitely want to let us know when."

"No doubt. Okay. I'll catch you soon, Captain. Thanks."

Dex headed back out to the barracks and checked out one of the environmental suits. He thought they would be bulky things that restricted movement but they reminded him of the outfits the aliens wore. They were formfitting and the helmets offered excellent visibility. The oxygen tanks weren't even that heavy.

This won't be so bad. Dex examined the tech attached to the tanks but he couldn't figure out what any of it did. *Some kind of reprocessing unit maybe? Who knows? I'll ask later if it becomes important.*

The rest of the men rallied outside and he joined them. "Okay, guys. Let's go over the plan and what we're going to do up there. I don't have a schematic per se but I'll tell you what I know and what's at stake. These aliens have zero empathy for us and they are only bringing people up there to kill them. You'll want to shoot to kill in *every* engagement.

"Here, I'll start from the top about what we experienced and go from there. Hopefully, we'll be ready to go at that point. My experience began when I got sucked into the ship by a strange, white light …"

***

Captain Micky Chilton flew the F Twenty-Two raptors for just over six years. That put him in the heart of multiple wars and police actions, thrusting his unit into intense aerial combat. He grew up with a military family, his father an airman while his mother worked as a computer technician.

Both his parents retired long before he took his post in Germany but they were both proud of his accomplishments. Earning his master's degree in aeronautics was one thing but when he got his wings, that was a real celebration. Eight generations of his family served the military and he became the first to fly.

His father tried but vision impairment kept him out of the program. The news broke his heart and his career stopped at master sergeant. Though he was able to put in his twenty, his zeal was sapped by having to work in fields that never interested him. The passion he showed for the sky drove Micky on, pushed him to do what his father could not.

When he received his deployment orders for a major fight in Southeast Asia, there were nerves at his going away dinner but his parents knew what it meant to be a soldier. They didn't throw out platitudes about coming home or being safe, merely kept him company for the night before he left.

Since then, he'd racked up near sixty kills along with countless hours of recon and escort duty. He rose to the rank of flight lieutenant, commanding his flight in the air. They had enjoyed peace time for the past several months but when the strange object came to Earth, his entire base was put on standby.

They were ready for a fight but Micky felt uneasy about going into battle with a totally unknown enemy. Their fights often came with questionable intelligence but no matter how bad their information was, they at least understood the basics of what they were getting into. The equipment they faced didn't deviate much from their own.

The opponents Micky faced tended to have inferior aircraft. Near enough that they could still be deadly but not so much that solid training and good maneuvers couldn't win the day. Fighting with aliens took on a whole different set of problems. No one on the base knew anything which meant a totally blind engagement.

Micky joked about such things while he was in school. Some of his friends applied for positions at the Space Agency and they talked about what it would be like to face down aliens. Their idle talk became a startling reality when the thing showed up and the smaller objects came to Earth.

When operational command confirmed the strange objects were flying around, every flight was put on high alert. Different bases even launched a couple of squadrons but none of them engaged. By the time they arrived, the things were already on their way back to space. The news stated that thousands upon thousands of people were abducted.

If they came back, Micky hoped he'd have a shot at them. The audacity of these creatures offended him. To come down, take people and simply leave? If that was the case, they treated the Earth like a grocery store … though that analogy suggested eating. He definitely hoped *that* wasn't the case.

Micky's unit consisted of three other pilots, each veterans of multiple conflicts. He'd known them for a long time, especially Dino Corelli. They attended university together though Dino was two years behind him. He'd just received his promotion to First Lieutenant and didn't seem to have any intention of slowing down.

Dino came from a humble home. His father worked as a painter and his mother stayed home. An only child, he joined the military right at eighteen to pay for college. He got a taste for flying, especially the speed. He talked about trying out for one of the stunt pilot programs but needed more time behind the stick before they'd consider him.

Second Lieutenant Donna Kendrick joined the team more recently, replacing a pilot who retired out. Like Micky, she came from a military family, following the tradition by joining the air force. She received her pilot's license before signing up in an effort to stack the odds in her favor for operating fighters.

Patrick Farmer came aboard just a month before Donna. He was an orphan from New England, quiet and unassuming but a hell of a pilot. His natural talent put him above and beyond some of the brightest newcomers Micky had seen in his short career with the air force. Having Patrick join worked out great for them.

"Micky!" Major Reilly shouted from his office. "Get in here!"

Micky didn't want to leave the TV in case they finally offered newer information. They covered responses from all over the world. Looting and rioting happened all over. He was able to contact his parents and found out they were alright, staying in their country home well away from any of the action.

The Agency's attempt to contact the aliens also held his interest. He wanted to know more, especially if they came back and started trouble. Anything he learned might help in an engagement with this new enemy. Then it dawned on him that Reilly might be putting his flight out there.

They've come back!

Micky hurried into the office, offering a crisp salute. Reilly returned it and pointed to the chair. "Sit down. I just got off the horn with Colonel Wyman Jacks. Do you know who that is?"

"No, sir." Micky shrugged. "Army? Name sounds army to me."

"Space Agency," Reilly replied. "He's already spoken with the brass here and has operational command of our unit. He's fielding us against those aliens when they return. And before you ask, he's convinced they'll be back soon. Some of the abducted people escaped from the aliens."

"Some?" Micky frowned. "What happened to the others?"

"Gone." Reilly looked away for a moment, shaking his head. "Anyway, these invaders will be back for more. Jacks has a plan to deal with this threat but he needs our help. We're going to be hitting those things with everything we've got, trying to commit some damage. He did say it won't be easy … or safe."

"When is combat safe?" Micky asked.

"This is different," Reilly replied. "These things have some kind of energy field around them and they're tough. Weapons *might* not penetrate them but the concussive force of our missiles and guns could get through. I don't think you're going to like the next part of this … I know I found it difficult to swallow."

"Can't wait," Micky muttered.

"We're not taking these things down," Reilly said. "We're supposed to cause damage but *not* destroy them. In other words, hit them with everything we've got until it becomes obvious we could knock it out of the sky then back off. It's instrumental to the plan to hurt them only."

"What kind of plan did they make? Because I don't think a bloody nose is going to do shit to these guys. If they're taking our people, we need to put those smaller vessels down the hot second they break atmosphere. Hit them with everything, full squadrons and anti-aircraft weapons if at all possible."

"Yet, the orders are to do what I said." Reilly shrugged. "I'll be honest, I don't get it but brass told me to trust him and I'm telling you the same. Agency guys have been working through the problem since the aliens arrived. I'm pretty sure they have a better idea of what they're doing than we do."

"I've seen what they can do." Micky pointed toward the TV outside. "Have you watched the news? They lost some space ships to that thing! If that's your idea of them doing a fantastic job … or even that they know what they're doing, I have to respectfully disagree. You really need to talk to the commander … or anyone … to get them to tell this … Jacks guy off."

"That's enough, Captain," Reilly said. "I get why you're pissed, it makes sense but this isn't the time to give me grief or for us to go against our orders. They have a plan, we're part of it and we *will* execute our part to the letter. Now, will you be able to follow these orders or shall I get someone in here who will?"

"Sir," Micky lifted his chin, "there's no need for that. I'll follow my orders as given."

"Thank you." Reilly sighed. "I'm sorry you feel this way, Micky. Believe me, I hope we find out what they were up to when they're all done but knowing our luck, all of this will end up classified and we'll never hear another word about it. Regardless, we will perform our duties as we always have: efficiently, honorably and expeditiously. You good?"

"I am, sir."

"We'll have a full briefing with the team in ten minutes. Until then, you're dismissed."

Micky headed back out to the others and sat down to watch the TV until the briefing. They'd be going up against the aliens after all, meeting the unknown threat. Part of him felt terrified at the prospect but the daredevil in him looked forward to the chance. Nothing on Earth would challenge them like this.

What a story we'll have when this is over.

***

Jacks sent a message to everyone involved in the operation, letting them know the key players were all in place. The engine ignition sequence started for the Leviathan and it would be prepared for launch at a moment's notice. Fighters all over the world sat ready to meet the alien threat and the marines armed themselves, prepared to infiltrate the mothership.

He addressed the press one more time and once again, they asked a question which could not have been known outside of his staff. They wanted to know about Avania, about what the aliens looked like and what motivations had been discovered already. He couldn't understand how it was possible they hadn't caught the leak yet.

So immediately after the conference, he dragged Madison into a conference room and closed the door.

"I assume you listened in," Jacks said, "heard their questions?"

Madison nodded. "Yes, sir."

"There's no way they should've known about our guest … except for this God damn leak! Tell me you have some information. I don't recall you sending me the investigators you put on this task either." Jacks paused. "Are you the one doing it? Is that why you've been blocking the investigation?"

"Sir! No!" Madison clenched his fists. "I've got people looking into it but it's not exactly easy. There are hundreds of devices in use here and they're not all locked down. People are doing research, communicating with colleagues and working through any of a hundred problems. Finding one person in that mess isn't simple!"

Jacks continued to glare at Madison, staring into his eyes. He finally looked away. "I've locked the Leviathan down as far as communications goes. Nothing's coming out of there. Of course, someone might've said something prior to the lock down but … I don't know. I can't see any of them doing it. They're soldiers and they all know better."

"I don't know what to tell you," Madison replied.

"Don't think you're out of scrutiny yet. In fact." Jacks gestured for the marines to come closer. "Guards, take him to the brig and confiscate any electronic devices he has."

"Sir! Are you kidding?" Madison eyes went wide and as the two guards grabbed him, he struggled against them. "This is absurd! You have no proof! No …"

"No proof?" Jacks lifted a brow. "Interesting conclusion to jump to there. I think you can sit the rest of this one out, Madison. We'll talk when this is over and if you're not the leak, I'll apologize profusely. If you are, then son … that will be a bad day for the both of us, I promise you that. Take him away."

"This is ridiculous, Colonel!" Madison yelled as the marines dragged him off. "I can't believe you'd do this! Come on, I'm in the middle of a lot of work! You can't just pull me out right now! You can't!"

"I just did!" Jacks shouted back. He took a moment to relax, drawing a deep breath before entering the control room. Fortunately, there was too much going on in there for anyone to have noticed or overheard his conversation. He took a seat, bringing up the most recent reports from all sectors.

Everything seemed to be going according to plan.

Jacks was torn about Madison. He wanted to be done with the leak question, wanted to know it was taken care of. At the same, the man had been his friend for a long time. The thought of him speaking out of turn killed him. If he hadn't exhibited so much suspicious behavior, Jacks never would've had him detained.

We don't have time for shady. Not in the middle of this situation.

***

Avania finished cleaning up then stepped into the bedroom to look at the clothes left for her. A bland pair of black trousers and a white blouse sat on the bed along with some socks. Her boots were on the floor and her jacket was hung up near the door. The rest of her clothes were gone.

I hope they know how to clean those properly. She got dressed, surprised to find the attire fit fairly well. Drawing on her boots, she stood before the mirror. Her hair was a mess from the shower but she didn't have anything to fix it. Combing her fingers through it helped a little bit. *I look terrible.*

A knock on the door drew her attention but she had no idea how to open it. The guards locked it anyway. "Um … come in? I believe you locked me in here so there's not much I can do to admit you."

The door slid to the left and Warren stepped inside. Avania sat on the bed, regarding him with what she hoped was a neutral expression. He didn't speak right away but stood there, looking her over in an appraising manner. *Perhaps he's decided to be somewhat more reasonable now that he's returned to the safety of his people.*

"I'd like to invite you to come up to the bridge," Warren said. "So you can become familiar with our tech before we launch. I'd also like to introduce you to the crew up there. Once things happen, we probably won't have much time for pleasantries."

"You're taking this vessel against theirs?" Avania asked. "Do you have a plan?"

"We do." Warren explained how they intended to use the marines and the shuttle they stole to plant the explosives. "There doesn't seem to be a way to do this without letting them take more people … and they must be preparing to do so if they've stuck around. That's your assessment, right?"

"Yes," Avania replied. "They have no reason not to, especially after losing lives and equipment. The more essence they steal here, the more they'll be able to salvage later. The owner will make a huge profit, the captain will walk away a hero regardless of the damage done."

"Then we have the advantage of them having to come to us." Warren gestured over his shoulder. "Shall we go?"

"Certainly." Avania rose, following him into the hallway. They paced down the hall to an elevator. The guards stayed behind. "You're not worried about me enough to bring the soldiers, hm? And here I thought I was dangerous. That Jacks fellow certainly seemed nervous."

"Dex vouched for you."

"But not you?"

"I'm not there yet." Warren looked over at her. "I'll need a better understanding of your culture and your part in it. Frankly, I don't trust you. Your casual disregard for our people up there made me wonder how you're any better than they are."

"Seriously?" Avania glared at him, struggling to keep her voice low. "I took a road of practicality and you wanted to throw your lives away. Perhaps your species hasn't matured to the point of understanding what it means to pick a fight you cannot win, but my people have learned that survival trumps empty sacrifice."

"What about when you suggested they had enough and we could just escape? What about all the people you wanted to condemn then?" Warren stepped close so their noses were nearly touching. "Then we went and proved we could succeed. What empty sacrifice happened there?"

"The one in which you threw lives away while charging the conversion station," Avania said. "They took nearly a quarter of a million people and we returned with less than a hundred and fifty!"

"Which is better than five!"

Avania stepped back. "I agree but had you left when I suggested, you would've been back here to confront them with your war ship sooner. We would've saved time."

"I suppose we're going to have to agree to disagree on that."

The doors opened. "If you wish." Avania boarded the elevator. "Shall we? I may not have agreed with your methods or your plan, but I'm going to do everything in my power to assist with its success."

"And why is that?" Warren joined her. "What's it to you if we succeed or fail?"

"Where do you think I'm going to be when this is over?" Avania asked. "Do you think I can teleport myself home? You're about to destroy the only wormhole capable vessel within ten-thousand light years. This place needs to be safe so we can collaborate. Your people have entered a larger world."

"I think we're ready for that."

"Not remotely," Avania said. "But you will be."

***

Meyers finished off another coffee, wincing as his stomach gurgled. He hadn't drunk so much since college and even then, he limited it to two full pots during a cram session. The caffeine didn't help anymore. Adrenaline did most of the work but his hands were starting to shake.

This is never going to happen. The thought made him slump in his chair. With the mothership quiet, he wondered if they might be stuck there. Did Captain Miller and his people do enough damage that the aliens couldn't leave? Maybe they were stranded. Unfortunately, the shield was still up.

Any direct attack was doomed to fail.

The council asked him about nuclear weapons. He talked them out of even trying it. Any projectile attack of such a nature could simply be knocked out by the EMP attack. At least, he was fairly confident in his assessment. Like so many political animals, they jumped to the nuke option entirely too fast.

Meyers sat forward, preparing to grab another cup of coffee when his computer buzzed. His eyes darted to the screen and he gasped. Several dots appeared near the mothership. The shuttles left the nest, approaching the Earth with an ETA of twelve minutes. They spread out, plotting courses to various continents.

"They're coming!" Meyers shouted. "The objects! They're on their way! Colonel! It's time!"

"We hear you," Jacks replied. "I'll get the fighters in the air. Give the Leviathan the launch order. This is it, people! We are operational status."

Meyers grabbed his head set and jammed it against his ear, connecting with the Leviathan. Excitement made him tap his foot. Years of work were about to be put to the test. Theories, countless meetings, and arguments all culminated to the order he was about to give. *Now to find out if we were as clever as we thought. Now, we earn our place in history.*

***

Warren gave Avania a quick tour of the bridge and let her sit at the empty science station. She logged in and became familiar with the computer. Part of him didn't want to give her unfettered access but he tried to get over his suspicion. The enemy was in space, not on his bridge. Regardless of whether she pushed his buttons, she was certainly on their side.

He sat in his chair, looking over all the reports that came in since Delgado started working on the launch sequence. The engineering staff went through quite a trial to get their department operational. Warren turned to Victoria, brows furrowed. *No wonder she was so excited about me getting back.*

"You just didn't want to contend with any more disasters, right?"

Victoria blinked, all innocence. "What? Me? Intentionally leave behind the absolute worst work for you? Nonsense. Really."

Warren chuckled. "Uh huh. Okay then."

"So … be straight …" Victoria glanced at Avania. She lowered her voice. "Do you trust her?"

Warren leaned close, whispering back, "if it hadn't been for her, we wouldn't be here. None of us knew how to fly that shuttle thing."

"How's the one we stole going back to the ship?"

"They're putting the module back in as soon as they get the go." Warren frowned. "Don't know who the hell they're going to get to cram themselves in there but I hope they pick someone thin. You haven't experienced claustrophobia until you've seen how the maintenance and manual controls are set up. Seriously, I'm going to have nightmares."

"I think I'll pass then." Victoria turned to her own screen. "I hate tight spaces."

"Captain," Madeline nearly shouted, "um … Doctor Meyers is on the line. He's said we should launch immediately!"

"What?" Warren looked over his shoulder. "Send him over here. Avania, can you check the scans? Did they launch their shuttles finally?"

"Checking," Avania tapped the screen on her console. "This equipment … so slow. Who designed this interface? Did they have any concept of intuitive control? And what about … oh. Yes. It appears they have launched the shuttles. If I'm reading this … thing … properly, they are on their way down."

Victoria smirked. "Apparently, our gear does not meet the standards of the princess."

"I guess not." Warren got on the line with Doctor Meyers. "We've confirmed the shuttles are on their way down and we're going to launch. Open the doors. The maiden voyage of the Leviathan begins now."

"Got it, Captain," Meyers said. "Good luck and Godspeed."

Warren clicked the com over to Delgado. "Chief, this is the captain. Mind igniting those engines?"

Delgado hooted into the microphone. "Been waiting to do that all day, sir. Get ready. This beast is waking up."

"Here we go, Victoria," Warren said. "This is it. This is the moment. How do you feel about it?"

"I'm sure I should be excited … afraid … nervous … but if I'm to be perfectly honest?" Victoria shrugged. "I think I'm just relieved."

"That'll do, Commander." Warren turned his attention to the screen as the hull began to tremble. The engines ignited. As the ship awoke, he gripped his chair tightly. He'd waited for that moment for years. It was supposed to be a positive experience, one for the whole human race to watch on television and cheer.

Instead, they raced toward a fight, combat with a new enemy. *Maybe this will unify the world against a common threat. Maybe we've found the one thing that will overcome all our petty squabbles. Causes like this often come with a heavy price. I hope we don't have to pay it all at once … or any time soon.*

If the Leviathan proved successful, if they destroyed the mothership and saved all those people, then the real work would begin. The fleet would need to be armed, people educated, personnel trained and the entire world prepared for the war to come. Humanity's arms race would shift into high gear.

Because if they did not gather the force of arms required to deal with this new threat, the entire world would be in jeopardy. First defense, then allies. There were others out there and Warren vowed to find them. A common threat might bind them together with other species and if those sick bastards were collecting other races, it wouldn't take much to rally them to the cause.

Chapter 10

Micky Chilton powered up his fighter and prepared for takeoff. He checked in with the others, each one taxied up. They received their go order to attack the shuttles descending on their area and for them, it meant a ten-minute flight to their destination before contact.

Rules of engagement were clear: hit them with everything they had and don't hold back. Unlike human targets, these opponents were to receive no quarter. He supposed the Geneva Convention didn't apply to aliens though he guessed some sort of resolution would have to be passed at some point if they truly went to war.

Then again, who's going to complain? Micky frowned at the thought. *I bet most of the fighting takes place far from here.*

"Phantom One," the ground control technician's voice squawked in his ear. "You are cleared for takeoff. Mission is go. Godspeed."

"Thank you, control," Micky replied. He pressed the throttle forward, his stomach dancing in anticipation and excitement. His guts always responded to the promise of action, to the thrill of flying at Mach two. Their most recent missions involved a lot of dogfighting, especially when they helped quell a well-funded uprising Southeast Asia.

The wheels rumbled on the tarmac then went silent as he lifted off, climbing toward cruising altitude.

Phantom Two was Dino and he followed with Dana as Phantom Three and Patrick rounding them out at four. They formed up in a vanguard and altered course, heading for their intercept point. The objective was to start hammering the thing before it got into a populated area.

In the event they put it down, no one wanted civilian casualties from the shuttle crashing into a city block. Their operational theater occupied a bunch of open fields with a couple farms. Chances of anyone dying in a crash were slim. If the aliens abducted more people, that represented another problem entirely.

I doubt we're going to knock this thing out of the sky. Micky thought. *But we're only one squadron going against this device. God knows how many units are being thrown at some of the others … and if other countries have decided to respond to this threat without coordinating efforts with us.*

"I saw this thing on TV," Dino said. "They're huge."

"That's what she said," Patrick replied.

Micky rolled his eyes. He thought to respond but he knew someone more qualified was about to.

"Not to you lately," Donna threw out.

"Ha ha," Patrick quipped over the laughter of the others.

"Big means you won't miss," Micky said. "Not like that sortie in the Sahara. Remember that? Couple buildings in the middle of nowhere. Nothing around but rocks and a couple of shacks holding radio equipment and you put that smart missile right into a sand dune. That was pretty spectacular."

"You know, as a leader you're supposed to build me up," Dino said. "I don't feel all that built up right now. I told you, the sand interfered with my visibility. I swore I was right on target."

"How was visibility?" Patrick asked.

"One hundred miles," Micky replied.

Patrick laughed.

"That's enough out of both of you," Dino said. "I'm done. Let's focus on the mission, huh? You know, fighting aliens so they don't come in here and take our people? Destroy our way of life?"

"Take our jobs?" Donna offered.

Everyone laughed again.

"You're a laugh out loud riot today," Dino added when they all settled down. "You ever think of taking that act on the road? Make a little extra money or something?"

"Can't." Donna sighed. "Gotta stick around here and make sure you guys don't get in trouble. I think that's why I was offered the job, come to think of it. Babysitting."

"Woman's work," Patrick said.

"I didn't say they gave the job to you," Donna replied.

"Okay, that's enough," Micky interrupted. "Remember the briefing about this thing. It may have a weapon that can knock out our electronics so go straight for manual ejection if you have to."

"I really like this fighter," Patrick said. "I will be so pissed off if those assholes knock this one out. I'm not kidding."

"Yeah, we're all attached," Dino replied. "Keep focused and moving. It might be hard for them to target us if we're hauling ass. Are we thinking we hit them with missile runs? A couple gun passes and call it?"

"We don't have much more than that," Micky replied. "We should see it shortly." They came over a hill and he gasped, eyes widening as the shuttle came into view. The rounded object was easily five times larger than their fighters and it moved seemingly without any thrust. He allowed himself a moment of awe. "Jesus Christ."

"Wow …" Dino breathed. "TV didn't do that thing any justice. That's intense. Can you even believe it? I mean, wow. And it's moving pretty fast too. Clearing some ground. We're going to have to hit it fast if we want to avoid the city. I honestly didn't think it would be able to go that quick."

Patrick added, "I can't wait to find out how the thing moves. What sort of propulsion is that? How does it stay aloft?"

"That," Micky said, "is for someone else to figure out ... a person not about to go toe to toe with the thing. Line up your attack run and let's get this over with. I'm going in first. I know it's probably tempting to give them all we have right away but I want to test the waters first then coordinate our strikes on the second pass. Here I go."

Micky pressed the throttle forward, engaging the afterburners. The fighter responded as extra thrust pressed him into his seat. The familiar sensation of heavy g force closed on his limbs, compressing his stomach. Every part of him trembled with the vibration of the aircraft, pushing full speed.

The object loomed ahead, rounded and menacing from its sheer size. He didn't want to know how much it weighed nor the measurements of its actual size. Massive was enough of a qualifier for him and as he rapidly approached, he knew he didn't need to be close to score a hit.

"Firing now," Micky pulled the trigger, letting his missile fly. He banked left to go around the thing, moving to another firing solution. His ordnance smashed into the shield of the thing, flashing brightly as it exploded. "Phantom Two, did you see any noticeable effect on impact? Did it cause any damage?"

"Negative, One," Dino said. "I'm dropping two."

Micky went wide, coming around just in time to see the two missiles hammer the shield close to where he'd fired a moment before. A green shimmer rippled over the hull but there was no other evidence they even hit the thing. It kept on moving, not deviating course or attempting to evade their attacks.

Donna dropped her payload next, firing multiple projectiles and even getting a good spray of guns in before she passed it on the right. Patrick followed closely and he managed to get one off. The hull of the enemy ship brightened, a brilliant light covering the hull the missiles just plowed into.

"Patrick!" Micky called out. "Hit it! I think we're making an impact!"

A tight beam lashed out from the surface, going straight for Patrick's fighter. He had half a second to respond, banking hard in an attempt to avoid the blow but it was too late. Sparks exploded from the engines as they shut down. The craft began to plunge toward the Earth and the canopy popped off, the seat blasted clear as the parachute deployed.

Jesus Christ! Micky shook it off. "Phantom Four is down, Control. Repeat, we have lost Phantom Four. Need immediate pick up."

"What's the plan here?" Dino asked. "Because there was no avoiding that beam."

"Better question," Donna piped in, "what prompted it to attack him and not me? Or either of you for that matter?"

"If they're remotely controlled, then they might be handling more than one," Micky suggested. "Regardless, it doesn't matter. We have to keep our distance and try again. Hit it with everything we've got. Dump the rest of your missiles and we'll get the hell out of here, I guess. We're clearly not able to handle that thing. Wait ... look!"

The hull brightened again.

"Fall back!" Micky shouted. "Get out of its range!" He hit his afterburners, throwing in some evasive maneuvers. It lowered his speed but he didn't want to be in line to be plowed by the thing. Thirty seconds of flight, he risked a glance over his shoulder. He'd put a lot of distance between him and it, plenty to feel safe. "Report in."

"Phantom Two here."

"Phantom Three ... God ... Phantom Four ..."

"What is it?" Micky flipped his fighter around, craning his neck to see what she was looking at. "What's wrong?"

"They fired again," Donna replied. "They ... got Patrick."

"What? Why?" Micky clenched his fist. "Is he ..."

"It ..." Donna's swallow was audible on the line. "He's gone, sir."

"No!" Micky cursed, fighting hard to keep a clear head. He hadn't lost anyone under his command. Yes, people had been shot down but they hadn't died. And that young man had only *just* joined them! He was new to the whole thing and this alien vessel annihilated him, after it had already rendered him combat ineffective.

"We have to try something." Micky muttered. "As I said, all weapons … deployed … then we go."

"Sir," Dino spoke up, "with all due respect, that may not be a good idea."

"Fire from distance … we won't get as close as he did." Micky scowled. "We're not going back with missiles. Even if we can't take it down … even if this was just a God damn distraction … I want to do this the way they intended. Now, come back around so we can hit it in the same spot. I can't imagine we'll have any luck anywhere else."

"Chances are we won't have any luck anyway," Dino said. "Forming up on you now, sir."

Donna joined him on the left just as Dino arrived on the right. They flew in a tight formation, lining up their shot with the object. It continued to lumber along, heedless of their approach or efforts. *This might be insane*. Micky hummed. "Guys, follow my lead. Let's hit the top of it."

"What's the point?" Donna asked.

"If it hits one of us," Micky pursed his lips before finishing his thought, "then we can crash our fighter into it after we eject. Buy us some time to get to the ground before … well … what happened to Patrick."

"I guess that's fair," Dino said. "A little morbid … but it makes some sense."

They climbed, gaining some altitude before redirecting and barreling down toward their target. The second he had range, Micky called out for them to fire, deploying the rest of his missiles all at once. Streams burst away from their aircrafts as they climbed, turning their backsides to the thing before witnessing the results of their attacks.

"Direct hits," Donna said. "Damn it! No noticeable damage again!"

"Control, this is Phantom One," Micky reported in, "we aren't doing any good out here. This thing is impregnable. We've hit it with everything we've had."

"Withdraw, Phantom," Control replied. "A Tens hit theirs out on the west coast and didn't do anything to it either. Russia pounded theirs with more than three dozen fighters. All these reports are coming in. I hope we bought the Agency the distraction they wanted. The cost looks like it was pretty high."

Micky thought about Patrick and scowled. "Yes, it really was."

"Um … Phantom One?" Dino jumped in. "That thing has changed course. It's coming our way."

Micky glanced over his shoulder and sure enough, it had decided to move. "Control, this is Phantom again. The bogey has altered course and is pursuing us. Repeat, it is in pursuit of us."

"We're seeing that." Control paused. "Fall out, Phantom One. Get back to base."

"The hull!" Dino shouted. "It's lighting up again!"

Micky's heart raced as he hit the afterburners. Dino screamed in the microphone. A light flashed to Micky's left but he didn't dare take a look. Donna caught up to him and they flew wing to wing, barely thirty feet apart. They were going full throttle, pushing Mach two but it still didn't feel safe.

"Dino?" Micky asked into the microphone. "Can you hear me? Dino?"

"He went down," Donna said. "Just like Patrick."

"Damn it!" Micky strained to look over his shoulder. They put quite a bit of distance between them and the ship. He throttled back but Donna kept going. Something slammed into his rear, causing the alarm to go off in the cockpit. "Mayday! Mayday! I've been hit!" His radio was down. He wasn't talking to anyone.

He reached for the ejection handle just as another blast took his ship, a final beam concluding the fight.

***

Dex oversaw the explosives being loaded onto the shuttle and even he started to feel nervous. They went big with five nuclear devices, enough to level half a continent. Each identical, shiny casing occupied a heavy-duty box and required four people to load onto the craft. They were unlocked as soon as they were on board, timers set and ready to activate.

They also brought some portable cover walls, waist high metal plates they could use to hide behind when the doors opened. Men set them diagonally away from the wall that opened, preparing their positions. They were even able to test the new weapons on them and the beams didn't go right through.

The smallest guy on his team proved to be a twenty-year-old kid named Red Jumera but everyone called him Jumie. He ended up with the unenviable job of crawling into the maintenance passage to plug in the remote module at the right time. He'd then have to wiggle out and put his environmental suit back on.

I still don't know how the captain and Avania were able to be so cozy up there. Dex peered into the hole, shaking his head. *Not that I'd mind giving that a try. She's pretty hot for an alien.*

Unlike Warren, Dex gave Avania an immediate pass when she charged the enemy ranks right along with them. When he saw her risk her own life to save a bunch of humans, he knew she was on their side and until she did something to lose it, she had his total respect. *Warren will come around when we've finished this fight.*

The marines lingered about with their helmets off. A couple of them perched on the bombs, making Dex frown. "You guys mind not using the nuclear weapons as your chill out spot? Just seems … I don't know … disrespectful. Or at least unsafe. If you wanted to sit on something, you should've brought some folding chairs."

The guys got down and leaned against the walls. It didn't take long before they became surly and bored. Dex hoped the aliens would make their move soon and just as he felt compelled to pace, he received the word that the shuttles were on their way. *Right about the time I started to wonder if they'd bother to come back.*

"We're go," Dex shouted to the men. "Jumie, get your ass up there to plug that module in. We'll want to do it when the first of those things starts to go up." He sent a message to control, letting them know they were in position and ready to go. "When this starts to move, everyone put on your helmet. Double check each other's seals too!"

Jumie crawled into the hole, disappearing a moment later. "I'm in position!" He shouted down. "Give me the word and I'll make it happen."

Dex forced himself to lean against the wall, waiting for control to update him. He turned to the others. "Be sure to stay near the cover. A good estimate is that it's going to take about fifteen minutes to get there. That's how long it took to get back. We were unconscious during the first trip so none of us had a good idea."

"Fighters engaged the shuttles," Control said. "Several of the objects seem to be fleeing back to orbit. Broadsword, you are go. Plug that module in and see what happens."

If we just sit here, we know we're screwed. Dex turned to the hole. "Go for it, Jumie! Plug that thing in and get your little ass down here!"

"On it, sir!"

Dex wondered if the Leviathan was already airborne. He wanted to see it go, watch the thing lift off from a distance and witness it dominate the sky before climbing toward orbit. One of the greatest wonders the world would ever know and he had to see it on a rerun after they returned from a mission.

Work gets in the way of some of the greatest things. Dex sighed, grabbing his helmet and sliding it over his head. He initiated the seals and contacted control to check his com volume. They replied an affirmative and he could easily hear. The others followed suit, each of them checking each other's gear.

Jumie came sliding out of the hole and started throwing on his gear again. Dex waited until he was done and checked his seals before letting the kid do the same for him. They all shouldered their weapons and moved behind the cover, waiting for the thing to take off. *Will this crazy idea work?*

Dex doubted it until he put their opponents in perspective. They were not soldiers, but workers doing a job. Automated systems were in place to ensure they did *not* have to worry about things such as piloting shuttles or repairing things. Their sole focus involved processing product.

The aliens were there to do grunt work, not be technological masterminds.

Ten minutes passed and Dex started to worry. He inhaled to ask control what was going on when the floor began to vibrate. The ship moved, climbing abruptly as it left the surface and headed back toward the mothership. *Oh my God, this actually worked!* The other marines hooted but he shushed them.

"Guys, save your oxygen. If things go south, we might be in zero G for a while. I don't know about any of you, but I haven't exactly been trained in how to maneuver in that. Just … be conservative and we'll be fine."

"Um … sir?" Jumie raised his hand. "These oxygen tanks reprocess and scrub. We've got six hours of oxygen in these."

"We do?" Dex huffed in surprise. "Well ... that's cool. I wondered what all the extra parts were on these things. Thanks for that. Let's keep it down anyway. We don't need to waste a bunch of time on celebration. There'll be plenty of time for that when we get home and that thing's blown up. I'll even pick up the tab for the whole night."

His offer made them cheer again but they cut it short, making him smirk. *Can't fault their enthusiasm, even if it is a little misplaced. Will adrenaline keep them from being scared when we get on board? I guess we'll see.*

***

The Leviathan rose from its perch, climbing sharply to attain orbit. Powerful thrusters compelled it forward, steadily ascending. Artificial gravity wouldn't kick in until they attained orbit so until then, they were pressed into their seats at an angle. Safety straps dug into Warren's shoulders, holding him firmly in place.

Nicolas tapped his console in a continuous state of motion, as if he were typing a dissertation. He had the most difficult job during takeoff, managing their trajectory to ensure a clean departure. If anything went wrong, Delgado's people wouldn't likely be able to correct the problem in time to avert disaster.

This meant navigating was of utmost importance. If the ship failed to break orbit, Nicolas would be the one to direct their crash to avoid civilian casualties. The thought of failure kept Warren up some nights, thinking about how damaging it would be to the Agency's reputation if the Leviathan did not work out.

No matter how many calculations were made or successful tests were performed, Warren knew he would not be satisfied until the ship survived its maiden voyage. As they rushed off to meet the collector ship, he wondered how long they would have up there before losing their flagship.

Think optimistic thoughts. Warren reminded himself of the EMP shields and tried to take heart in them. He didn't mean to be negative but it seemed more responsible to consider the problems rather than dismiss him. Unfortunately, he didn't have solutions for them yet. *Soon. I just need some more time*.

The ship shook violently as they reached the upper stratosphere. Wind speeds topped over a hundred kilometers per hour and the turbulence knocked them around. Madeline cried out and he checked to see she was okay. She closed her eyes tightly, holding on to her chair. He understood her worry.

Briefings didn't do departure justice. Saying it would be rough didn't click with people until they were involved. Warren, Nicolas and Victoria all went into space on the smaller vessels. Madeline had not. The Leviathan took the punishment far better than their other ships, that was for sure.

Warren nearly threw up the first time which said a lot considering his prior profession. He turned his attention to Avania who sat with her arms crossed, wearing a bored expression. *I wonder how many times you've been into space*. He turned back around and settled into his chair. *Their advanced ships might not suffer from this type of departure.*

If so, he would've sworn such shaking would've woken him up on the shuttle as they left Earth before. *Maybe that's how Dex woke up*. Warren had been the last person to be caught by the aliens and likely suffered from the effects of their strange beam for a longer period of time.

It dawned on him he didn't understand how exactly he'd been brought on board the shuttle. Was it a form of teleportation? Did they simply drag him up there with a tractor beam? The latter was theoretical from the perspective of the Agency but the former had been ruled out almost from the beginning.

Avania would know and when they had a moment, he'd ask.

The shaking slowed down, finally stopping and a low hum filled the bridge. Warren checked his monitor for system status, noting that the artificial gravity was online. He looked forward to testing it. The smaller ships didn't have it installed yet. Each module was much too big to fit but engineers were working on reducing the overall size.

Nicolas turned, grinning at them. "Welcome to space, everyone. The Leviathan has broken Earth's gravitational pull. All systems are operating in the green and we are free to maneuver."

Warren clapped Victoria on the shoulder. "There you go. I told you, didn't I? You made it up here. It just took a while."

"A very long while," Victoria said. "Longer than any of us anticipated to be sure." She turned to Nicolas. "Bring the screen online." It flickered on, revealing the dark of space with the moon to the left. She disengaged her safety belts and stood up, taking a couple tentative steps forward. "This is incredible … every aspect of it."

Her wonder made Warren smile and he joined her, placing a hand on the back of Nicolas's chair. "Turn us about to the port. Get the mothership in our line of sight and let's take a look at our target."

Nicolas engaged the thrusters and as the ship moved, Warren felt it through the deck. A vibration tickled his feet, settling into something so subtle he had to concentrate to know it was happening. He returned to his seat, leaning forward as the view on the screen shifted slowly to the left.

Twenty seconds later, the mothership filled the screen, the giant orb sitting out there near the moon. Warren narrowed his eyes as he took it in. *Our next meeting will be quite different, I assure you*. He gestured to Madeline. "Inform control we are in position to engage the enemy."

"Yes, sir." Madeline started speaking quietly.

Avania joined him, staring at the screen. "Congratulations. I expected this ship to not have gravity. You're further along than I anticipated."

"I'm glad we've managed to impress you," Warren replied. "I'm guessing that's hard."

"I don't know." Avania shrugged. "Your people have shown many qualities that make me better understand why the collectors consider you such a high value target. Your spirit alone sets you apart though this ingenuity is also impressive." She clasped her hands behind her back. "What sort of shields does this thing have?"

"Environmental," Warren replied. "We use sonic noise to repel debris. That's … pretty much it."

"That might be enough to build on." Avania hummed. "Our own technology in that regard isn't too different."

"You mentioned spirit," Victoria said. She didn't turn around as she spoke, maintaining her focus on the mothership. "Is that why they came here? Why they picked humans at all? Willpower?"

"Absolutely," Avania replied. "Your kind has always been special. Disciplined, strong, perseverant. The process requires vitality and vibrancy. To be honest, our people would work as well but of course, none of them volunteer for such things. The hypocrisy of the privileged, trickling down until your kind suffers for it."

"Sounds sick," Nicolas muttered.

"It is," Warren replied.

"Update from control," Madeline said. "The shuttles are returning to orbit. Several of the flights took heavy damage and losses. They …" She paused, clearing her throat. "Sixty percent casualties."

Nicolas turned in his seat, eyes wide. "Jesus Christ, those things really went crazy then! Sixty percent?"

"I know." Warren held up his hand. "Stay focused. Madeline, did they say the stolen shuttle launched?"

"Yes, sir. It's on its way."

"Then our distraction needs to begin now." Warren nodded toward the screen. "Engage engines, Nicolas. Close on the ship and get ready to hit it with everything we've got. Madeline, remind everyone to keep their environmental suits handy. If those EMP shields don't work, we're definitely going to need them."

"Are you ready for this?" Avania asked. "When you start shooting them, they'll direct their weapons your way."

"And hopefully ignore the shuttles."

"This thing isn't going to be able to evade anything." Avania moved to look over Nicolas's shoulder. "We're going to pretty much be entering a punching contest. I'm going to run some scans over their ship and see if my parting shot did any damage we can exploit. Just on our way out, I sent a shockwave through the hangar to give them something to do."

"Repairs?" Nicolas asked.

"Essentially," Avania replied. "Nothing too bad, but something to prevent them from trying to wormhole out of here. Some types of damage are severe enough that using a wormhole can tear the ship apart. We've seen it during combat when a vessel desperately attempts to escape only to destroy themselves in the process."

"Sounds … dangerous," Victoria added. "Is there any way around that?"

"Seal the damage," Avania explained, "and perhaps pray. On occasion, fortune has provided." She sat down and started tapping away at the console. "I'll let you know what I find momentarily. Um …" Warren looked back, noting her furrowed brows and frustrated look. "*This* is your scanning software? My goodness …"

"Let me guess," Warren said, "not up to your standards?"

Avania sighed. "Antiquated, that's all. It will take a few minutes more but I'll get it. If there's a weakness, I'll help you exploit it. For now, the distraction will be enough. Besides, they've got a lot on their minds at the moment. Adding more to it will definitely test their powers of observation."

"Nicolas," Warren said, "tell me when we're in range. Power up the weapons in the meantime and Madeline, ensure our shuttle pilots are ready to go to get those people out of there. We'll get as close as we can but they're going to have to move fast. This is why we're out here, folks. Make it count."

Chapter 11

Dex checked his watch for the tenth time since they felt the shuttle start to move. Tension filled the room, getting worse with every passing minute. Approaching the mothership held a number of unknowns. Did the aliens know they were there? Could they open the door when they arrived? Would the Leviathan's pilot help them escape in time?

More importantly, would they detect the bombs? Their technology was ridiculous and might easily put them in a position to catch on to the radiation. None of the people on Earth know one way or another. Dex tried not to second guess it, tried to brush it off as pre-combat nerves. He rarely suffered from such things but he gave himself a pass this time.

They hadn't even been on Earth for five hours before he was heading *back* to the one place he never wanted to go again. Had the aliens not killed Gary, Jake, Debra and countless others, he might not have volunteered. This was a matter of honor. He owed the aliens for what they did and, to be fair, he was the most qualified to lead the attack force.

"The vibration stopped!" Jumie shouted. Dex smirked, remembering the moment they figured it out the first time. Then, they were armed with desperation and anger. Now, they carried their own weapons and enough cover to protect themselves in a lengthy fight. "Does that mean we've docked?"

"It sure as shit does," Dex said. "Stay in cover. If the door doesn't open right away, I'll take care of it. You've already heard it before from me but these guys have solid weapons and you can't rely on headshots. Their helmets will probably absorb concussion damage. Aim for center mass. Kill shots only."

"Is there any other kind?" Someone asked, drawing a chuckle from the crew.

Dex drew a deep breath, aiming his weapon at the door. He counted to thirty in his head before slipping out of cover and pressing himself against the wall. Inching his way along, he let the rifle hang from the shoulder strap and extended his hands in preparation of pressing them against the two plates to open the thing.

Just as he arrived, it started moving. He cursed under his breath. If he ran, the aliens would hear him and if he stayed there, he'd be directly in their line of fire. After what happened before, they would definitely be on the lookout for wily humans ready to jump them. Surprise wouldn't be on their side.

Dex crouched and shuffled backward, once again aiming his rifle. Jumie muttered into the com, "how many will there be?"

"Three to ten," Dex whispered. "Have I cleared your line of fire?"

He received a quiet affirmative.

The door reached Dex's head. He drew a deep breath. Several targets presented themselves, six aliens in all, each armed and at the ready.

One looked in his direction just as Dex depressed the trigger, riddling his target's torso full of bullets. The alien danced backward and flopped on the ground in a pool of blood. Chaos erupted as the marines all started shooting. Each burst drowned out the buzzing hum of the beam weapons, echoing in the tiny room.

Fortunately, the helmets suppressed some of the noise, preserving Dex's hearing. He redirected and fired again and again. The aliens stayed in motion, making themselves moving targets but it didn't help. Their beams splashed against the mobile cover, harmlessly leaving behind black stains.

Someone screamed, one of the marines went down but the aliens fell back toward the door and the hallway. "Take them!" Dex shouted. Jumie and three others charged the door, blasting away. Only one alien made it out and he favored an injured leg. Dex raced over slammed into the wall near the opening, waiting for backup.

The other two joined him and he nodded to them. Jumie threw a flash bang grenade into the hall. It made a dramatic pop and the three marines burst out, Dex going right while the other two went left. The injured alien was maybe twenty feet away, fleeing down the hallway directly in front of Dex.

He fired twice, popping his target in the back. Red mist exploded in front of it as it fell to the ground, twitching before lying still. "Clear this side!" Dex shouted.

"Clear," Jumie added. "Looks good through this hall."

"I want a perimeter," Dex ordered. "Thirty yards in both directions. Get those bombs out of there." He boarded the shuttle again. Two marines were down, one dead with a shot to the face and the other wounded, a blow to the shoulder. "Damn it. Soldier?" He knelt in front of the injured one.

"Yes, sir?"

"What's your name?"

"Corporal Corbin Derreks, sir."

"Derreks, I need a no bullshit assessment from you right now. Are you still combat effective?"

The man's left shoulder was blackened but he appeared to be right handed. Derreks nodded, clenching his jaw for a moment before replying. "I can and I will, sir. Whatever it takes, I won't let you down."

"I'm leaving you with one other person to guard the bombs until we're ready to get the hell out of here. You get me?"

"Yes, sir!" Derreks fought to claim his feet and moved out into the hallway.

Dex found Jumie in the hall. "We need to get on with this and get the bombs in position as well. I'll take point. This hallway is a circle, it loops around to all the shuttles that connected up with the mothership. The aliens must be grabbing our people now. You're with me as we blaze the path. You ready?"

"Always, sir," Jumie said.

Depositing the payloads by the converters might've done more damage but Dex felt it would be impractical to move the things around while trying to recover prisoners. Spreading them to different parts of the ship made sense and they'd tear the hull open anyway. The goal of destroying the place wouldn't be a problem, not with that firepower.

"Listen up," Dex addressed the rest of the crew. "We're falling out. Jumie and I will sweep and clear. The rest of you bring the bombs. If you have to engage, drop your payload and shoot back. We're going to rally at the entry point when we have the hostages. So grab some shit and fall out, boys. We've got some work to do."

***

Avania struggled an overwhelming desire to slap the console and curse at the slow software the humans used to run their scanning suite. She sat watching it compile data for nearly two minutes before it began to deliver information. If everything operated at such a speed, they would never get anything done.

The returned data seemed to be missing well more than half of what she expected. Structural integrity of the collector was blocked by the shields. Previous damage, also blocked. She knew for a fact she'd caused some trauma and yet it didn't show up. The information felt like an incorrect report, a halfhearted attempt to deliver important messages.

I'm not going to be able to give them anything with this. Avania stood. "I need to get to your engineering section right away."

"I thought you were going to tell us about the weaknesses of their ship," Warren said.

"I tried but the shields are blocking your scans," Avania explained. "So if I'm to be useful, I need to be down there. I would like to check out the EMP shield I heard about. I should be able to tell if it's going to work and believe me, at this point, we want to know. There may be no reason to get any closer."

Warren frowned, glaring at her for a good ten seconds. "Alright. Commander Serling, please escort our guest to engineering."

"Sir?" Victoria asked. "Are you sure? I believe she knows the way."

"I'm sure." Warren nodded. "Turn her over to Delgado and come back up."

Victoria sighed. "Yes, sir." She stood. "Let's go."

Avania followed her onto the elevator, taking a moment to appraise the woman. Short brown hair, blue eyes, a bit plain but on the prettier side, she carried herself with an obvious confidence. Something about her screamed competence, the type of military leader who would've gone far within the alanta military.

And clearly, she's done well here as well. It seems to be a male dominated military.

"Have you served a long time?" Avania asked.

"I have," Victoria replied. "What about you? Did you join your armed forces for a time?"

"Everyone in my culture is bound to government service," Avania replied. "Nobility has their own unit … but we weren't treated all that differently from the commoner troops. It was determined a long time ago that we were a distraction to some of the lowest born individuals so we were segregated."

"Seems like there wouldn't have been enough of you to make that happen," Victoria said. "Were your units small?"

"No, there are many noble families." Avania tilted her head. "You don't have royals here?"

"We do, but the civilized nations have turned them more to figureheads than actual people of power."

"Ah. Our culture discussed that before I was born. It was turned down by the common folk, if you can believe it. They said they wanted to continue to trust in our judgement, in our wisdom." Avania scowled and looked away. "Little did they know my cousin would rise to power and make them regret *that* decision."

"I'd love to hear more about that when we have time." The elevator doors opened and Victoria gestured outward. "Here we are. Just down this hall to get into engineering. Chief Delgado's in charge down here and I'm going to warn you in advance, he's been a little stressed all day. We've had a lot of challenges."

"I understand. To the best of my ability, I won't annoy him. I just want the opportunity to look over what's been done to see if I can assist in some way."

"Good luck." Victoria led her into the engineering area. "Delgado! I've got a visitor! Where are you?"

"I'm busy!" Delgado shouted back. He emerged at the catwalk just above them. "What's going on?"

"You should tell me," Victoria replied. "Is something the matter?"

"Yes, the artificial gravity modules are operating at different settings than expected. We're looking into it now. Couple that with those EMP shields drawing more power from the generators than the engineers told me they would and you've got a real shit show." Delgado paused, eyeballing Avania. "That the guest?"

"Yes, this is Avania …" Victoria gave her an apologetic look. "She'll tell you the rest of her name. Anyway, she's going to take a look at those EMP shields really quick to see if they'll genuinely help. Afford her every courtesy. She's down here with the captain's permission. If you have any questions, contact him."

"I don't have time for a tourist!" Delgado complained.

"I assure you," Avania said, "I'll be able to help. Just show me where they were installed and I'll look now without getting in your way."

Delgado grunted and crawled down to their floor. "Fine, just … come with me then." He gestured at two black boxes on either side of the room. "They're inside those casings. They were pretty delicate. They essentially use magnetics to cast a field around our electronics that should, in theory, absorb EMP."

"I'm heading back to the bridge," Victoria said. "You'll both be alright down here?"

"Fine." Avania waved at Victoria to leave and approached one of the boxes. "They did a good job by keeping it surrounded. If they're doing what you say, that's why they're pulling so much power. Magnetics require a great deal of energy to be at all effective. We experimented with them for artificial gravity years ago."

"Really? We tried that. It proved to be too heavy to be effective."

"Exactly!" Avania smirked. "Is there a way to see the components inside? Even if it's with a computer?"

"Yeah, there are these panels on the sides." Delgado showed her on the one to the right. "You just tap here and you can access the diagnostics."

Avania watched the screen come alive, displaying a high definition view of the components within the box. She tapped through each one, reading what the humans called them. Unfortunately, the parts were so unnecessarily large, they might've been particularly fragile. *Hopefully, we don't take damage to this section.*

The ship rumbled and she had to grab the device to remain standing. Delgado shouted for everyone to hold on. Technicians scrambled about, strapping themselves into seats or grabbing rails depending on their current location. Avania made her way to the edge, near to the chief.

"What just happened?"

"Felt like we hit something," Delgado replied, "but to be honest, I've never been in space before. I don't know what happened."

I think we just experienced our first attack. Avania didn't want to announce that too loudly. It might cause some unnecessary panic. "Do you have scans down here? Something we can use to see?"

"Yeah, I've got a view screen with a tap into the main cameras. It's in my office over there."

"May I?" Avania gestured.

"Yeah, go for it."

She rushed across the way, hurrying inside and sitting down. Engaging the com link, she made a request for the bridge then tapped at the screen until it came on. Outside, they were still approaching the collector's ship. Only a few shuttles hadn't docked yet and they were closing in quickly.

The marines may already be on board. They might be engaged with the enemy.

"This is the bridge," Madeline's voice greeted her.

"This is Avania in engineering. We just shook. Can you tell me what happened?"

"We're not sure," Madeline said. "It was like … turbulence."

Hm. Avania shook her head. *They have a great deal to learn about traveling in space*. She continued tapping at the computer until she found the same pathetic scan suite they used upstairs. Bringing it online, she noted they had indeed struck an object, a large rock that was damaged but remained intact.

She found it, some thousand kilometers behind them and scanned it. The composition was not entirely natural. *Garbage*. She recognized the metal and radioactive bits. *That thing was jettisoned from the collector's ship. Did they do it on purpose in order to slow this ship down?* Avania didn't know what they'd do when they saw the Leviathan.

While the human vessel wasn't quite as large as the collector, it was built for battle. That probably intimidated the mercenary bastards. Would they toss out garbage to hide something else? She wouldn't put it past them. It would be an obvious ploy to a space faring culture but to the humans, making their first forays into space, they might not think about it.

And fly right into a bomb.

Avania scanned ahead, finding a cluster of junk coming up fast. "Madeline, order your pilot to go up. We have a considerable amount of space debris off the bow and I assure you, we do not want to run into it. Make it happen right away!"

"Um … I'll try, ma'am."

"Do more than try!" Avania clenched her fists. *These humans are so stubborn!*

The ship rumbled and the artificial gravity struggled to keep up with the sudden course change. Avania held tight to the desk, staring at the scans. The Leviathan would *just* miss the largest cluster of debris. Scans flashed red when she focused on the next floating chunks. Most of it was made of metal, large enough to be visible with only five times magnification.

Unstable mass. Avania frowned at the readings. She had to think back to her school days, time spent in the royal military. *Wait. Extreme radiation.* A quick adjustment brought back more data showing a volatile substance encased within the metal. *That is a bomb.* "Madeline, are you still there?"

"Yes, ma'am."

"Full stop and reverse," Avania replied. "We are approaching a bomb. I can't tell how potent it will be so we should definitely avoid it."

The device exploded as she spoke, causing the Leviathan to shake again. Delgado started shouting for a damage report. Lights flickered for half a moment. Avania cursed and left the office. She thought to check in with the engineer but he was already doing his job. She needed to get back to the bridge.

Hopping in the elevator, she tapped her foot, willing the thing to go faster. The collectors were definitely worried about the Leviathan or they wouldn't have thrown out booby traps in their way. If they had more of that type of thing, they could destroy the Earth vessel but it would take time.

They're trying to delay us, Avania realized. *They want us to slow down and not get close enough to attack. They think they can escape. That means those marines need to hurry or they're likely to become humanity's first intergalactic travelers. Hurry, elevator! Hurry!*

***

"Damage report," Warren said. "Did our shields deflect any of it?"

"Most, actually," Nicolas replied. "Minor surface damage to the hull. Our environmental shields are holding. However, I'm picking up more of those devices." He turned to look back at them. "Without altering our course, we would've struck that thing. Just a quick calculation indicates closer proximity likely would've caused a breach."

"Understood." Warren rubbed his chin. "Continue to climb and get us clear of those ... mines, I guess. We should be able to fire now, correct?"

"Weapons are charged and ready. Enemy shuttles are all docked."

"Fire when ready."

Nicolas tapped his console and spoke into his microphone. "Engineering, be advised, I am firing all weapons." A low grind of metal sounded on either side of them from the bowels of the ship. The weapons discharged, hurling rockets toward the collector ship along with dozens of cannon rounds.

Avania stepped onto the bridge just as the first of their attacks struck the shielded surface of the collector's vessel. The resulting flash of light made Warren look away for a moment, rubbing his eyes. He half expected there to be no reaction but then again, the sheer amount of firepower they threw might've been overwhelming.

"Direct hit on all shots," Nicolas said. "Not sure about damage but look at the surface of the object."

Warren squinted, leaning forward in his seat while the image magnified. The area they hit seemed to be glowing brighter than the rest of it, as if the shields themselves were injured and throbbing. He tilted his head, puzzling out what might've happened. He finally shrugged and turned to Avania.

"Any thoughts about that?"

"The shields are trying to recharge," Avania said. "Hit them again. Target the same location."

"You heard her," Warren added. "Go for it, Nicolas."

"Firing a second volley." The grinding happened again and another series of missiles launched from the ship. They sped toward their target, tearing through the open space between them. Seconds before impact, a beam of light lashed out, ripping the ordnance into pieces. Debris struck the hull along with the cannon shot.

"Did you see that?" Victoria pointed at the screen. "Why didn't they do that the first time?"

"They didn't think they'd be a threat," Avania replied. "That's a good sign. It means your weapons are far more potent than I thought."

Another section of the collector ship began to glow and a beam blasted through space, striking the Leviathan on the starboard side. Warren gripped his chair, nearly being tossed from his seat. Avania slammed into Madeline's chair, grabbing hold to keep from hitting the ground. She sat down and strapped herself in.

"That was something," Warren muttered. "Keep hitting them with the cannons, Nicolas. What about our missiles?"

"They're still reloading," Nicolas replied. "Cannons are firing again. I'm adjusting course to get a better angle on that damaged section though it seems to be clearing up."

"You'll have to be faster," Avania warned. "Those shields can regenerate quickly while they have power."

"Don't let up." Warren turned to Victoria. "Get the weapon crews on the com. They have to be hurry on the reloads."

"Yes, sir."

"Damage report?" Warren asked.

"I'll get it," Avania replied. "That wasn't the EMP weapon. They did a pure beam attack. Your Deck Seven is severely damaged. Bulkheads have locked down the area to prevent decompression." She looked up. "What's in Deck Seven?"

"Living quarters," Victoria said. "No one should've been down there so at least we're save there. Their beam weapons cut right through the shields. It doesn't sound like they were slowed down at all."

The Leviathan fired again, cannon shot hammering the shields for a third time. Missiles went out in a spread formation, which made Warren respect Nicolas all the more. The collector ship destroyed a few but at least three of the missiles collided with the surface. Their shields began to throb in a hexagonal pattern.

"So they've got sections," Warren said. "See that? We can tear through different *parts* of their defenses."

"They'll try to divert power," Avania added. "But I'm not sure it'll help if you keep at it. Excellent aim, by the way. I'm impressed. You're not using your computer to lock on the target?"

"Doesn't work for cannons," Nicolas replied. "And the missiles were but I had to program their paths manually to make them spread out to counter their defense. Seemed to work. They weren't prepared for a wide spread. At the last second, I had them all shift and dart inward."

"And they can't maneuver quickly," Victoria said. "Which gives you that advantage."

"To be fair, neither can we," Nicolas replied. "Hang on!"

Warren gritted his teeth as the shields on the collector began to glow again. Another beam shot out at them, white with gold sparks dancing along the surface. It hit them but there was no rumble, no motion. The lights flickered, went out and remained dark. He slapped his knee, turning to Nicolas.

"The EMP! Did it take out everything?"

"Negative, sir." Nicolas chuckled. "Computers are still online. Don't know what happened to the lights. I'm switching to emergency now."

"Wait!" Avania called out. "Hold on. Shut down all non-essential systems! Now!"

"But …" Warren stopped himself, catching her idea. "Do as she says. Right away. Madeline, announce to the crew to use their environmental suits and shut down. I think I know what she's getting at and this might buy us an opportunity." He got up and donned his suit. If the ruse worked, they might break through that defense in a few moments.

And if not, there was no way the collectors would leave when they could destroy the human flagship. Warren had to buy any amount of time he could for the marines to finish their part. One way or another, he'd keep his enemies there for as long as it took and by the time they'll tried to get away, it would be too late.

***

Dex led the way, jogging down the hallway toward the next shuttle bay. At thirty yards, he saw the aliens wheeling out unconscious humans, piled up like sacks of grain. He slowed, taking aim then firing a couple of controlled bursts. The weapon fire echoed off the walls, reverberating with the percussive intensity of a marching band.

His first target he caught fully in the chest, dropping him in a second. The second took three rounds to the side. The others scrambled for their weapons, dashing toward the door for cover. Jumie blasted one, leaving three targets. They tore off down the hall just as the other marines caught up.

"After them!" Dex shouted. "Don't let them get away!"

Blue beams flashed past them, five and six at a time. Dex tossed himself to the floor, returning fire but aiming high to avoid the racks of people. Other aliens joined their companions, at least seven of them coming upon the scene. The marines fired in unison, filling the hall with enough bullets to cut down the contingent of enemies.

Buzzing stopped and Dex called for a cease fire. He didn't rise, opting to take aim for another moment to ensure the fighting was over. When he felt certain they were okay to rise, he crawled to his feet and motioned for Jumie to accompany him. The two arrived at the humans, pausing when they saw some of the aliens writhing about.

"Live ones," Jumie said. "Are we taking prisoners?"

"Don't got room for them," Dex replied. Those who were alive wouldn't be for long. They were covered in blood, massive holes in their suits indicating the severity of their wounds. "Won't matter anyway. These guys are done." He turned to the hostages. "These people are why we came. I need two escorts to get these people out of here!"

Three marines started rousing the victims, getting them on their feet and ushering them back down the hall. Dex checked the shuttle to see if any had been left behind. When he found it clear, he started on his way back. A buzz made him wince and he heard someone scream. Jumie cried out, "contact!"

Shots were fired as another exchange took place. Dex moved to the door and paused, leaning out to take a look at their opposition. He couldn't get an accurate count but there were at least another seven aliens, possibly more. Grabbing a grenade from one of his pouches, he pulled the pin and cooked it for a moment.

"Frag out!" Dex shouted, tossing it toward the enemy. It clattered on the floor only twice before exploding. A wet splatter made him wince and he glanced again. Three of the aliens had collapsed, lying still on the floor. Another wallowed against the wall, holding the stump of his left leg, blown off just below the knee.

Those who survived continued to shoot but they were no longer aiming. Blue beams slapped the ceiling and walls, seemingly fired at random. Dex hit the deck, narrowly avoiding a blast that would've taken his face off. "Everyone stay down!" He shouted the words, even though the com was half an inch from his mouth.

Jumie joined him, firing a couple shots down the way. Dex tossed another grenade, hoping it might suppress their attackers again. He knew they didn't have time to brawl with this one group, not if they hoped to save additional people before they were taken to the converters.

The grenade popped followed by a single scream. Blue beams ceased. Dex risked a look. Only two of the aliens appeared to be alive, sitting up against the walls. They were badly injured, holding their weapons in their laps. They looked in his direction, struggling to lift their arms but they couldn't seem to do it.

Jumie finished them off with a single shot each. Dex looked at him.

"Sir?" Jumie asked. "They were still a threat."

"Yeah, I know." Dex slapped his shoulder. He turned to the others. "We've got more people here but we have got to pick up the pace!" The collector ship shook, a minor tremor he felt through the floor. "That might've been the Leviathan taking some shots at us. It's definitely time to pick up the pace."

"They're putting up quite the fight," Jumie said, "was that expected?"

Dex nodded. "Yeah, big time. They might not have been prepared for us specifically, but they were definitely prepared for another group of guys to burst out of the shuttle ready to throw down. They weren't going to let that happen again and as a result, our job became harder." He considered the enemy weapons for a moment, looking down at one of the pistols.

They could come in handy. Dex didn't know if it would be a good idea to switch out familiar gear for the alien. When they were in a pinch, with no other option, it made perfect sense but this time, they brought their own toys. *No, now is not the time to get creative when things are working.*

Another marine was out of action, dropping them down to seven guys. Dex didn't like the attrition but they were facing a desperate, well-armed opponent. Caution wasn't an option. They had to press on, to get the work done with what they had. Sooner or later, the aliens had to run out of bodies.

Unfortunately, the same could be said for Dex's side.

Chapter 12

Commander Avery Harden started with the Agency a few weeks before Captain Miller. He was given command of the *Seeker*, a research vessel intended to take trips back and forth to the moon. A crew of thirty piloted the vessel but they could accommodate up to a hundred people if necessary.

The cargo hold would allow them to take on the rescued people from the mothership when the marines finished their operation. After Singer's ship went dark, the Seeker was the only other vessel that would be capable of holding so many, though getting them aboard might've been quite the challenge.

Avery felt like they wouldn't have any trouble getting the hostages on board but they still needed to assist the Probity. Singer hadn't been able to communicate out, hadn't said anything since the ship went dark. If they were still alive and unable to communicate, they definitely needed help.

Powering up the engines wouldn't be a huge deal if they weren't damaged but considering how much time passed, Avery doubted it would be so easy. If their situations were reversed, he wondered about Singer's course of action. Would the man have come for him already?

Orders told the Seeker to hold their position, to remain in place and standby. It felt like a waste of time. When the Leviathan took the field, Avery received instructions to rescue the people from the object when the marines were ready for exfiltration. However, that still left the Probity in a tough spot.

I suppose when the object is dealt with, we'll have all the time in the world to mount a rescue operation. The problem was that the Probity needed assistance right away. Those on board had a limited amount of resources to survive on before they'd be lost. Oxygen had to be the chief concern. Their tanks would only last so long.

The concern was losing four ships, Avery thought. *With the object distracted, I should be able to mount a rescue attempt.* He reached out to control. "This is the Seeker. We're ready to get in there and help the Probity. Permission to break standby."

"Hold one moment, please."

Avery bit his tongue. He felt like he'd called to pay a bill. *They put me on hold?* Yes, they were in the middle of multiple operations but granting him permission to take care of their own didn't seem like a tall order. *Maybe something else is going on, some other catastrophe I'm not privy to.*

"This is Meyers," the voice made him jump as it blared over the speaker. "You are authorized to move in on the Probity and see what you can do. Note that you might have to disengage suddenly to get the marines out of there so make it fast, Harden. Know that I haven't asked Colonel Jacks about this. If you want to do it, better hurry."

"Thank you, Doctor." Avery felt a sense of relief wash over him. "We'll make it happen right now." He killed the connection and turned to the helm. "Get us over there. We've got people to save."

The view screen showed the Probity. Fortunately, the ship was far enough away from the Earth to not be in jeopardy of burning up in the atmosphere. At least that countdown wasn't ticking by but it was a small favor. Avery checked the scanner, noting it would take just over three minutes to reach them.

Not too bad, all things considering. When they were close enough, personal coms might work. If so, they could at least reach out to the crew of the Probity, see if any of them made it. A morbid thought hit him, mostly due to the assumption that accompanied it. *They can't all be dead.*

As they raced forward, another communication came through. He picked it up. "This is Harden."

Jacks's voice blared in the speaker. "What're you doing up there?"

"Taking advantage of the distraction," Harden replied. "We're checking on the Probity while we have the chance. If I can get them out, I will. We can salvage the ship later."

"Those marines will be counting on a pickup!"

"And they'll get it," Harden replied, "but the Probity is counting on some assistance. They don't deserve to die in there because we refused to act. Now we can discuss this in an official capacity when I return but I'm going to move in and save as many lives as I can. If it helps, Doctor Meyers gave me authorization already."

"He did, did he?" Jacks sighed. "Harden, I want those people saved too—"

"With all due respect, sir, it doesn't seem like it. You're pushing back on my attempt now."

"There are thirty people on the Probity," Jacks said. "We're saving over a hundred on that ship. Your standby order was to recover a larger number of people."

"And I'll still take care of it." Harden tightened his fist and let it out along with a deep breath. "Sir, I'm saving those people and I'll be there for the marines. What happens after is up to you but for now, I'm in the field and I'm calling this shot. Is there anything else you'd like to add before I go?"

Jacks didn't respond for several moments and when he finally did, he grunted first. "You're a stubborn man, Harden but I understand. I hope you're right that you'll be able to take care of both. If that ship shoots at you while you're closing in on the Probity though, you're going to condemn a lot of people."

"I'm assuming you're watching the exchange between the Leviathan and that thing," Harden replied. "They're far too busy with a bigger target to be multitasking right now. Harden out." He killed the connection. His pilot turned a concerned look at him and he smiled. "Don't worry about it. In the end, he's going to see that I was right."

Both missions are important and I'm not letting one stand in the way of the other. Harden turned to his com and started sending a signal out to the Probity, requesting that anyone pick up the line.

"Sir," Ensign Ruth Cole caught his attention from the scanning station. "The Leviathan took a blast from the enemy ... like the one used on the Probity."

"Oh no." Harden's heart hammered his chest and cold sweat broke on his palms. "Are they ... is their ship still powered?"

She didn't answer right away, finally clearing her throat. "I'm afraid not, sir. I'm not picking up any power readings at all. It might just be distance but ... I'm changing the view screen so you can see for yourself."

The Leviathan appeared on the screen, all the lights out on the hull. As the Seeker drew closer to the Probity, Harden knew they would be within range of the enemy attack again. He couldn't risk it, not with the battlecruiser down. *Damn it!* He clapped his leg in frustration. *We were so close!*

"Break off and withdraw," Harden announced. "Do it quickly before that thing hits us too."

The ship banked and turned, moving back to their position where they'd be standing by before. *What are we going to do now?* Harden thought, staring at the dead battleship outside. *How are we ever going to defeat this thing if our most powerful warship was taken down so easily? God help us. This may be the end.*

***

Victoria sat in silence, staring at the view screen. She tried to guess the next action of their enemy, playing the game several moves ahead. Did they believe the ruse? If so, what would they do about it? Blast the ship to bits or try to leave? Warren played a dangerous game, gambling big but what outcome did he predict?

Avania came close to them, leaning in to whisper. "Your scanners use so little power there's no way they would be able to detect them. I've done a quick sweep and their shields are still down. I'm fairly certain they will not be paying us any attention. If I were you, I'd hit them with everything you've got before they fully recharge their defenses."

"Nicolas," Warren said, "are all missile batteries loaded?"

"They are, sir," Nicolas said. "They're ready go to and I've programmed another course for them … this one far more random."

"Perfect." Warren turned to Victoria. "Shall we give these guys a quick surprise?"

"Know that when we do," Victoria said, "that they won't fall for that again. We're going to have to finish the fight when we fire."

"Yep, I'm counting on it." Warren gestured to Nicolas. "Fire when ready. Once the missiles are deployed, kick the power back on and get us in motion again. Madeline, contact the Seeker and let them know that we'll need them to be ready to extract those marines soon. They have to be close to completing their mission."

"I wouldn't go that far," Victoria muttered. "Avania, if we break through that shield, do you think we'll be able to communicate with our people over there?"

"The interference would be diminished," Avania said. "I can work with Madeline here to see about breaking through it at that point. We may simply have to intensify the signal but it would also be nice if we were closer. Once you deploy your weapons, I recommend we charge them, providing this thing can slow down quickly enough."

Nicolas clicked his tongue. "This is the first time I've flown this thing. I can't tell you how fast it'll stop … or even slow down. I'd recommend we be cautious when we talk about things like *charge*. That could quickly turn into *ram* and I'm pretty sure the hull wouldn't take that kind of abuse."

"Either way, we're not finding out," Warren said. "Still, I agree with Avania about getting closer. That'll increase our chances of getting a communication out. I was thinking we were going to have to let them find a way but this helps even more. Alright, if we're ready for this, fire away, Nicolas."

Victoria winced as the gears of the weapons started grinding. *We need to have those looked at. I'm not sure they should be making that much noise.* The lights popped on along with the screen, catching all the missiles as they sped off toward their destination. Nicolas counted to five out loud then fired the cannons.

The floor rumbled again as the engines came alive, propelling them forward. "Three quarters thrust," Nicolas announced. "Retro in … twenty seconds to avoid collision."

Beams from the shield burst in several directions, catching some of the missiles. Three got through, pounding that same tender point on the alien defenses. The cannons battered it a moment later.

They returned fire, beams lashing out. Two missed, the third clipped them by the rear thrusters. "Firing another salvo," Nicolas called out. "Retro thrusters in ten seconds."

Cannons lit up the shields again. This time, the throbbing shield changed from red to white then winked out. The section dropped, revealing the bare surface beneath.

"You're through!" Avania shouted. "Madeline, reach out to them! Quickly, while we still have time!"

The retro thrusters kicked in. Safety harnesses bit into her shoulders as she was shoved forward. Warren huffed beside her. The force of the reverse motion stabilized as inertial dampeners kicked in. She sat back, only just then noticing the lights flickered when Nicolas engaged the thrusters.

That's probably a bug we're going to need to look at. Victoria made a mental note. *I bet engineering has a novel of issues to go through.*

"Leviathan to Lieutenant Pollard," Madeline said, "please respond. This is Ensign Blanchard calling on all channels. Do you read?"

"Leviathan!" Dex's voice burst over the speakers. "You have no idea how good it is to hear your voice! This is Pollard! Are you the ones making this place shake so much?"

"I've got this, Madeline," Warren said. "We've taken down a section of the shields!"

Another series of blasts came from the enemy ship, hammering the hull of the Leviathan. Avania returned to her station. Victoria didn't need her to run the damage report this time. Delgado sent it in almost immediately. Hull breach on deck seven and eight, crew quarters and the mess hall, based on the exact section.

"It was bad," Victoria muttered to Warren. "Bulk heads have closed over the areas. We still have compression in the rest of the level."

"How close are you to leaving that place?" Warren asked. "We're keeping their attention but I can tell you right now, we can't keep it up. Their weapons are punching through our environmental shields and the hull can't take a lot more. If they get lucky and find the right place to shoot, we're done for."

"We've cleared several of the shuttles but the last one we checked was empty. We're heading to the collectors now." Dex paused and they heard gunfire over the com. "Contact left! Get that guy! Leviathan, we're under fire but several of the bombs are in place! Withdraw. We can take it from here and get back to you. Don't risk the ship anymore."

"We can't just leave you to deal with them on your own!" Warren shouted. "How much longer, man? We have to distract this thing so your ride can pick you up!"

"We've got a bit more to go, sir." Dex stopped abruptly as more gunfire went off. "Maybe we can take their weapons off line or ... something. It seems like it might be the only way to make this work!"

"I can try to guide them," Avania said. "Patch them through to this ... head piece thing you have. I'll talk them through some activities which might help us out."

Warren nodded. "Do it, Madeline. Get him over there and let's see what we can do from the inside. Nicolas, bank left ninety degrees. Full thrust. We'll loop around and keep hitting them. Dex, we're getting you some navigation help and we'll still keep them busy out here. Good luck!"

Victoria held on to her seat as the ship shifted to the left. Nicolas fired again as he made the navigation. She had to give him credit for his ability to multitask. It was stunning. Tapping a message to Delgado, she let him know the plan then turned her attention back to the screen. The next ten minutes would tell whether they won the fight or lost everything.

***

Dex spun to the side, slamming into a wall. Avania's voice filled his helmet but the buzzing of enemy weapons drowned her out. Jumie fired several bursts before taking cover beside him, shouting that he needed to reload. The converter was just down the way. He could see the familiar yellow glow.

"Avania, come again? I didn't copy."

"I asked where you are, Dexter. I can't help you anywhere without your present location."

"We're at one of the converters now," he replied. "There's no way they could've plugged anyone in them yet. We've been pressing hard on these bastards."

"That's … lovely. Truly. When you've finished your conflict, I'll direct you on how to use the control panel to disrupt some of the systems."

"Okay … I'll help with that while the others check the other converters, I guess. This will be interesting."

"That's not the word I would technically use but I suppose it applies," Avania said. "Just let me know when you're done firing weapons."

Easy for you to say. Dex crouched and leaned around the corner. The world swam, adrenaline gripping his chest. A blue beam whizzed by, blacking the right side of his helmet. He fired two shots. His target dove to the side, a bullet tearing through his foot. Another alien shouted, taking aim.

Dex redirected. Falling back wasn't an option. He was unlikely to get his shot off in time. Shell casing bounced off his helmet from above as Jumie unloaded half his magazine. The alien began dancing backwards and his weapon went off. A marine behind him cried out.

"Get back!" Jumie grabbed his arm, dragging him around the corner. Two blue beams flashed past where he'd been a moment before.

"Thanks," Dex said. "Was that the one I got on the foot?"

"I think so." Jumie looked across the way at the others. "He's on the ground to the left, lying on his side!" Another buzz sounded as beams cut through the air, forcing the marines back down the hall. "I don't think anyone's got line of sight on that prick and I'd hate to waste a grenade on one guy."

"I've got it," Dex replied. He took several deep breaths. "If this doesn't work, be ready to put him down, okay?"

"What're you going to do?" Jumie asked.

"I'm curious about that myself," Avania added. "I'm not even there and this sounds like it might be a bad idea."

"I'm going to solve the problem." Dex set his rifle down and drew his sidearm. Holding it up, he spun and threw himself out of his cover, firing the pistol the second he had a clear shot. The alien returned fire but missed as Dex landed on his side.

He rapid fired, planting five rounds in his target's chest. The alien's body jerked a couple times and fell still, blood pooling on the floor beneath him.

"Solved." Dex muttered. He crawled to his feet. They'd brought several people down to the area and put them on the conveyer belts. *Jesus Christ, these guys are industrious and fast! This is ridiculous!* "Lock this area down and rouse those people. I'm going to need a team to clear the next converter which is that way." He gestured.

"What about you?" Jumie asked.

"I'm going to … do something with this control panel thing." Dex shrugged. "Watch my back." He cleared his throat. "Avania, I'm near the control panel. What do you want me to do?"

"The first step you have to take involves bringing up the menu. Tap the upper left corner of the screen."

Dex looked at it, frowning at the squiggly lines under several boxes. They didn't have pictures, just glowing blue shapes. He didn't have any idea what he was looking at and the language certainly wasn't anything he'd seen before. He complied with the order though, tapping the box on the upper left.

"Just so you know, I have no idea what any of this means." Dex sighed. The screen changed, showing a dozen boxes with three columns. More of the strange language appeared on the right of each. He described what he saw, drawing a look from Jumie. "Oh, you just keep an eye out for me. I don't need you giving me a hard time right now."

"Sorry, sir."

"We've roused these people!" One of the marines shouted. "I'm going to escort them back to the rally point while the others get to the next converter."

"Sounds good," Dex said. "Avania? What the hell do I do now?"

"Count three rows down and tap the second box from your left."

Dex did as he was told and the terminal began to flash. He took a step back. "Is it supposed to be blinking? Flashing? Flickering? Whatever the hell it's doing."

"Yes, that means it's looking for the data you requested. Remain calm. It will only take a few moments."

"Easy for you to say," Dex muttered. "You're not standing in the middle of a conflict zone with enemies just itching to turn you into blue goo."

The captured people were escorted away from the converter. A couple of the men rushed off to the next converter. Dex wished he could go with them. He would've thought alien computers didn't have to spend so much time loading. Anyone who mastered interstellar travel should've done away with loading screens.

"Contact!" Jumie fired his rifle and Dex leaned over to see what he took a shot at. Another alien body hit the ground, sprawled out with a hole in its chest.

"Nice shot," Dex said. "What the hell was he doing down here alone?"

"Probably thought you all moved on," Avania said. "Has the screen stopped flashing?"

Dex sighed. "Not yet." The floor trembled and he had to grip the console to remain standing. "What the hell was that?"

"We're keeping those shields down so you and I can continue to talk," Avania replied. "The Leviathan cannons are sufficiently taxing their shields, which means they can't recharge the section that collapsed. It also means they have to decide whether they want to shoot at us or defend themselves."

Dex considered what they were up against. The alien weapons were only pistols. He hadn't seen military grade equipment from these people yet. Add to that the ship they arrived in. It counted as a civilian ship. Yes, it was a match for humanity because their technology hadn't advanced far enough.

What would a destroyer be like? Or a battleship? Their military vessels may well be far more than Earth could handle, especially when the collector ship was able to cause significant damage to the Leviathan. Their EMP shut down a ship in their fleet with a single shot. He imagined the damaging attacks would be far more devastating.

And that didn't even begin to touch on their ground forces. What type of armor did they employ? How nasty were their weapons? Hopefully, Avania could give them this information. She'd be busy for quite a while after the operation ended. He hoped she planned to cooperate.

Gunfire echoed off the walls, coming from far down the hall. Dex hoped that meant the marines had arrived at the other converter. They might have their work cut out for them, depending on how many aliens were down there. He couldn't understand how they were so zealous. What compelled them on past any self-preservation?

The screen stopped flashing and Dex practically cheered. "Hey, the screen's done." He frowned at the new display. A series of strange symbols dominated the four quadrants. Squiggly characters sprawled across the top, like a title of some kind. There were no more boxes this time, just a circle, three lines close to each other, a hexagon and a plus.

"Great. Look for the palanta."

"The what?" Dex shook his head. "Please tell me you didn't just use some weird ass word in your own language."

"Sorry, it um … looks like a circle?"

"Really? Why not just say a circle?"

"Because it's a palanta." Avania cleared her throat. "Anyway, do you see anything like that?"

"Yeah, it's right here. Do I tap it?"

"No, you trace your finger around it starting in the lower right. There should be a small dot. It may be difficult to see."

Dex leaned close, squinting until he saw what she was talking about. Pressing his finger into it, he paused. "Which direction do I drag?"

"Right to left."

"Clockwise?"

"No, Right to left."

"That's clockwise!" Dex started moving his finger. "Never mind, I'm doing it now."

"Hey," Jumie said, "we've got trouble. I just received a report that the aliens were shooting the unconscious hostages. We lost *dozens* of people."

"Are you kidding? What the hell!" Dex finished the circle. "Hurry up, Avania! They're killing the hostages now!"

"We're almost there," Avania said. "We are breaking into a system that you have no business even getting into from where you're at. It's not exactly easy."

The screen changed color, glowing purple. Dex turned to Jumie. "Get down there and help them. I'll be fine."

"Are you sure?" Jumie asked. "You're kind of busy to be watching your own back right now."

"We don't have the luxury of you hanging out here when they need the firepower. Make sure they're arming the able-bodied hostages we saved. Part of this plan relied on the fact that we'd be able to boost our numbers by saving people."

"I'm on it." Jumie jogged off down the hall, leaving Dex alone.

"Okay, the screen is purple," Dex said. "Also, I'm alone so I need to make this quick. I don't want to be hanging out here longer than I have to. What's next?"

"When it turns back to blue, you're going to see two squares at the bottom. The one on the left will be flashing. That's what you want to hit." Avania paused. "Essentially, you're confirming that you want to put the shields into maintenance mode."

"I'm tricking it into thinking we're going to fix it?" Dex smirked. "I get it. That's why we were able to do it from this control panel?"

"It wouldn't have mattered which panel you did it from. This one was near you so that's why we went with it." Avania paused. "We won't have a lot of time when you do that before they try to restore the shields. I'm thinking you're not interested in standing there trying to counter them so when you hit the button, get everyone ready to leave."

"That's easier said than done!" Dex cursed. "Damn it, Avania!"

"Do what you can."

The two squares appeared. Dex hovered his hand over the flashing one. "Attention, all units. We're about to be on a tight time limit. Get your hostages to the rally point and start the bomb countdowns. I've got an easier idea about how to get these people out of here than trying to dock the Seeker. Load them on a shuttle and I'll meet you there shortly."

Dex hit the button, turning to dart away. He stopped abruptly, staring at an alien aiming a pistol at him. *Sneaky bastard!* The helmet hid the thing's features but he imagined an expression of fury, eyes burrowing into his. There was no way he could get his rifle up to take the thing out before it pulled the trigger.

A quick draw of his pistol might've been possible but even that motion would take longer than the twitch of a finger. They stood there for a good five seconds. *What's this thing waiting for?* The ground trembled, far worse than before. The alien stumbled forward, his weapon buzzing as a beam lanced out.

Searing pain danced along Dex's leg as the beam grazed him just above the knee. He fell to the right, drawing his pistol as he went down. Two shots caught the alien in the hip and a third got him in the stomach. When Dex landed, he fired again, getting his target in the chest. As it flopped on its back, he crawled to his feet and limped toward the hallway.

The wound on his leg had been instantly cauterized but every step sent a shock of pain along his nerves. *I don't have time for this!* Dex pushed himself, doing his best to ignore every agonizing step. They would be off the ship soon enough but before he could enjoy that taste of freedom, he had to get back to the others.

A task that seemed easier said than done.

***

Micky Chilton woke up to the sounds of gunfire erupting around him. A strange buzzing made his skin crawl, like thousands of bees raging in half second intervals. Blue lights flashed here and there. He didn't dare sit up but rather took in his surroundings with only his eyes, listening intently to the chaos.

Metal walls and ceilings surrounded him. He was lying on a hard surface and as he scraped his fingers over it, he noted it was some kind of rough rubber. Focus began to return to him, a sense of what happened before he woke up. He'd been in his fighter, attacking the strange alien shuttle when it shot him from behind.

I thought I was dead. The thought made him realize they must've captured him. *That's how they grabbed the first round of hostages. Holy shit, I'm in space!* Turning to his left, he saw a strangely clad man holding an odd pistol. The weapon turned out to be the source of the buzzing as it belched a blue beam from the tip.

Oh my God, that's an alien. More gunshots went off, the familiar sound of an assault rifle. He'd trained with those but just then, he was unarmed. *Is this a rescue attempt? Have our people come to save us?* He was having a hard time remembering the full extent of the operation he'd been involved in but it didn't matter just then.

I have to help somehow!

Micky tested himself, flexing his arms and legs. Everything worked. He wasn't hurt. Getting into the fight made him nervous if only for the fact there were so many unknowns. However, if he didn't stand up, he should remain out of the line of fire. A plan came to him, something that could help without endangering himself.

He rolled off the platform, slamming his body into the thing's legs. It stumbled but didn't fall. Micky grabbed hold of its ankles and yanked hard, making the alien topple to the ground. It landed on its back, losing the pistol as its hand slammed into the ground and bounced.

Micky rolled on top of it and beat it in the chest several times. It struggled to grab his throat and he leaned back, gripping it by the hand and wrenching hard to the left. He felt the break, heard the thing scream in pain before rough hands grabbed him from behind. Struggling, he threw his elbows out and tried to kick backward.

"Relax!" Someone shouted. "I'm a marine! Slow down, Tex. We're here to help!"

The marine let him go and he stumbled away, staring wide eyed at the man. His savior wore an environmental suit and carried a rifle. He turned it on the injured alien and executed him. "We have to get the hell out of here, buddy. It's just me and Gordon over there on this particular one. Help us rouse these people."

"How?" Micky asked.

"Slapping seems to work best." The marine shrugged. "I'm Denton. What's your name?"

"Captain Micky Chilton of the—"

"Dude, save the formalities," Denton interrupted. "Just get these people up. We're on a time limit. Nukes are armed and we're trying to get the hell out of here. If you don't want to find out what five big ass bombs do to an alien facility first hand, you'll want to move. Hey, grab one of their weapons too. You can help."

Micky turned to look at the various people lying on what appeared to be a conveyer belt. It fed into a large device with something glowing yellow inside. Chains hung over it, like what he'd seen at a butcher's shop when he was a kid. *Were they planning on cooking us or something? Christ in heaven, this is insane!*

The marines were slapping people, rousing them from their slumber. Micky did the same, helping through the first few moments of disorientation. "It's okay," he said. "You're going to be fine. Just get up. Marines have come to help us. Can you walk? We really need to get moving."

Micky grabbed one of the weapons as the last of his people got to their feet. He wondered if any of his other flight made it onboard. Were they dead? The marines wouldn't know. There were too many operations for a couple guys to be privy to the status of one fight in Germany.

"You guys all ready?" Denton shouted.

The people replied, though not nearly so enthusiastically. Micky felt their fear, saw the terror in their eyes. Many of these people hadn't been fighting the enemy when they were taken. They simply had the bad luck to be caught. *At least they're free now*. Micky waited for Denton to lead the way.

"Follow me, everyone! We're getting you out of here but move your asses! This is *not* a place you want to be left behind! Believe me!"

Micky did. Still, he took up the rear, watching their backs with his new weapon. It felt insanely light in his hand, practically like a toy. He'd seen it in action though didn't know how devastating the beams could be. He wanted to try it but discharging the thin might panic the other people.

I hope I don't need this thing. Micky admired his surroundings, the smooth metal walls and ceiling, the matching floor and the darkness of the corridor both ahead of them and behind. The sterility of it gave him the creeps, the fact they were about to do something terrible to a bunch of unconscious people would likely haunt his dreams.

If these men hadn't arrived, I really would've died in that aircraft. The sobering thought made Micky grimace. He'd been in several near misses in his life as a pilot but never one so horrifying as whatever he found himself in on that spaceship. The menace of the aliens made a lot more sense to him as he hustled down the hallway.

And the absolute need to destroy their ship became quite clear as well.

Chapter 13

Another blast slammed into the Leviathan, cutting through one of the main thrusters. It immediately went offline. The view screen flickered but remained on, showing their target and the many shield sections that throbbed red. They were on the verge of dropping if only they could continue to fire their weapons.

"Bank hard right," Warren ordered, "give them another target to shoot at."

"Unnecessary," Avania said. "And ... prepare for a glow."

The enemy shields turned white, increasing in brightness until Warren had to look away. Five seconds later, the light was gone and when he looked back at the ship, nothing flashed on the surface. The shields must've been down completely, all sections, not just those they'd been damaging for the last several moments.

"You did it?" Warren asked. "Dex was able to get them down?"

"They're in maintenance mode," Avania replied. "That buys us a little time but they *must* get off that ship pretty much now ... before they turn it back on."

Warren turned to Madeline. "Get the Seeker on the horn and have them head in for pick up."

"I think Lieutenant Pollard has a better idea," Avania said. "At least, he said something about that on the com."

Warren tapped into the marine channel. "Dex, what's going on? We're about to send the Seeker in to pick you guys up."

"I think we can steal another shuttle," Dex said. "That would be easier than trying to dock our ship on short notice, don't you think?"

"Who's going to pilot it?" Warren asked. "Avania brought it out the first time."

"When we're on board and away from this thing, we'll meet up with the Seeker then."

"That's wise," Avania added, "because once the collector ship is down, the shuttles might lose navigation."

"If you think that'll work, Dex. Get those people out of there any way you can. We'll coordinate with the Seeker to ensure they're ready to help." Warren tapped the arm of his chair. Something didn't feel right. "Do they still have offensive capabilities? Or are all their weapons based on those shields?"

"They may have installed turrets," Avania said. "Such equipment is not standard to these vessels but you never know how paranoid the average captain will get. Most places they visit don't try to stop them. In some sectors, there's even a fine for obstructing their duties. A couple systems leave people in designated areas, like sacrifices."

"A fine?" Victoria blurted out. "You must be joking! A fine for defending your own people? Please tell me that's not real."

"I assure you, it is." Avania sighed. "These ships travel under the flag of royal protection ... a hotly sought-after commodity and privilege for these mercenary animals. My explanation does not, in anyway justify them. I'm simply telling you the facts. I would love to see them all put out of business and thrown into prison."

"Captain," Madeline said, "there's something interfering with communications again. A massive signal ... like a power surge or ... or deliberate noise. I can't tell which."

"Avania?" Warren asked.

"I'm looking." Avania spun in her chair suddenly. "They are preparing to wormhole out."

"Wait, what?" Victoria looked at Warren. "I didn't think they could just ... do that. And if they could, why haven't they already?"

"They were still collecting goods, remember?" Warren frowned. "What do we do about this? We have to stop them?"

"Target the upper part of the sphere." Avania gestured to the screen. "Hit them hard. Open the hull. It will force them to cancel, even if it's only temporarily, while they get a safety precaution in place."

"Target it," Warren said. "Fire when ready. But why is this going to work?"

"Because going into a wormhole with a hull breach is practically suicide," Avania replied. "Especially in larger ships. If they can seal it quickly, they can still escape but they won't go until they've got a physical obstruction barring the hole." The cannons discharged, peppering the enemy hull. "We have to buy time for those people get out."

"Madeline," Warren said, "can you reach Dex?"

"I'm trying, sir."

"Repeat a message to him. Let him know what's about to happen. Tell them to hurry."

Nicolas fired again, this time causing a blue-yellow bulb to burst from the hull of the ship. "Direct hit, both salvos! Look at that! Breach!"

"Good work," Avania said. "Let's hope that will buy enough time and that they don't manage to get their shields back online. Though I suppose that won't matter if they steal a shuttle. This is going to be very close, captain. If you have divinity in your culture, you may wish to consult it … or them."

Warren shook his head. "I don't think we need to rely on luck here. As long as they hurry, we should be good to go."

The ship shook violently and safety straps kept Warren from being tossed out of his seat. He grunted from the shock of it, the pain of nylon biting into his flesh. "Report!" He coughed several times after shouting. His chest burned and as he looked around, he saw the others didn't fare much better. "What the hell was that?"

"We've been hit with a laser blast," Avania said. "It seems they do have turrets after all. Nicolas, if you wouldn't mind targeting the coordinates I sent your terminal, you should be able to take them out. As far as our damage is concerned, the concussion seems to have caused a breach outside of engineering."

"Is everyone okay?" Victoria asked.

Madeline answered, "medical bay has a number of casualties. There are some people cut off from the rest of the ship in that section. One of them … had a malfunction with their environmental suit. They're gone, sir." She drew a deep breath. "I'm waiting for a tally of the dead. But there are at least six. Likely more."

"Damn it!" Warren slapped the arm of his chair. "Take out those turrets, Nicolas. Fire!"

"I am sir," Nicolas replied, "I needed to divert some power but we're letting them go now." The weapons let off their familiar grind as the projectiles were hurled toward their destination. Another blast flew toward them, causing another massive tremor throughout the Leviathan.

Lights flickered and stayed out. The bridge was lit by the glow of consoles and the view screen. Smoke poured out of a panel to the right. Avania unfastened her harness and hurried over, disengaging the safety clips to pull the metal section off. She winced, withdrawing once them grabbing it again.

That thing must be scorching hot! Warren popped the belts off of his chair and rushed over to help her. When he pressed his fingers against it, he withdrew swiftly from the searing heat. Gritting his teeth, he helped her pop it free. A fire licked the wires and he grabbed the emergency fire extinguisher, blasting the flames with it.

Avania returned to her post as the weapons started grinding again. "We're losing power!" Nicolas shouted. "That's the last volley I'll get off without help from engineering."

"Do what you can," Warren said. He returned to his chair and clicked on the com. "Delgado, do you read me?"

"I'm a little busy!" Delgado shouted back. "We've got a real mess down here!"

"How bad is it?"

Delgado shouted indistinctly for a moment before responding. "Systems are going down all over the ship. It ain't pretty but we're doing what we can. Generators are holding, artificial gravity is okay and life support too but we're struggling with power relays. Several sections of the ship are dark but we're working on it."

"Can we get back to Earth like this?"

"Only one engine's operational," Delgado replied. "And we can't analyze the other but a massive chunk is missing. I guess to answer your question, yes, but it won't be a fast trip. I need to get back to this. Some of my men are trapped and we're trying to get them out through maintenance passages. Delgado out!"

"Shit." Warren turned to Madeline. "Were you able to get through to Dex?"

"Still working on it, sir. The interference is lifting though so I imagine I'll be through in a moment."

"Good." Warren clenched his fist. "Those turrets down, Nicolas?"

"Yes, sir. Unless they've got more, we should be good."

"Pull us back. I want to have some reaction room in case they decide to do something insane like ram us."

"Which is a possibility," Avania said. "They have no reason not to at this point."

"You're full of great information," Warren muttered. "Full speed, get us out of here."

***

Micky nearly ran into the person he was following when the line abruptly stopped. A crowd milled about a large case and two marines were ushering people into a room. They shouted in an attempt to make them hurry but some seemed dazed, stumbling into the chamber while others anxiously tried to push their way in.

He hurried to the front of the crowd, tripping on someone's legs just as he approached the marines. One of them lifted his weapon and aimed it at him for half a moment before shaking his head and turning away. Everyone was on edge, especially the soldiers who came to get them.

I can't blame them. Micky looked down at the person he'd tripped on and gasped. They had to be dead. Half their face and chest were melted. Someone put its arms over its chest. He swallowed hard, fighting back an urge to be sick. *That's what those beams do to people. Dear God in heaven.*

"You ready?" The voice made Micky jump. "We're boarding this shuttle to get the hell out of here, you ready to go or do you want to stay?"

"I'm ready," Micky nodded, moving into the room. "How … how's this thing going to leave?"

"I have no idea. I'm waiting for the LT to come back. He's been on one of these things when they've flown before so I guess we'll find out soon. Hang tight." The marine dashed off, leaving him amongst the crowd. The area was packed full though there was just enough room to mill about.

"Captain Chilton?" A familiar voice shouted his name and a moment later, strong hands grabbed Micky's arm. "It's you! God, it's good to see you!"

Patrick stood there, holding him tightly. "I thought you were dead!" Micky hugged the man. "When you ejected, we saw that thing shoot you! We swore you were gone!"

"Me too! There was a bright flash … and I blacked out. I swore I died. I mean, seriously, there was no way I didn't bite it, right?" Patrick stepped back, bumping into someone as he shrugged. "But here I am! It wouldn't be a miracle without those marines, though. If it hadn't been for them … hell, I don't know what would've happened but it didn't look good."

"No." Micky thought about the body outside that had been burned up by the blasters. "This shuttle thing they've piled us on is interesting. I have no idea how it works. Did you find a cockpit or anything?"

Patrick shook his head. "No, and I was one of the first people on board so I got a good look before it got crowded."

"Lieutenant!" Someone shouted outside, a sound that chilled Micky.

"I'd better check that out." He paused. "Look for the others. Dino … Donna. Maybe they got grabbed, too."

"I will! See you in a minute."

Micky hurried off the shuttle and found two of the marines surrounding a third, trying to help him. It took a moment to see what was wrong but the light made his leg glisten. Part of the environmental suit had been seared into the flesh, melted into him. *Another one of those beam weapons. He's lucky it didn't take the whole limb off.*

"Excuse me," Micky stepped forward. "I'm Captain Chilton, USAF. Is there anything I can do to help?"

The wounded man looked him up and down. "I'm Lieutenant Dexter Pollard, marines. You a pilot?"

"I am."

Dexter nodded. "Then maybe you can help. We've got to get this shuttle out of here." He turned to one of the other marines. "Jumie, how long before the bombs go off?"

"Less than twelve minutes."

"And we're sure we have everyone on board?"

Jumie frowned. "There might be people left but we had to hurry. This was a smash and grab, sir."

"I counted just over a hundred and fifty people," Denton stepped forward. "There … likely were a lot more … but this is what we could get."

"Are we it?" Dexter asked.

Micky counted four marines, five if he included the dead one.

"Yes, sir." Denton nodded. "We got hit hard on that last push. I don't know what happened to Derreks. He was right here."

"He's gone," Jumie said. "Came to help at the last converter … took a shot to the head and another three to the body. Went down … in … well … he's done."

"Couldn't bring him back?" Dexter asked.

Jumie shook his head. "Sir, he was pretty much melted."

Dexter cursed. "Understood." He looked at Micky. "When we get on the shuttle, Jumie will pull the remote module. We have to launch the thing and get the hell out of here. Hopefully, we can land it on Earth again.

"I can try to help …" Micky shrugged. "How different can it be?"

"Oh, you'll see." Dex sighed. "Get on board, guys. Let's do this."

"Get them!" Buzzing weapons barked down the hall, blue beams cooking the air around them. Jumie returned fire as he withdrew toward the shuttle. Denton grabbed Dexter and dragged him on board while Micky laid down suppressive fire, sidestepping for cover. The aliens seemed to be making a last-ditch attack, an eleventh-hour assault.

"Close the door!" Jumie shouted. "LT, get the door closed!"

"I'm trying!" Dexter shouted. "Keep them back!"

People started shouting inside the shuttle as the aliens appeared before them, five in all. They unloaded into the room. Men and women hit the deck, those that weren't quick enough were cut down. Jumie and Denton blasted away. The final marine took a volley to the chest and legs, ending him in a second.

Micky went prone, shooting the aliens in the legs. Each time he scored a hit, one of them collapsed, screaming in agony. The marines finished them off. The fight lasted thirty seconds, possibly less but when the noise stopped, the cries of the wounded replaced the gunshots and buzzing.

Jumie helped Micky to his feet and they turned, looking over the corpses of several fallen allies. Some were injured, others unconscious but they lost at least fifteen in the sudden and final assault. The doors began to close, sliding up from the floor. Dexter shouted for Jumie to get into the maintenance hatch.

The doors sealed shut, locking in the cries of the wounded and the stillness of the dead. Micky found Patrick, thankful to learn he'd survived. He found Dino who was on the floor, unconscious with a graze to his left arm and right leg. A nurse moved amongst them, checking people over.

"Thank God we made it," Patrick muttered.

"Not quite yet," Micky replied. "When this thing is on the move and we're well away from that … shop of horrors … then we'll have made it. Until then, we're in trouble still."

"Bombs go off in six minutes!" Denton shouted. "Move it, people! Get this thing rolling!"

Micky let his head droop. "See what I mean?"

"Bombs?" Patrick called out. "What bombs?"

"We didn't just come here for you guys," Denton said. "We had to take that thing out, too. And believe me, what we brought will do the trick, but if we're not gone soon, we'll go with it."

"Fantastic." Patrick looked at Micky. "You'd better go see about trying to get us launched, sir. I kinda doubt these marines have any clue about what they're doing. At least with flying."

"I'll see what I can do." Micky headed over to Dexter, clearing his throat as he approached. "Did he get that module removed?"

"Yeah, you think you can get this thing out of here? Cause I sure as hell can't squeeze up there and Jumie's already complained about the ideas of hitting the wrong button." Dexter grunted, leaning against the wall. He favored the injured leg. "I can get you on a com link for some help if you want a try."

"I'd love a shot," Micky said. "Just get me up there."

"Jumie!" Dexter shouted. "Hurry the hell up, man! Time's wasting!"

"It was stuck!" Jumie called back. "I didn't jam it in there that tight … anyway, it's out now. Step aside. I'm coming out."

Dexter pulled off his helmet and pulled off his headset, handing it over to Micky. "The person on the other end of that should be able to help you. I hate to put pressure on you, but we really need you to hurry. Everyone in here, those who are left, their lives are in your hands. Good luck."

Jumie slipped out of the hole and stepped away. "All yours."

"Thanks." Micky rolled his eyes, put on the headset, and pulled himself into the tight space. If he'd been any larger, there was no way he'd have fit up there but as he drew closer to the controls, it widened enough for him to move about. *Who the hell maintains these things that's so damn small? Seriously, how's this make sense?* "This is Captain Chilton. Hello?"

"Captain Chilton?" A woman's voice sounded surprised. "What happened to Lieutenant Pollard?"

"He handed this to me so I could get some help launching this shuttle," Micky replied. "Time's of the essence. Are you the one who's going to walk me through this?"

"Hold on, I need to transfer you."

Micky laughed at the comment while taking in his surroundings. A panel to his left was open, revealing some sort of electrical board. When he looked up, a video screen lit up the area with a map of the Earth. Levers stuck up on either side with buttons at the end of them. Waiting killed him inside and he whispered for them to hurry.

"Hello, this is Avania. I'm on the Leviathan and I'll do my best to help you launch that shuttle. Are you there?"

"Yeah, I'm here," Micky said. "Go for it. What do I do? I see two levers and a screen. Pretty much all I've got."

"The screen should be showing you an image of the Earth. Tap it."

Micky did, causing the screen to flash. "Um … it's flashing."

"Good. Grab the two levers. There are buttons on top. Hit them both at the same time and hold them down."

"What's that going to do?" Micky complied, his thumbs hovering over the buttons.

"It will override the clamps holding you in place. Hit them both and you'll be dislodged from the vessel and start toward Earth. I recommend you hurry."

Micky pressed the buttons. A cold breeze hit him in the face and the shuttle began to rumble. A moment later, the marines cheered.

"You did it!" Dexter shouted. "You launched this thing! Way to go! Thank God!"

We're not out of this yet. Micky thought. "What do I do now?"

"The screen should now change and show you the direction you are going."

Micky looked up and saw the open space. He guessed the next part, shifting the controls in the opposite directions. A marker on the side of the screen showed they were going down. *I get it. These are basic maneuvering controls.* He leveled them out and continued going straight. "What's minimum safe distance from that thing?"

"I can't be sure," Avania said. "I've never seen your weapons at work. However, we have moved some distance away. The moment it goes up, you will likely lose power. At that point, you'll be waiting for a rescue. Good luck and we'll see you soon."

"Wait!" Micky shouted but the line already went dead. *What the hell did she mean about* our *weapons?* He shook his head. *That's the least of my worries right now.* He swallowed hard and kept them steady, flying away from the mothership. He allowed himself to feel some relief, some sense of accomplishment.

They managed to escape after all but the bodies below, the death toll sobered any sense of real accomplishment. *Such a cost.* Micky wondered what the next move was, what humanity planned to do. He wanted in. One way or another, he intended to be involved in the response to these aliens and the war they brought to Earth.

There was no way he was going back to his flight after what happened. No, he needed to see this through to the end.

***

Avania turned to Warren. "The shuttle is away. They've escaped."

"Yes!" Warren clapped Victoria on the back before standing up. "That's great news. Thank God. How long before the bombs go off?"

"Less than five minutes," Nicolas said. "Why aren't they abandoning ship?"

"Because they don't know what's about to happen," Avania said. "When we fell back, they must've felt like they'd driven us off. They have time to finish their repairs and get out of here." She shook her head. "Pathetic … they should have been better about their scans. These fools really are the bottom of the barrel."

"Not that they could do anything about the bombs now anyway." Warren motioned to Nicolas. "Switch the screen to them. I want to see this happen."

Nicolas changed the camera and Avania watched as it zeroed in on the collector ship. Purple and yellow globes dumped from the hull breach which they still hadn't sealed. She frowned at that, surprised to see it. They must've been too busy to bother, thinking they had to deal with their intruders.

First they tried to flee then they went to deal with them? What are these maniacs doing?

It dawned on her that they might not have had any idea how to contend with the things thrown at them. They never ran into opposition. Firing on the Earth ship was clumsy. Yes, they did plenty of damage but they could've destroyed the ship with some thoughtful targeting. Instead, all they managed to do was hurt the Leviathan, not even cripple it.

Their EMP toy failed so they didn't know what to do. "Truly, these mercenaries were not the best. That's how we succeeded. They're little more than hired hands. Basic workers and lapsed soldiers." Avania shook her head. "Incredible. I suspect they've long since forgotten the discipline of whatever military training they had. Fortunate for you in many ways."

"Not so fortunate for all the people who died because of them," Warren said.

"I do hope you know what I meant by my comment," Avania replied. "I was not undermining the losses but stating that the collectors made many mistakes … the biggest one being that they came here in the first place. If any of them lived to tell the tale, they would lament this visit for the rest of their lives."

The collector ship burst, pieces flying in all directions. Massive chunks spread out as a secondary blast tore the rest of it to pieces. Some drifted, others rocketed away but nothing could've survived the blast. Shards of metal turned red temporarily and winked out as the cold of space quelled them all, swallowing the fury of the destruction in the silence of the void.

Avania expected the humans to cheer, to carry on and show some level of excitement but they remained solemn and quiet. She didn't know what they were feeling or thinking. Was this a lamentation for their dead? A moment of silence for their success? She didn't want to intrude and merely sat there, watching.

Warren finally spoke up, sitting down. "Tell Commander Harden to finish rescue operations. We'll provide support. Inform control of our success ... though I know they just saw it themselves. Congratulations, everyone. We just won our first battle. Let's hope we have as much success in the future."

Epilogue

Dirk Reidel sat in awe with everyone in the news center as they watched the destruction of the massive object that had menaced Earth for the better part of the day. The threat appeared to be over. When word got out to all the places without power, maybe the violence could finally end.

Humanity survived a hostile encounter with alien invaders. Nothing could be more inspirational than that. The Agency stepped up and proved themselves with a victory. After a harrowing day of uncertainty, terror, and finally redemption, the roller coaster ride came to an unsteady halt.

But this was not the end of it. Anyone with half a brain realized that much. The aliens would be back eventually and when they came, it would not likely be so easy to put them down. People might take a deep breath of relief but they would quickly follow it up with questions of what happened next.

The military and the Agency would need to partner, to prove to the world that they were ready to protect the planet and the whole of the human race. Dirk doubted they'd have any shortage of volunteers. The event might even bring nations together who fought for generations, though that might be more optimistic than realistic.

Wyman Jacks promised a final update for the day about the events but he let them know that the Leviathan did its duty and they were conducting rescue operations for the ship that had been hit with the EMP earlier. They'd all be returning home soon and from there, the next steps could begin.

Dirk finally felt as if he could take a break and he left the anchor desk to use the bathroom and stretch. As he paced down the hall, his colleagues clapped him on the back and congratulated him on handling himself well. It had been a grueling day but one of the most rewarding of his career.

He looked forward to covering the next part of the story, the next thing that would catch the world's attention about the aliens. But hopefully, it could wait for another day. Just then, he wanted to crawl into bed and pass out for the next twelve hours. Someone else could cover the aftermath. He was there for the real story.

And I'll be here for the next one, too. Good night, world. You made it to see another day.

***

Warren sat in the briefing room with Avania and Victoria. They waited for Jacks to come on the line to discuss the concluded rescue operations and next steps. The Seeker saved the Probity and ended up needing to get the marines off the shuttle. The thing lost power immediately upon the collector ship going up in smoke.

The Probity suffered a tragedy. While they were able to save five of the crew members, twenty-five perished when the EMP attack struck the ship. The ship itself could be repaired but almost all hands were lost in the process, including Commander Singer. Warren knew the man well. He'd be missed in the fighting to come.

One hundred ten people survived the escape of the collector ship, leaving countless dead. Warren had hoped for better but the situation was tough. The marines did what they could, brought as many out as possible. When the aliens threw a parting shot, they did the most damage. It was a cheap stab by those who knew they'd lost the fight.

The Leviathan lost ten crew members with another twenty requiring medical attention. It was better than Warren thought but still painful. Their first time out should've been a celebration, a major success of humanity but instead, it turned into a blood bath of human lives and destroyed alien technology.

Jacks came on the line, "can you guys hear me?"

"We hear you," Warren said. "Have you received our report?"

"I did. I know it probably doesn't feel like it right now, but good job. You've given humanity a lot of hope with what you did today and saved a lot of lives to boot. Now we can lick our wounds and move on. Any thoughts about what that means? Now that you've been up there and given the ship a shake, I thought you might have some insight."

"If I may," Avania said, "the first step that needs to be taken is to study the chip I gave you. Then, send your smaller ships to salvage as much of the technology as you can. You've proven to be clever enough to build this ship, and it is a marvel given what you know now, but you can learn a great deal. Especially with my help."

"What exactly can you do for us?" Jacks asked.

"I can assist with interpreting the data," Avania replied. "I'm not a technician but all of us learn the basics of maintenance for our technology. I have a fair understanding of how wormhole drives function. That may be able to assist you with the construction of such a device.

"Furthermore, we can improve your artificial gravity and, more importantly, get proper shields working for your vessels. I assume there are more ships like the Probity and Seeker?"

"Six," Jacks said, "in total."

"Then we'll need to upgrade them and prepare them for the fight to come." Avania clenched her first. "Reach out to other planets, other people and bring them together. With allies, we can win the fight to come. Without them, we may be able to fend off another collector ship, perhaps a small party … but if the full might of my people arrive, we will lose."

"Grim." Jacks sighed. "What do you think, Warren? What's your opinion about all this?"

"We've got a lot of volunteers," Warren said. "And I think we need to take one step at a time. Salvage, learn, push as hard as we can to get things moving in our favor. Once we've got that going, we can think about finding help. The only trouble is, we don't know how much time we've got before someone comes back."

"I'm sure we'll find their schedule," Avania replied. "And when we know where all they were going, we'll have some idea when to worry about someone looking for them."

Victoria cleared her throat, "we have an intact shuttle. That should tell us quite a bit as we reverse engineer it. I'd pull in more technicians, more scientists, even Delgado and get them to work. We'll need to be doing this around the clock if we hope to succeed. I hope you're all ready for some long nights."

"We are," Jacks said. "Okay, I'll set up a schedule and get people in action. I'll let you guys determine who's coming here and who's staying with the ship. Hop a shuttle and come on down. We'll need some brainstorming in person. And let's not forget that the world fell to shit during this event. We've got a lot of clean-up to do."

"Did you ever find your leak?" Victoria asked. She explained to Warren, "someone was leaking information to the press."

"Yes, I think we did," Jacks said. "One of my personal aides. Madison. We're still investigating and we'll know soon. That doesn't matter as much right now. The council's talking about being transparent with our course of action, rally the people. You know the drill. We have some hearts and minds to win over, especially considering the riots and other violence the general population got up to."

Warren rubbed his eyes. "Thanks, Colonel. We'll talk soon." He killed the connection and looked at the others. "Sounds like we've got at least a semblance of a plan. You think we've got this?"

Avania shrugged. "It will all come down to how much time we have but I believe we need to try regardless."

Warren smirked. "The one thing you're going to find about humans is that we don't give up. We're a tenacious lot. It's pretty much in our DNA."

"Believe me, I know," Avania replied. "It's why your essence is so valuable … why they wanted you so badly. They will learn exactly what that means. My people should have left you alone and now, due to their disregard for your fortitude, they're going to pay dearly. I will certainly see to that."

Victoria's brows lifted as she looked at Warren. "I'm glad she's on our side."

"Yeah." Warren nodded, squinting at the alien woman. "Me too. Get on up to the bridge and let Nicolas know to bring us about. Course set for Earth orbit. We've got a lot to do. I think it's time we got about it."

Printed in Great
Britain
by Amazon